DEATH BY CHOCOLATE

Julie Anne Lindsey

The Killer Confection Series
Book 1

KNIGHT ROMANCE

This is a work of fiction. Names, characters, places, and incidents are products of the author's imagination or are used factiously and are not to be construed as real. Any resemblance to actual events, locations, organizations, or person, living or dead, is entirely coincidental.

kNight Romance Publishing
Port Richey, Florida

ISBN-13: 9781937629267
ISBN-10: 1937629260

Library of Congress Control Number: 2012933896

Knight Romance Publishing , March 2012
www.knightromancepublishing.com

SPECIAL THANKS

Special thanks Carolyn's Kitchen for the use of her Pink Dorothy Apron on the cover!

-?-

This is the story of one beleaguered housewife in desperate need of a shiny, white knight. Unfortunately those were in short supply. In her fairytale, men acted their age, women dressed theirs, and nosey neighbors were put in the stocks.

Sadly, her life wasn't a fairytale…

CHAPTER ONE

"Mr. Russell, I know you're in there."

Ruby Russell squirmed against the wall beside her front door, attempting to squeeze herself in behind a large potted plant. She cursed her husband under her breath as the pounding on the door continued.

"Mr. Russell, your van's right here in the driveway." Ruby could hear the pacing on her front porch. "I'm not leaving until I get an explanation for this account."

Her eyes rolled beneath her bangs. *As if the three-year-old minivan in the driveway belongs to my husband. That's a laugh.* No, Ken had a sales floor model of some foreign number she wasn't even allowed to ride in, let alone drive. Kenneth. He'd corrected her a thousand times in the past few years. Kenneth wouldn't be caught dead in her rickety van.

"I'm not leaving, Mr. Russell," the voice threatened, making her escape by avoidance an impossibility.

One hot puff of air escaped Ruby's lips and lifted her bangs briefly, sending flour into the air. She was in a real pickle. Undecided, she watched the ticking clock and prayed.

She prayed the man would give up and leave.

She prayed her thoughtless husband would show up sooner rather than later.

She prayed no one in her neighborhood was witnessing this show.

It was already two thirty in the afternoon and a school day, a very bad combination. Busses would bring the neighborhood children and their adults out very soon to scoff and stare. Ruby desperately wanted this gentleman off her lawn before that happened.

The Russells didn't need any more attention, especially not of this sort.

The entire situation was absurd and unfair. It was Ken's midlife crisis. Yet somehow, he managed to avoid the associated humiliation. The gawkers and rubberneckers admired him and his shiny new toys. They loved the ridiculous and he fit the bill perfectly. His incorrigible behavior these past few years had made him more popular, not less. Since the day her precious angel baby boy had left for college, all of the humiliation was saved for Ruby.

She grew more and more uncomfortable while debating her next step. The plant sharing her hideout was quickly becoming inhospitable. Scratchy leaves left marks on her silk blouse. Small snags and tugs appeared with her every twitch. Her blouse was all but ruined.

As soon as she was free, the infuriating ficus was going the way of Saturday's leftovers. It had never been happy in that corner anyway.

With a hiccup of despair, her eyes caught sight of the Queen Ann mirror in the next room, which grandly reflected her demeaning situation. A perfectly shameful image of her hiding behind the prickly tree pinked her cheeks.

Absurd. Where had the confident young woman of her youth gone? She barely recognized the full blond hair and big blue eyes looking back. So much had changed. Everyone used to call them Ken and Barbie.

Ruby sucked in a breath and squared her shoulders. Yes, her waistline had grown and her bust line had fallen, but hardly enough to justify the Plastic Surgery brochures Ken had brought home. *Pish.* She shook her head and swiped flour from her cheek with the back of one hand.

Who was she kidding? Barbie had been replaced long ago by a suburban Mrs. Doubtfire. Even plastic surgery couldn't remedy that.

Her posture deflated with a gush of released breath, like an icing bag devoid of its creamy filling. Something had to be done about Mr. Harmon. She wished she were anywhere but home. *If only I had somewhere to go.* She watched the oversized clock in their hallway. She'd gladly have stayed away everyday and avoided these situations if only she had a destination. Sadly, the opportunity never presented itself, and Ruby was trapped. Pressed quite literally into a corner, she made a brave decision to choose what was important. Her dignity.

Ruby rubbed her hands roughly against her apron and smoothed her platinum hair.

Pound. Pound. Pound.

"Who is it?" Ruby's voice was shrill. She was going for casual, but her nerves were fraying, and her pitch was off. A growing tremor convulsed her lungs with each and every breath.

"It's Phil Harmon, Mrs. Russell, from ITRUST Bank and Loan."

Ruby tugged sharply on the heavy wooden door with one round fist. She dabbed perspiration with the other. Sunlight twinkled in brightly, reflecting tiny rainbows from the beveled glass onto her apron. Her sensible size fourteen blouse lit up like a disco ball. She tried to overlook the fact. It would do her no good to dwell on the fact she probably looked like a giant, lite-brite. No, it was definitely not a good idea to think about that. It didn't help her nerves at all.

"Hello, Mr. Harmon." She felt as if she'd been running instead of cowering. "I've been baking." This was clearly evidenced by the flour, fast becoming paste upon her forehead. *Gracious and blameless. Concentrate on being gracious and blameless.*

"Would you like to come in?"

"No, ma'am." He looked over Ruby's shoulders into the house. "What I would like, is to talk to your husband. Is he home?"

She opened her mouth to say he'd be arriving any minute, when she heard the roar of Ken's engine. He turned into the cul-de-sac as if on queue, and she was overcome with relief. Finally Ken could put an end to the whole sordid mess. He could redeem himself by playing the hero to her damsel in distress, as he had once loved to do.

Ruby saw his carrot-orange tan and arrogant smirk as he rolled down the street into view. His ultra white teeth reflected sun into his mirrored aviators, and his overpriced hair plugs blew carelessly in the wind.

Her gut burned with embarrassment to see him enjoying himself while she neared a blackout, trying to maintain some form of composure in the face of such a humiliating situation. She suspected she should be used to feeling humiliated by now, but it wasn't something she could get used to. *It surely isn't fair.*

Even with his shirt shamelessly unbuttoned, Ruby was glad to see him. Ken could put an end to the fiasco, and an end was exactly what she desired at that precise moment in time.

Let Mr. Harmon direct his ire to the true culprit here, and hopefully do it out of sight of the neighbors.

Predictably, the apple red sports car pulled smoothly into the drive beside her van and stopped. Ken glanced at the pair on his porch. Then, as if he were no more than a lost commuter in an unfamiliar location, he promptly shifted into reverse. In a flash, the sleek new machine was gone, along with its pretentious, middle-aged pilot.

Ruby's heart fell. Air whooshed from her lips. She'd been abandoned. Again.

"I-I- ," she stuttered, fumbling for the words. He'd left her. In the middle of a socially catastrophic mess of his own making, Ken had slithered out, leaving her stranded. She was stunned speechless for a moment. *How could he do this to me? What will the neighbors say about us now?*

With a shocking surge of will, Ruby squared her shoulders and faced the problematic Mr. Harmon. Ken might have abandoned her to suffer his disgrace alone, but that didn't mean she had to let it play out on her front porch for all to see. Mr. Harmon needed to go…now.

"He's at work, Mr. Harmon." Covering for him seemed the appropriate thing to do. After all, she was his wife. Till death do them part. Without loyalty, what did they have?

Ruby braced herself against the doorframe with one weakening arm. Her trousers caught on the rough wooden edges. They'd likely match her tattered blouse before this was over.

He'd looked right at her and left. She still couldn't believe it. Her chest tightened, and she began to wonder how many people had seen his performance. The neighbors hadn't stopped staring since the day Michael left home. They had openly gaped at her when she'd returned from the hospital too. Nosey busy-bodies, the lot of them. Pardon her if she needed a break from the judgmental eyes on their street. Every mother deserved some time to herself when the one perfect piece of heaven she could lay claim to tore her heart out and called it "going away to college"

From her periphery, she saw her neighbor, Tillie Tanner, emerge from her home. Tillie had no doubt witnessed every humiliating moment of the horror. Of all the societal corruption on her block, Tillie took the cake. She kept her eyes upon Ruby as she crossed her perfectly manicured lawn to the mailbox. Her three-inch heels stuck in the grass with every step. Her hot pink leggings showed more thigh than the designer probably ever intended, and her own white blouse was in need of a few more buttons. Tillie didn't say a word, but her bright green gum was visible with every exaggerated movement of her otherwise puckered up lips. Ruby rolled against her door, feeling more ill with every passing second, while Tillie chomped, stomped and stared. Ruby prayed Mr. Harmon didn't notice Tillie. It took all the concentration she had to keep her horrified gaze from sliding over to her neighbor.

Surely Tillie knew glitter on wrinkled cleavage was a sin. Stilettos and hot pants belonged on a street corner. Her false lashes reached out to tap her spray-tanned forehead. Ruby was certain Tillie thought she looked glamorous. Disgust rose in her throat and a bitter taste crept over her tongue. Tillie Tanner loved to stare and spent more time on French manicures than good old fashioned American manners. Ruby would have been hard pressed to find a worse person to witness the demolition of her reputation.

"Mrs. Russell," Mr. Harmon's voice startled Ruby. Clearly bored and evidently unaware of their audience, he continued to complain. "Don't you think I would have stopped there first? His boss already told me he was working from home today."

Irritation peppered the words. His eyes refused to give

Ruby release, and she was certain she would collapse at any moment; adding insult to her already grievously injured self-image.

She leaned more heavily against the jamb for support and refused to look Tillie's way. Beads of sweat rolled at her temples, and the porch began to move slowly. "Oh dear," she breathed.

She'd seen Ken leave for work that morning.

What does it mean? It doesn't make sense. If he isn't at work, he should be at home. None of it made any sense.

If he hadn't been at work all day, then where had he been? Why would he lie about going to work? If he had a day off, why hadn't he spent it with her? She barely saw him lately, and what else would one do with a day off if not spend it with one's spouse? Golf? *Inconceivable.*

She hoped he hadn't lost his job, but he'd been working too much for that, even on Sundays. Questions and confusion stalled her panic, but the pinch in her chest increased anyway, and all she wanted to do was lie down. Her hands began to slide against the door's casing as the phone rang. The whole situation was simply impossible to bear. She needed to get away from Mr. Harmon before she took her humiliation to a whole new level and lost her composure in full view of her neighbors.

"Mr. Harmon," Ruby forced a whisper from her lips. "That's my phone. I need to answer it."

Ruby struggled to smile though she felt her eyebrows knit together. Her bottom lip quivered against her will. The familiar sting of tears crept into her eyes. It couldn't be helped and she really hoped Mr. Harmon didn't notice. A quick glance at his face proved otherwise. She'd seen his expression many times before. The look was pity, and it hurt every time. Blessedly, without further protest, Mr. Harmon left Ruby to tend to the telephone.

Ruby shoved the door closed and leaned into it, steadying herself. Her vision shimmered around the edges. After the awful encounter, she really needed a moment to regain her composure, but her phone continued to ring insistently. Breathless, she propelled herself along the back of the couch in an exhausted slide towards the kitchen. Her eyes burned from the double dose of midday sun and emotion. She was a hot mess. The last thing she wanted to do was speak to someone on the phone in such a condition, but answering was the only way to make it stop ringing.

"Hel-lo?" Ruby choked, wiping her hands and face with a dishtowel. She wanted the voice on the other end of the line to be Ken's and she wanted him to be proffering the most sincere apology of his life. She deserved an apology.

"Ruby! Thank Goodness!"

Ruby recognized the voice at once. It wasn't her husband. Instead, a frantic Betty Bates blathered on the other end. Betty managed the youth shelter where Ruby volunteered.

"We need you! There's been a mistake! We don't have any cake, cupcakes, dessert or anything for the benefit luncheon tomorrow!" Betty's pleading, high-pitched tone grated on Ruby's already frazzled nerves. While Ruby appreciated being the person Betty called when she was backed into a corner, dealing with someone else's crisis was the last thing Ruby needed at the moment.

She poured a tall glass of water and sat precariously atop a stool near the counter waiting for her vision to return. She wiped away the few tears insistent upon making an appearance.

"This isn't a good time for me," she croaked.

"Please! Please! Ruby, we'd owe you forever! The children need the money this benefit can bring. We have to show we have reliable volunteers supporting us!"

There it was. Betty's secret weapon and Ruby's Kryptonite.

Guilt.

If she didn't do this for Betty, then she wouldn't show herself to be a reliable volunteer. Knowing she wouldn't be turning Betty down, Ruby let her forehead hit the counter and slide against twenty-year-old tiles.

"How many?" A sob escaped with the words.

"Twelve dozen by ten o'clock tomorrow." Betty sounded victorious. She'd known Ruby wouldn't say "no." Ruby never did, of course. "The luncheon will begin at eleven… Actually, nine thirty is better, so we can set up properly."

Ruby muttered something incoherent and said good-bye.

As the panic and stress of the day mounted, her chest grew hot. She tried in vain to rub the heat away. *Twelve dozen cupcakes delivered by nine thirty.* A tiny groan escaped her neutrally painted lips. It was already three o'clock. What about her dinner? What about her housekeeping? What if she had plans or business to take care of? What about HER?

Betty disconnected while Ruby glared at the phone in disbelief. Indignant, she stripped the apron from her waist and seized her purse from the counter to take stock of the funds she had on hand. Seven dollars. *Crepes*. That would never be enough for the supplies she needed. She sighed heavily and trudged upstairs to the master bedroom.

Ken had to keep cash somewhere in the house. He always had some on him. But in all their years of marriage, she'd never asked about his stash or looked for it. Before now, it had always seemed disrespectful to do so.

However, recent events had changed the situation. Ken owed her. A little pocket money to cover the baking supplies was a small step towards repaying her for the predicament he'd left her in with Mr. Harmon. Mind made up, the only question remaining was, where to look. *It has to be the bedroom. No one ever goes in there but us.*

She threw open his drawers in search of money, turned over shoes in his closet and checked every suit pocket she could reach. She was fast running out of places to look. Then she spotted a large box of ski boots on his top shelf. Ken had planned a ski retreat to celebrate their empty nest after Michael left for college. That hadn't gone as planned, and though they never went on the trip, he'd also never returned the gear. It seemed as good a hiding spot as any. Better probably, because her five-foot two-inch frame couldn't reach it. Determined, she dragged a suitcase from her closet to his and wobbled up onto it for height. It still wasn't tall enough. She stretched hard, smashing her bosoms into the custom shelving, wrinkling her already ruined blouse and possibly damaging the luggage.

"Retrieving this box better be worth the dilapidation of my best American Traveler rollaway," she growled in consternation, if only to herself.

Back on solid ground, it took a minute for her to right herself. Then she studied the large box. It was much too light to contain a pair of size twelve Snow Masters. A familiar heat returned to her cheeks as she considered her behavior. She was not a nosey woman, and certainly not a thief. If the box did hold money, how could she take it?

Scolding herself for even considering it, Ruby lifted the box to return it, but she just couldn't quite bring herself to put it back on the shelf. She had always prided herself on being the perfect housewife and stay-at-home mother. Reputation and attention to detail were important, and she'd always striven hard for perfection. She had thought her son and her husband appreciated the effort. Of course, that was before her son had shattered her world by going AWAY to college and Ken started dressing like a gigolo.

She'd reluctantly accepted that her wonderful, brilliant, studious boy was away at college and doing fine. But the changes in Ken were more than she could understand. It was jarring to realize he'd become a stranger to her. Her Ken would never run away and leave her to clean up his mess. She'd been married to the man for umpteen years! How could he have changed so much? In a flash of impulsivity, she lifted the box's stiff blue lid.

With that one, relatively benign action, her world tilted on its axis.

She dropped the box on the bed and sat next to it in stunned silence. An inspection of the contents sent her swimming against an invisible tide of disbelief, shame and embarrassment. Her heartbeat echoed deep in her ears, throat and head, pounding like a bass drum. Inside the box were photos of *Kenneth* and a woman whom Ruby had never met. The woman was young, barely more than a girl compared to Ruby, and certainly of a more spirited disposition by the looks of things. She was tall and thin with olive skin and flowing dark hair. If there were a polar-opposite of Ruby Russell, this girl fit the bill.

Beneath the photographs lay condoms and a prescription bottle for male performance enhancers. Ruby's hands flew to her mouth. She shut her eyes tightly, hoping to un-see the sights she knew would surely kill her. For the second time that day, the periphery of her vision shimmered and she waited for the floor to meet her face.

Instead, something completely different happened.

The scream that began in her toes climbed powerfully through her entire form. Like the thunder of a thousand Sioux chefs, it filled every curve and fold of her with heat and vengeance. Her stomach rolled into her back, tightening everything as it went. The scream finally caught in her throat by an invisible switch.

Ruby would no longer worry about where Ken had been all day. The man in those pictures wasn't her husband. That man was an imposter and a lunatic. Her husband was no middle-aged hipster. She'd married a decent and honorable man, not some derelict nincompoop who showed chest hair and dated young vixens! He wasn't a hero, wasn't the man she married. Nearly thirty years together, and he rewarded her like this?

"Ha!" She hacked a throaty noise into the air. Ken was gone and she had no interest in his doppelganger. No, she had other, better deserving, things to be concerned with, like cupcakes.

She removed the cash lining the large box with one strong rip and neatly returned the box to its shelf. Ken certainly couldn't ask her if she'd taken any cash from there. Not without admitting the box existed, which of course would lead to other, more uncomfortable confessions. She was certain this shell of her husband lacked the backbone to admit any of it to her face. Carefully, she climbed down from her perch once more, squared her shoulders and headed for her vanity.

She fluffed her blond coiffure nervously in the mirror and applied fresh powder to her face. Her blue eyes were still wide with shock. She looked a little too intense to go out in public. She'd have to wear dark glasses. She glossed her lips and left the room before she changed her mind. Ruby might not have been twenty-three any longer, but she was an appropriate, dignified, proper lady and worthy of much more than Ken had given her. With that, she straightened her spine, pushed her shoulders back and strode forcefully to the door, trembling inside the whole way.

Ruby had baking to do.

Montrose Hills was a bustling community of mixed

generations but hopelessly devoid of cultural diversity. Men pushed mowers, and women planted roses. Chemically-treated lawns glistened like a treasure trove of emeralds in the hot summer sun. The upper middle-class citizens of Montrose Hills clamored collectively to get a home in Ruby's neighborhood. It was the best, mostly due to the people who populated it and most of those individuals were currently in view.

Her quiet street increased in decibel by the second. Locking up behind her, Ruby saw the neighborhood gossips gathered in the cul-de-sac. Mothers and grandmothers made their way back from the bus stop with children trailing behind them.

In an unusual stroke of luck, it seemed most of the neighborhood had missed the spectacle of Ken's desertion. The blue sky and warm weather warned her to get it all settled soon because the school year was at a close. She couldn't risk a repeat of today's events, unless she wanted her humiliation to be broadcast publically to every man, woman and child in Montrose Hills.

The women in the cul-de-sac stared as Ruby secured her sunglasses and chiffon scarf. She was in no mood to be neighborly, and she prayed silently they'd let her leave without any pleasantries. Her prayer was only half answered.

"Ruby!" Tillie's incessant gum chewing implied an accent, but there was none. It was simply the cud between her teeth playing tricks on the ears. "Hey, I saw what that son-of-a-gun husband of yours did to you today." Every word was loud and overly enunciated, making sure everyone in the neighborhood could clearly hear and understand. Everyone looked; adults and children alike. Ruby's eyes rolled heavenward behind her dark glasses. *Is there no justice in the world?*

"I heard every single word, and I was just telling the ladies about it." She threw a thumb haphazardly across her shoulder towards the group, who in return smiled slyly and nodded, confirming Ruby's fears. Her private shame had in fact been a very public humiliation.

"They all do it," a voice called back from the pack. "I just spend his money and indulge myself. I mean, we deserve something for keeping them, right?" The speaker wore black pedal pushers and heels with feathers across the open toes. The neighborhood cliques were as mean as any group of high school girls and immeasurably gaudier, which was probably why they never included her. It was easy to see Ruby didn't fit in with their group. She was of a different strata entirely. "June Cleaver" wouldn't waste her time with all those "Peggy Bundys".

They may have had a point, but it wasn't feasible for her. Ken's new lifestyle had driven them into the poorhouse. Ruby had been tightening her belt for the last eleven months. Spending was absolutely not a viable option for the Russells, or at least not for Ruby.

"Not like we can start over at our ages," another voice announced pensively, causing the group to turn in on itself. A round of catty laughter and vulgar stories of retribution began. Ruby fanned her flushed cheeks and said a hurried prayer for the lot of them as she hastened to her van. Then she drove rather wildly to her favorite baking outlet.

The soft yellow glow of the Cutie's sign soothed her nerves. Ruby took a minute to fix her face in the rearview mirror and sighed with relief. She was home. It was her haven, a place where like-minded, sensible bakers came to prepare. A smile broke through her melancholy.

Cutie's Cupcakes was the nicest baking outlet in the state and they'd opened a store right inside her township's limits. A blessed event. Cutie's was the kind of place where Ruby could lose herself for hours, and most definitely the best thing to ever happen to Montrose Hills in her modest opinion. As she hurried across the lot, her pulse raced. Being there was such a thrill, and she felt her feet skipping along the pavement as she went.

The enormous glass doors opened majestically at her presence, inviting her inside. Cutie's welcomed her with open arms, shimmering gourmet utensils and an air of productivity that Ruby thrived on. Beyond the sparkling glass doors stood a row of shiny silver carts. They waited for her, looking for all the world like a freshly halted parade of tiny chariots. Ruby smiled widely and chose a cart with a yellow seat and a chocolate cupcake stenciled inside. The little peach painted tag on the cupcake read, Culinary Queen.

She marched, almost pranced, into the place she considered her sanctuary. Ruby Russell, Culinary Queen, had come to buy and browse, buoyantly, upon the heavenly aromas within the castle. Scents of sugar and icing wafted outward to meet her, and she spun the little chariot into the heart of the store. Unbridled pleasure spread over Ruby's round face, and she nearly tiptoed up and down the enchanting aisles. Inside Cutie's Cupcakes, she was a ballerina on point, living a delectable dream.

The outlet was utterly intoxicating, and Ken's money would allow her to be indulgent for a change. Ruby sucked in lungfuls of joy as she shopped. Along with supplies for the twelve dozen cupcakes, she chose stencils, pans and pipers she never would have been able to justify buying before. She even bought a carousel of flavored extracts for her countertop. *Apparently, vengeance really is sweet.*

"Hello, Mrs. Russell!" A pert voice called from behind a glass barrier.

"Claire Cummins," Ruby answered. "How are you?"

Claire had been a long-time friend of the Russell family. Michael had brought her home from middle school after her family moved to Montrose Hills. The following year, Ruby taught the young lady to bake while Mr. and Mrs. Cummins battled through a bitter divorce.

It took.

Claire now attended a very prestigious culinary school in Kensington City only a few miles away. Though the city was riddled with crime and overstuffed with people and pollution, it was an opportunity Ruby would have killed for.

"I'm super." She loped around the counter to embrace Ruby. Ruby had been a mother to Claire when her own mother had been too absorbed in her own drama to do right by her. In the end, it benefitted both Claire and Ruby. Claire had gotten the love and support she needed and Ruby rather enjoyed having a daughter.

"How's school?" Ruby narrowed her eyes. It seemed too early for Claire to be home for the summer.

"Excellent!" Claire beamed. "I'm at the top of my class. We let out yesterday for summer break, and I drove home last night. I hoped to come over and catch up. I miss you." She kissed Ruby's cheek and hugged her tightly once more.

"Well," Ruby patted her hands. This wasn't a great time to have company. She needed to talk with Ken, and that might take a while. "Give me a call and let me know what your work schedule's like. I'd love to have you over for a proper tea."

Claire nodded sweetly and made her way back around the glass. She went back to decorating an elaborate four-tier cake. It was grand enough for a wedding, but the tiny princess on top told another story. Ruby suspected some little girl would be getting the birthday cake of a lifetime.

Several other enthusiasts spoke to Ruby as she shopped.

They called her by name, and one even asked her opinion on fillings for an upside down cake. She'd easily been there an hour when it was time to move towards the checkout.

Her spree completed, she went reluctantly to stand in line at the only open register. The standing was far less exciting than the shopping. As soon as she brought her chariot to a halt, reality returned to her in all its ugly, emotional glory. Images of the pills, the young woman, the neighbors and Mr. Harmon swirled through her mind. She tried to shake them away. She wanted to remember she had choices to make. Her mother once taught her to make lemonade when life brought lemons, but she was just so angry. Her blood boiled in her veins.

For the very first time in her life, she understood why they sold wine at Cutie's. Ruby left her cart in the line and hustled away on impulse. She grabbed a box of Chardonnay from a nearby end cap and tried to be stealthy as she made her way back to her cart.

It was an impossible combination. The box thumped against her thighs, and she lifted it to her chest, only to feel like a burglar trying to escape with booty. She hoisted the wine into her cart and attempted to conceal it beneath her other supplies. Another exercise in futility.

Back in line, Ruby tried paging through *Cupcake Cuisine* in an effort to divert her thoughts from the day's events, but it was useless. It was hard to accept that in a single day she'd been publicly humiliated, abandoned and betrayed, and now stood in line to make purchases with money from her husband's "box of sins." The alcohol hidden in her cart only made everything worse. It wasn't long before the magazine became rather tattered in her shaking hands.

An enormous pink clock above the exit said five o'clock when her turn to check out finally arrived. It was dinnertime, and Ruby had no idea what she'd make for dinner. Her brain was wrecked. Her focus was gone, left behind in a nasty ski boot box with that child and those pills.

Her eyes jumped as her patience dissipated. She had to peel the sticky magazine cover from her sweaty palms to place it back on the rack. She unloaded her cart's contents onto the conveyor, but her eyes were glued to the magazine. On the back cover, where she'd propped it against the gum and breath spray, three small words leered back. Lush brown frosting formed the suggestion, *Death by Chocolate.*

Maybe I'll have to try that. Ruby allowed herself a private joke before paying her bill with Ken's dirty money.

CHAPTER TWO

At home, Ruby hefted the box of wine from her hatch and hauled all of her supplies up the steps to her front door. Ken still wasn't home. There was too much to do for her to dissolve into a pool of tears and emotion, and it wouldn't matter anyway. So she went straight to work, trying in vain to keep her despair at bay.

She emptied the canvas bags from Cutie's, placing each new item in its home. Supplies for her cupcakes were organized near her sink, and she moved everything else around to make room for the shiny new carrousel of extracts. Space was a commodity on Ruby's counter, and it took extra effort to accomplish the task. Then it was time to find her bowls, spoons and muffin tins which took quite a bit more re-arranging.

At last, it was time to bake.

Working so hard not to cry had an interesting

consequence. She was quickly becoming livid, and also quite uncomfortable with the carnal emotion. Anger had never done Ruby any favors. Fortunately, it was nothing a few glasses of chardonnay couldn't cure. She really wasn't supposed to drink. It'd been years since she'd had a sip of anything stronger than coffee. She poured a glass and swirled it before her eyes.

The last time she drank was the year Michael left for college. Since then, she'd become eternally thankful for coffee. Ruby knew it was reckless, and the box was overkill, but these were desperate times. So she baked and drank, and all the aggression seemed to fade.

Ruby enjoyed the baking, the measuring, the pouring, the sweet predictability and absolute control. Working in her kitchen was like a well-rehearsed dance, where she sashayed into a happier place and made magic from ordinary white paper bags and little plastic bottles. The smells were invigorating. The control was exhilarating, and after a night like that, she'd be sure to receive accolades for her work. Acknowledgement and perhaps a bit of envy were in her future. Everyone loved Ruby's treats.

Very soon she was happy. Heartaches forgotten. She danced with her wine and turned the radio up a little louder than usual. She felt rebellious that way. Probably from the wine. She even took the pins out of her hair and just enjoyed the baking. Ruby rocked her sizeable hips to the tick tock of the black cat clock, whose tail and eyes swung in time.

At midnight she stopped to admire her creation, concentrating on the fruits of her effort and trying not to think of anything else. Ken hadn't come home. Dismay tainted her satisfaction. Frustration returned to Ruby in a slightly fuzzier manner.

Ken was out making a mockery of their marriage, in his goofy new getup and overpriced crowns. All while she was at home alone getting drunk. She mashed the back of her hand against her lips to suppress a giggle and control a wild new impulse. The funniest thought she'd ever had slipped into her head, and she couldn't wait to get started.

She wiped her hands on her apron and then ran to get the hidden box . She stumbled on his shoes and fell from her luggage more than once before she succeeded, but the retrieval was worth the effort.

A handful of his happy pills will give him an evening to remember. Laughing aloud the entire way, she stumbled back to the kitchen where she whipped up some chocolate mousse for her beloved husband.

She imagined his humiliation when the pills began to work, and then when they wouldn't *quit* working. A wicked noise erupted. Wine threatened to escape her nose when she pictured him in that...condition. He'd have to tell her what was happening then, *and I will only take him to the hospital* after *he's told me everything*. He'd have to go in her van, too. *That will suit him just fine. Perhaps he'll get a lady doctor.* Ruby snorted and giggled. Mostly, she wanted his confession and an apology. She deserved that much. She must have for all she did, and also, he really should have to pay for what he'd done.

The thought of Ken's repentance spawned an abrupt calm, which quieted her nerves and her laughter. It was a new and brilliant feeling for Ruby. She hadn't been truly at ease in a very long while. The calm was nice, and so before she lost the incredible feeling altogether, she went back upstairs to bed; no longer interested in waiting up for her husband.

Ruby woke to the sound of her alarm at quarter after six. Her head felt as if it were filled with lard. She shoved weakly against her pillow and shifted upward in bed. Their white eyelet duvet and fluffy down pillows were untouched where Ken should have been. Sunlight trickled in through the sheer draperies over her window, and a sick feeling overcame her. He hadn't come home. Or worse, he'd come home and then gone back to the girl so he could enjoy the condition Ruby put him in. Her stomach coiled with anxiety.

Familiar waves of guilt crashed over her. With the presence of the morning sun and the absence of the wine, her ever-pending stroke returned. Predictable as pie.

Ruby slipped her swollen feet over the bed's high edge and into her most well-worn slippers. She donned her housecoat on her way into the hall and padded down the stairs for her morning coffee and some aspirin. Shuffling along, she imagined all the things she'd say to Ken, if he were home, and if she were that kind of lady.

From the foyer, she saw the light in the kitchen already on. Two steps further and she saw Ken asleep at the counter. *He probably had too many and passed out. Serves him right. He couldn't seriously expect to keep up with such a young girl.* She shuddered hard and swallowed – her pride.

"Ken." Ruby was sure she didn't want to have this conversation, but she couldn't leave him sleeping on the island. The tile must be awful for his chronic neck pain, and he looked rather pathetic in that position. She resolved to argue later, when they both felt better.

"Ken." She spoke his name softly at first, trying not to startle him.

There was only silence.

"Kenneth?" She raised her voice a fraction more. It cracked.

Still silence.

Finally, Ruby laid her hand on his shoulder to wake him, not really wanting to touch him, but needing to rouse him sooner rather than later.

He didn't rouse.

Instead, he rolled.

Kenneth toppled off the stool and flopped hard onto the marble floor like a two hundred pound sack of flour. His head smacked stiffly against the stone, and yet, he made no sound. Ruby stared blankly as her mind struggled to connect what she saw and what it meant.

Ken's face was covered in chocolate mousse. He wore a large round oval from his forehead to his chin, much like one of her facial masks, but undoubtedly more delicious. Stiff spikes had formed on his nose and eyelashes. It occurred to her he looked a bit like a clown at a cookie convention.

She puzzled over what she saw, unable to right it for herself. It was the condition below his belt that brought all of the ingredients together. The bulge in his trousers sent her flying backwards into the living room. It'd been years since she'd seen it, but she definitely knew how it got there. Ruby gasped, clutching her throat in shock and remembrance. Her mind scrambled and then began to shut down, like the lights in a bakery at closing time. Flick. Flick. Flick. Darkness.

What have I done?

"Ma'am, I just have a few more questions." Officer O'Leary stayed behind to talk with Ruby. The scene had been completely surveyed, and the coroner's office had finished their work. Kenneth was gone. Only the two of them, Ruby and Officer O'Leary, remained.

Still sporting slippers, a few curlers and her housecoat, Ruby offered him everything from sweet tea to croissants. She couldn't manage to sit still. Surely, any officer worth his salt could see she'd killed Ken.

Darn that cheap wine. There must be a lawsuit in there somewhere. An image of herself dressed in a black and white striped prison uniform trying to file a law suit against the wine company popped into her mind. She twisted her hands and kneaded her fingers. *There should be a warning on the box.* This wasn't her fault. She was a fine woman and an upstanding citizen!

"Ma'am, this wasn't your fault." The officer captured Ruby's erratic train of thought. "You shouldn't blame yourself."

Without speaking, she looked curiously in his direction. Officer O'Leary wore a suit, tie and hat. He didn't look like a policeman. He could have been just visiting, if it hadn't been for the murder. She wondered idly if Tillie Tanner and her cronies were on the front lawn, gleaning for gossip and propositioning paramedics.

"Ma'am, please." He nodded towards the sofa.

She conceded, moving slowly towards the sofa. This was the part where he should've been reciting her Miranda rights. In a minute, he'd ask her and she'd admit what she'd done. Her chin lifted a fraction of an inch. She wouldn't deny it. There was nothing worse than a liar, and if he didn't ask she'd confess.

"Ma'am, were you aware your husband had been taking male performance enhancement drugs?"

"What?" Ruby swayed in her seat. *Of course they'd know that.* Embarrassing.

Lie or no? Lie or no?

"The coroner…," the officer shifted nervously, "expects to find large amounts of Viagra in his blood. We believe the medication was the cause of his heart attack."

"He had a heart attack?" she squawked. *Oh, definitely lie.* What good would confessing to the drugs be if the man had a heart attack? She could hardly blame herself for that.

"No. No. My husband, he didn't…We didn't." She was unable to look directly at the officer. That was more information than the gentleman had requested and certainly more than she'd ever in her life felt compelled to divulge. Her face burned. Under normal circumstances she would never even have stumbled near a conversation along this vein. The situation had her so flustered that if she didn't watch herself she'd next be telling him exactly how much she weighed and that she'd never worn the negligees in her trousseau.

"We understand, ma'am." He looked completely unmoved. "We see this more often than you'd think. Men believe they need to hide the things they do to feel young, virile. You knew about his recent hairline implants, we assume." He scratched his pen over a small blue notepad.

"Yes. Of course." *Who wasn't aware of those? Perhaps the blind couple on the corner missed them, but surely the gossip has made it that far anyway.*

Ruby cringed. She resented the plugs. She'd been denied a new stove for her baking because Ken had to have those plugs. It was for his self-esteem, he'd argued. He *needed* them for his self-esteem. *Moron.* Fat lot of good they'd do him now.

"The drugs he was taking in conjunction with the drugs for the implants, to fight infection, promote new hair growth…we suspect, they interacted poorly with the other medication. Taking them with this much Viagra in his system was a very unfortunate decision."

"I don't understand." Ruby let the words sink deep. "He had a reaction between medications?"

"Yes. It's likely the doctor who did the plugs," cough, "implants, was unaware of the other medication. Men don't tend to mention these things, Mrs. Russell. The doctor had no way of anticipating this. I don't see a lawsuit here." The officer looked at her with the look she'd seen all her life. Pity.

She turned away. Had she killed him or not? Was a confession still in order? She hadn't known anything about the other medications but did that make her culpable or not?

"Ma'am, one more thing, before I go." He moved towards the door.

Where was he going? Did he truly not understand what she'd done? "Yes?"

"Do you work outside the home?"

"No." Ruby's hands clutched at her own shoulders. How *would* she survive now? All his debt was on her.

"What will happen, financially?" He pressed.

"I – I don't know. We have funeral plans in place. The house has some equity…"

She quickly ran over what would happen to her. She could live with Michael until she got on her feet. They'd always been the best of friends. Charlotte would do what she could. There was no better girlfriend on earth. That was a fact.

Ruby leaned forward onto her thighs. Her blood pressure plummeted. She groaned when her ugly house shoes came in to view. Two curlers rolled out.

"Don't worry." Officer O'Leary's gruff voice replied. "You'll be taken care of, ma'am. I just wanted to get your reaction."

"What?" Her voice muffled beneath her bosom. She twisted her face upward to look into his.

"Your husband had insurance policies on you and also on himself, each worth more than a million dollars, and both were current. You'll be fine. Good day, ma'am. I'm sorry if I worried you unnecessarily." He shoved the silver pen into his notebook and tipped his hat to her before securing the heavy door behind him.

Ruby stared after him dumbly, replaying the words in her mind. *A million dollars, drug reaction, not my fault, a million dollars…a million dollars.* The horrendous morning combined with the after-effects of an entire box of wine made it impossible for her to concentrate.

She screwed her body around on the couch until her feet arched up over the arm, and she saw the pristine white ceiling aglow in the morning sunlight. She regretted not seeing Officer O'Leary out properly, but she didn't trust her legs to carry her. Instead, with great effort, she pulled an afghan over her head and prepared to sleep off her hangover. An insurance policy like the one he mentioned could make up for Ken's misgivings. She'd pay off his debt and have plenty left over to donate to charity. Or maybe she'd use the money to do something amazing like buy a Cutie's Cupcakes chain, or at least a new stove. Images of Ken's chocolate mousse mask played in her mind as she drifted to sleep.

Ruby woke a short time later with a start. The cupcakes! She ran for the phone as she took the stairs almost two at a time. Tripping slowed her progress dramatically. Inside her closet, she pulled on the first thing she saw and left a message for Betty Bates. She managed to do this as she brushed her teeth. Ruby doubted the message was coherent, but it was something.

Back downstairs, she moved more methodically, loading the cupcakes into four carriers. Each one held three dozen cupcakes in three tiers. Each also had a handle, but Ruby only had two hands, so she had to make two trips. She threw her purse over her shoulder and her glasses onto her face. In the van and on her way, she left another message for Betty. This one was more appropriate and apologetic, though Ruby's head was still in a thick fog.

The luncheon was almost twenty minutes away with traffic, and it was ten thirty The cupcakes were already an hour late and she had just left her development. Traffic was a nightmare. Summer Saturdays in the nearby city were something to be avoided. Street fairs, art shows and tourists had everything backed up all the way to the suburbs.

Ruby put her mirror to use. Her face was a pale mess. That wouldn't do. She rummaged for makeup in her oversized bag as she crept along. She found an old compact with powder, a tampon which she tried to apply to her lips accidentally and nothing for her eyes. At every light she tried her best to erase the circles and anxiety, but the effort was futile. Eventually she found a lip shade she hadn't worn in two seasons and tried it. The tampon had done a better job.

When Ruby arrived at the luncheon, the parking lot was full forcing her to park along the road and haul the pastries. Unfortunately, she still only had two hands and four large cupcake carriers.

She slung her bag over one shoulder and tucked one carrier between each bicep and her bosom. Then, she took another bundle in each hand and ran. The van door stood wide, but she refused to look back. Even if Ken had splurged for the automatic door shutter button, she couldn't have reached that either. Ruby tried to move swiftly. She was horrendously late and every moment counted. The carriers squeezed into her underarms threatened to jump with every step.

Betty stood at the gate glaring. Ruby knew she probably looked like someone who'd broken free from an outing of mentally retarded children. Her hair was a mess. She had on a sweatshirt, despite the day's warm temperature, that said I heart NY and green culottes with socks and track shoes. She was tilted forward unnaturally and huffing as she went. Betty looked horrified to be waiting for *her.*

When Ruby drew near, Betty snatched the carriers from

her hands. Ruby hurried along behind her with the final batches, unable to dislodge them without dropping them, and worried all the while they might fall. Her cheeks flamed with humility, and her arms bulged over the enormous cupcake containers. Her eyes brimmed with regret as Betty suddenly turned on her.

"I asked you to have these here two hours ago," she barked from between her teeth, unhinging the oversized carriers. Her smile was for show, in case anyone watched them.

"I-I'm sorry," Ruby gasped, catching her breath from her short run.

"Well, I hope whatever kept you was worth ruining my luncheon. I hope you realize how selfish it is to make a promise and then let everyone down like this." Betty unloaded the cupcakes onto several large trays for the tables outside.

Ruby leaned against the nearest work space and relieved her arms of their burdens. Betty didn't look in her direction.

"Ken died," Ruby whispered. It was the first time she'd said it aloud.

Betty looked her over and pulled her red lips to one side before speaking again. "I'm sorry to hear that." She lifted the trays and moved away from Ruby. As she exited onto the patio she added, "Charlotte would have delivered these on time if it were impossible for you to be here. Given the circumstances, you shouldn't have come."

Tears pooled behind Ruby's lids. She considered overturning every platter still waiting to go out. Instead, she turned away and walked slowly back to her van.

She was relieved to see her van still there, despite the open door. She didn't know how she would have gotten home otherwise. Leaving the door like that was irresponsible. She was on a roll, making rash decisions. It never ended well for her. Her skin crawled with memories of other rash decisions and she rubbed her sleeves roughly, fighting chills despite the warm, summer day. Ruby secured the rear door, climbed into the driver's seat and sat there.

Several minutes elapsed before she could start the engine. Ruby allowed herself to cry into the steering column under cover of her large brown sunglasses. They'd reminded her of *Charlie's Angels* when she bought them. She'd wanted Ken to notice. He hadn't, but how could he after looking at that girl all day?

Once again, her mood shifted from despair to defiance, and she started the van. Ruby wiped her face with the back of her sleeve and pulled erratically into traffic. Tires squealed as she cut off an oncoming ice cream truck. The little Jingle Brothers' bus swerved and beeped. Ruby didn't bother to look. She had calls to make at home.

"Michael?"

"Mama!" he cooed. "How are you? I missed your call last night, but I was planning to call this afternoon. What's going on?"

"Oh, that's alright, sweetheart."

Ruby didn't recall phoning him the night before, and she shuttered to think of him answering with her in such a wine-colored frame of mind. She probably would have told him everything, and then this morning his father would be gone. None of it mattered now. Michael didn't need to know.

"I was just thinking of my son."

"Well, it sounded like a party."

"No, no. Just the radio."

"Well, what's going on today, Mom? What's on your calendar?"

"Honey, I'm afraid I have terrible news."

She had run through a myriad of ways to tell the same

story and none of them were right. It wasn't a natural conversation. It shouldn't have happened. The call shouldn't need to be made, but it did.

After a long silent pause, Ruby spoke with her son. More than an hour passed before he agreed to say good-bye. He promised to be home in two days. He needed to get time off from school and work and arrange airfare. Until then, he said he'd check in regularly for support and encouragement. Michael had always been a godsend. He was sincere, respectful and courteous. He put others first. She could hear in his voice how his heart was broken for both his loss and for hers.

Ruby picked at the loose grout and chipped counter tiles as Michael told her he couldn't begin to imagine losing the love of his life. She looked at the lackluster cabinetry and linoleum flooring and heard little of what he said after that. The love of her life had left her long ago. She'd always been thankful Michael never doubted her affection for Ken or his for her, though, it had seemed an impossible façade to maintain as of late. At least he lived far away. *It is best for a child to believe in the strength of their parents' union. It has been a lie worth living.*

Ruby scowled at the wallpaper border over the cabinets while Michael agreed to call the extended family for her. She thanked him and was relieved to say good-bye.

Ruby needed her girlfriend.

"So, he's dead?" Charlotte tossed her bag onto the couch and tilted her head like an antenna trying to get in the clearest signal. She had been given that information over the phone, but apparently Charlotte still felt it necessary to get clarification.

"Yes." A smile slid across Ruby's face.

"Ruby!" Charlotte scolded.

"I'm sorry. I'm sad, too. He was Michael's father. I just – I hated him so much! He was mean and – and – a cheater!"

That would get Charlotte on-board. Ruby knew how callous she must sound, but after the original shock wore off, she was kind of pleased with her loss. Ken's death actually fixed a great many problems, not the least of which was getting rid of Mr. Harmon and Ken's debt. *No more public humiliation!* Ruby was elated with that. She knew she shouldn't be. People would think she was wicked. But she couldn't help it. She needed Charlotte to back her on it.

"What?" Charlotte exclaimed. Her husband had cheated on her a decade ago and she'd never gotten past it, even after his death. Considering those circumstances, Ruby knew getting Charlotte on her side was a foregone conclusion.

She set her wineglass down and grabbed Charlotte by the wrist. "Come on."

Charlotte was a tiny thing. Her hair emphasized her slight size. It was long and dark, and hung youthfully down her back or over her shoulders. Her wide brown eyes held secrets Ruby would never understand, and that was perfectly fine with her. She'd been a dedicated friend since the day they met, and Ruby couldn't possibly have found a better or more genuine and supportive companion. But Charlotte's trials and tribulations had always topped Ruby's, so having a kind of adventure of her own was exciting.

Together they raced to the closet. Ruby retrieved the evil box of curses and sat cross-legged on the bed like a schoolgirl. Charlotte joined her, and Ruby told her everything in complete confidence. Charlotte appeared appropriately horrified.

She hugged Ruby tightly and pressed their foreheads together. This was the way Charlotte always reacted when promising her undying loyalty.

"Well. That certainly changes things," she whispered. "I

suppose I'm not here to comfort you, like I planned. So, what do you want to do?" Charlotte eyed Ruby cautiously. She had to wait a bit while Ruby composed her thoughts.

After some deliberation, Ruby said "Shop."

CHAPTER THREE

The funeral was an awful affair. Thanks to their pre-planning, she couldn't change anything. The casket Ken had chosen was as obnoxious at his car. Which she'd quickly sold to commission the remodeling of her kitchen. The casket was maroon, the closest thing to red the funeral home had available. *Fortunately, it will soon be buried.* Meanwhile, she was required by etiquette to mill around it, comforting their family and friends.

Of course, everyone had heard, by then, how his death had come to pass. The crowd behaved as expected. Small cliques of men snickered in the more dimly-lit corners. Women smiled slyly and watched their husbands a little more closely.

The preacher, on the other hand, was a complete surprise. He was a local television personality, and most of the viewing area watched his show. He was almost as much an eye sore as Ken's god-awful casket. In her opinion, Reverend Flynn wasn't old enough to be a proper man of the cloth, but Ruby doubted it mattered. The whole event was nothing more than a formality. She kept her eyes on the preacher. It was irksome he didn't wear a collar. In fact, he wore a suit like everyone else. If she hadn't recognized him from television, she wouldn't have even known he was there to perform the service. He could have been a car salesman or Officer O'Leary, for that matter.

She still didn't know why he'd called her. She and Ken had never attended his church. They didn't know him. Truthfully, the Russells hadn't attended any service in years, but they were Catholics, if they were anything.

Reverend Flynn was not.

Ruby had purposefully stayed involved with St. Peter's Cathedral over the years, mostly as a volunteer. Despite the effort, her affiliation with the church was loose at best. She hadn't been in a hurry to call Father Frank and ask for representation. She knew she'd have to answer all of the tough questions about where they'd been all those years and why he never saw them. He'd want a promise from her to attend mass again regularly, and she was afraid to lie to a priest. Then there were confessions, tithes, penance, Hail Mary and rosaries. She was immobilized by the thought. What kind of penance would she get for what she had done to her husband? Ruby shivered and glanced around the room. When the coroner's report confirmed O'Leary's suspicions, drug interaction, she hadn't felt any better. She had been the one to give him the pills, even if he hadn't known it. Ruby still half-expected Officer O'Leary to come bounding in to arrest her. The fact it never happened only made the anticipation worse. And now here she was, doing her best to keep up appearances while inwardly she was about to go to pieces. Sweat stung her neck and back, threatening her new silk blouse. No one noticed. The only one watching was the preacher.

That jokester, Flynn, had called and offered to perform

Ken's service for free. It was an impossible offer, a sign. He wasn't a proper Catholic priest, but little could be done about that. It just so happened Reverend Flynn's asking price was the exact same amount Ruby hoped to spend, so they made a deal. She regretted the necessity of that bargain, and she cringed when he stood to begin the service.

"Friends," he began. "We're gathered here today to pay our respects to a beloved member of our community." Ruby coughed and shifted in her seat. She should have asked to see his little speech before he began. Ken had done nothing to contribute to the community, ever. Unless the community counted the amount of money he'd spent in it. If that were the case, he should have been the crowned ruler of Montrose Hills.

She glanced beside her to the empty chairs where Michael and Charlotte should've been. Charlotte, bless her heart, had tried to attend the funeral, only to wind up in the bathroom hyperventilating five minutes after seeing Ken in his casket. The last funeral she'd attended had been her own husband's, and being there with Ruby for Ken proved to be too much. Ruby sighed for her loss, thankful at least to have Charlotte waiting at the house when guests began to arrive.

"Kenneth Russell was a man of honor, trust and integrity." Reverend Flynn blathered on, adding inflection to the lies for interest's sake. She *had* told him her husband's name was Ken. Revered Flynn kept saying "Kenneth". She shifted in her seat as she pondered the strangeness of it all. Laid out in the ugliest casket ever created, "Kenneth" did seem to fit. She may as well have been crashing the funeral of a total stranger. Ruby's eyes rolled into her head behind the smart black veil of her mother's pillbox hat. *Who was he kidding? Maybe this was the standard speech for any funeral service.* Ruby considered preachers like him might have prewritten occasion and speech templates. This was the funeral one. She pictured him donning his suit that morning and thumbing through a large recipe box looking for the Fs. *Festivals, Frittatas, Funions. Oh, here it is, Funerals.* She rolled her lips together. That made sense. Wherever he found the speech, it certainly didn't apply to the stiff in the casket. *Stiff. Oh boy…*

Ruby shifted some more. She shut her eyes to remove the images gathered there and shielded her face with her right hand. Onlookers would think she was crying.

She wished Michael could have made it in on time. It seemed all things had conspired against him. First, his flight had every imaginable delay including weather and engine trouble. Then the rental place lost his car reservation, leaving him to drive a car he told her much resembled one of his high school sneakers. That was all before his luggage out and out vanished. So Ruby sat alone, fiddling with her pearls and waiting for Michael's arrival.

He'd phoned an hour before, but she still watched the door for him. She knew he'd be there as soon as possible. Reverend Flynn offered to postpone the service, but she opted not to wait. She and Michael could catch up at the wake. Besides, Michael would have been mortified by the whole spectacle. The man in the casket was nothing like the man Michael had called father. Combine that with the gaudiest casket ever made and the officious television preacher and it seemed best that Michael not bear witness to the whole mess.

"Today we're comforted with the knowledge that Kenneth Russell is in a much better place than the one from which he has transcended." Reverend Flynn was laying it on thick when Ruby tuned back in.

She couldn't believe he was still talking. She'd known Ken most of her life, but had she been speaking, she would've been done by then. *The reverend couldn't know what he was saying.* "A better place." *Dubious.* Ruby had her own ideas about where Ken woke up after enjoying her mousse. She covered her lips with a gloved hand as if to stifle a yawn and snickered. The black satin gloves served a dual purpose. They looked lovely, and they also covered the fact she had left her wedding rings at home.

"Though his death came as a surprise to us all, the pain of his loss is eased when we think of the way in which he passed," the preacher continued. "Happy." An unease crossed the chairs behind Ruby, and she rubbed her face to cover her own humor. "...at home and enjoying a special dessert made by the loving hands of his adoring wife."

Adoring? Ruby's eyes jumped to the face of the minister. The look he returned wasn't compassionate. To Ruby, it seemed cold and accusatory. Their silent exchange lasted long enough for Ruby to wonder if he'd also like to try her mousse.

He returned awkwardly to find his place in his notes, and he wrapped up the commentary without any further glances in Ruby's direction. A poem was read by someone on staff at the funeral home and one of Ken's cousins from Greenville sang a hymn to end the service.

When the theatrics were finally over, the spectators stopped briefly at the cemetery with the "fugly" casket. Ruby didn't condone profanity as a rule, but in this particular instance, the word fit perfectly. Michael arrived in time to say good-bye at Kenneth's graveside. Ruby was elated.

"Mom, I'm so sorry." He pulled her to him.

"Don't be silly. I'm just glad you're here."

"Okay, well, I'm here now, and I want you to let me handle things." He pulled her back to look into her eyes. "Mom, while I'm here, I want you to try and relax. Let me do what I can. I know crowds aren't your thing. You've already had to do so much on your own. Let Charlotte and I take care of everything." Michael arched his brows awaiting confirmation.

Ruby nodded dutifully. It wouldn't be a hardship on her with Michael "at the helm". He was such a good boy. She knew he'd take care of all the things she didn't feel like doing.

The group returned to the Russell house together for lunch. Ruby had taken each guest's preferences carefully into account. She had worked all night on the food, display and decor. Countless hours were spent before that perfecting the menu and making certain she'd thought of everything. This was her time to shine.

During the wake, she ate little and drank much.

"Mom," Michael rubbed Ruby's shoulders near the end of the wake. "You're doing great. Hang in there, okay? We're in the home stretch." He winked lovingly at her, offering reassurance, and went back to mingling with the crowd.

She saw him fidget with his phone as he mingled. Ruby had taught him to multitask and apparently it took. She missed seeing him. Michael had always been a good-looking kid, friendly, too. His honey brown hair and crystal blue eyes reeked of nobility. To Ruby, he was a prince. They were in sync, and undoubtedly, he was as ready as she was for the guests to leave them alone so they could catch up.

It had been too long. Michael told her there was something new going on in his life. They needed to have a heart-to-heart. She hoped he'd gotten a job offer closer to home. Then she could see him everyday again. She'd make him breakfast each morning before work and pack his lunches and prepare a new meal every evening. It'd be perfect, and they'd be able to really talk. Ruby loved their talks. Michael always seemed to value her opinions and insight. She knew she was the most important lady in his world. It was a sublime feeling, one she missed. Until then, she would have to wait for her guests to go home.

Hopelessly bored and torn between her guilt for contributing to his death and anger over his betrayal, Ruby decided it was time to check her meticulously planned spread. Nothing good ever came from dwelling. There were probably compliments waiting for her. She slid off her chair and moved in amongst the crowd. Everyone seemed to be in good spirits and the food was definitely disappearing. The two days she had spent in preparation were being rewarded.

Ruby wanted this event to be something people would remember. She'd gone to great lengths with the details. There'd never been so many people in her home before, and it was quite nice. Ken had never liked company. So until now, Ruby had only been able to imagine how nice it might be to feed a crowd and hostess an event. If it weren't for all of the black attire, no one would have ever guessed the purpose for her gathering. *It will be nice to do this again sometime, now that Ken isn't around to mind.*

"Well, I see you finally got those new appliances you've been wanting." The snappy voice was like fingernails on a chalkboard inside her head. Ruby jumped as she refilled trays of fruit and sandwiches. She turned carefully to see Tillie, flanked on either side by her cul-de-sac crew. None of them had actually been invited but she wasn't about to make a scene and ruin her shining moment.

"Hello, Tillie," Ruby offered. "I'm glad you could make it."

She lifted the empty bowls from the table and nestled them in her arms.

"We heard you're set for life now," Tillie blurted. "You get insurance cash and no more no-good-cheating husband. What luck for you, huh?" Tillie's eyes were speculative and

Ruby began to sweat. Every smack of the obnoxious green gum felt like an accusation.

"Excuse me," Ruby smiled and turned to escape the woman whose perfume was already permeating her draperies. She'd have to replace those. Even a good dry cleaning couldn't help them now.

"We understand." Tillie trailed behind Ruby with her girls in tow, like a mama duck with her ducklings. "We understand plenty about your situation. What I don't understand is why there are no sugar free desserts here? You should be more considerate of your guests." She anchored one jewelry laden hand on a slender hip.

The combination of Tillie's announcement of Ken's indiscretions and the insinuation Ruby had in any way failed to provide the best in her efforts for the reception had her immediate and full attention.

"What do you understand about my situation?"

"We've all been here. We're all divorced. You know that."

"Divorced?" Ruby hissed.

Tillie nodded.

"Divorced and *widowed* are different. Don't you think?" Ruby's lungs burned. All the air had been vacuumed from the room around her. She'd worked very hard to consider each of her guests. Tillie was not one of them.

All her hard work over the last two days and she hadn't gotten even one compliment. Instead, Ruby had gotten a complaint. A complaint!

Oblivious, Tillie quacked, "My healthy diet and exercise routine is what keeps me fit. Maybe you might want to think about something like that…now you'll be on the prowl." She slurped white wine from a plastic cup and elbowed the nearest duckling.

Ruby's cheeks flushed red. She mostly certainly would

not be on the prowl. She wasn't some kind of animal. She'd married for life, unlike Tillie and her pack of tarts. She wouldn't expect them to understand. But she'd be damned if she let Tillie undermine the hard work she had done to turn out the gourmet spread.

Ruby struggled back through the crowd to her kitchen. If she didn't unload her arms soon, she'd drop everything on the floor. She didn't suppose Tillie would want to clean that up.

"She should have gotten a coffee cake from Treeline." Tillie turned to her cohorts. "Their coffee cake is amazing, sugar free, made with organic ingredients, and much better, not this dry..."

Ruby heard Tillie insulting her buffet as she and her entourage dispersed with plates full of veggies. Tillie's behavior deserved rebuke. It was thoroughly unacceptable, rude and inappropriate. Ruby placed the bowls in her sink and returned to her previous post. She was thankful to find her wine where she'd left it. She filled the glass dangerously full and decided to watch the crowd from her sunroom instead. Sulking away, she carried her drink in one hand and the bottle in the other.

Tillie had ruined her husband's wake and insulted her cooking. Someone needed to teach Tillie Tanner some manners.

News crews gathered in the cul-de-sac. Ambulances, cameras and a rather large crowd trapped Ruby's van in the driveway. Ruby hid on the floor behind her sofa, peeking over the top occasionally to monitor the scene outside. Though she knew what she'd done, she hadn't anticipated the over-the-top response.

She could see the television in the kitchen from her hideout on the living room floor, but the remote was out of her reach. It was difficult to hear the news anchor, and she was awful at reading lips. Ruby was never good at making plans, either, but she needed one to get that remote, so she gave it a shot. Shoving one house shoe off using the opposite foot, she retrieved it awkwardly with her hand.

Three. Two. One.

The slipper catapulted over the island, rapping the television sharply. *That was a stupid plan.* She shoved the other slipper down over her heel and pulled it between her big and first toe until her fingers could reach it. *Biscuits.* It was no use. She didn't bother tossing it. She just dropped the slipper and turned onto her knees again to watch out the window. She couldn't raise the volume on the television by hitting it with something.

If only she could hear what was being said, she might survive the pending stroke. Ruby's heart skipped and jumped in her chest. Only a few feet separated her from the action, but she heard nothing. Ruby cursed her energy efficient windows for their silence. She was stuck. Opening a window was impossible. It would draw too much attention, so Ruby sat alone, silently assaulting her stubby fingernails.

When she'd snuck onto Tillie's porch that morning, she hadn't expected such a brouhaha to ensue. She'd gotten up before dawn to create her mama's three pound sugar-laden perfection. Her mama's coffeecake beat any she'd ever tried, hands down. Nothing else came close. The day was perfect. School was out and there would be no early risers catching busses or chauffeuring children. Ruby waited in the mudroom for more than thirty-five minutes for Tillie to take her tiny rat-dog for its morning walk around the neighborhood. It was infuriating, that Tillie had run so late on a day when Ruby had worked so hard. She'd even begun to worry the Treeline coffee cake might arrive before Tillie ever left home. Luckily, Tillie was around the corner before the bakery truck pulled up. *It* was right on time.

Ruby watched the man dressed all in white, climb the stairs to Tillie's porch, rap twice on the door and leave the perfect white pastry box on her swing. Ruby waited until the brake lights were out of sight. Then she slid from her hiding place, replaced the Treeline coffee cake with her own and returned to her kitchen for a fresh pot of coffee. All-in-all, she had felt that it had been a successful mission.

Ideally, Tillie would have eaten the entire cake herself and gained ten pounds, but she'd settle for running into her later and asking about the cake. Once she and her lackeys raved about it, Ruby would whip out the true Treeline cake and show Miss Skinny that it wouldn't be a real coffee cake without sugar. Instead, Ruby sipped espresso and watched as car after car arrived and the occupants were welcomed in again and again. She considered the coffee cake might be a prop, a formality for skinny people. Maybe it was something they set out on the table for show, stared longingly at but never touching. Perhaps no one would eat it at all. From Ruby's dining room table, the ladies seemed to have been having a gay old time together. With her windows cracked, Ruby listened to their catty laughter and the shrill annoying pitch of Tillie's voice. The radio in Tillie's kitchen window played bandstand, and Ruby swore the women danced between rounds of cards.

Overcome with impatience she shut her own windows tight to snuff out the merriment, and went to take her shower. She trudged upstairs annoyed and disappointed. Half an hour later, she returned to chaos. If only she'd left her windows open.

Tillie Tanner is an unscrupulous tart. Ruby scratched remnants of polish from her nails. *A waste of perfectly good oxygen. Sadly, there is less and less clean air. But there are more and more people like Tillie.* She probably knew what Ruby had done and called the police. O'Leary would be back in no time asking her if she knew how long she'd go to jail for theft. As if she hadn't done them a favor. The twelve dollar cake was not worth all this nonsense! She had every intention of playing the grieving widow card. *I wasn't thinking clearly, Officer O'Leary.* Then she would return the inferior pastry to its rightful owner. *Silliness.*

The confounding and astronomically infuriating part was the media presence. Channel 3 hadn't shown up to document Ken's death, and that was a Death with a capital D! This was just the case of one neighbor doing another neighbor a delicious favor. What the ambulances stayed for was beyond her. Yes, call 9-1-1 and everyone under the sun shows up, it was only natural she supposed. Everyone was curious. It wasn't often emergency vehicles came to her neighborhood, but having them line the street was embarrassing. She supposed the ambulances were meant to assure the safety of all the home's occupants -- from the deadly confection. She rolled her eyes. Montrose Hills was a respectable neighborhood, not Compton.

Then again, Tillie always drew a crowd. Ruby rolled her eyes.

It was a complete waste of taxpayer dollars for so many emergency vehicles to loiter as they were doing . Tillie had hosted her Tuesday morning card club for years. She and some friends played Bridge every week. She'd never invited Ruby, not once. It was like some exclusive club for the same five women. Ruby wondered which of them had called the police.

While she struggled to remember which car had arrived first and tried to figure out if she had been somehow caught in the act, her stomach growled. She wished she had some of her coffee cake while she waited. She spent the next few minutes thinking of what she'd make to eat, when she was able, and contemplating the carpets. They were in remarkable condition considering their age. It was a testimony to her dedicated housekeeping.

Finally, the stretcher rolled out. "A stretcher?" she whispered. Ruby held her breath then, hoping it was nothing serious, Tillie was awful, but one death was enough for the week. Ruby's heart leapt into a frenzy. The person on the gurney was covered head to toe in a white sheet. "Oh dear." What on earth went on over there during their wild parties? Maybe it was a good thing she shut them out and went to take a shower. Whatever she missed must've been vile.

Ruby scooted on her backside over to the kitchen island and fished around with one hand over her head for the remote. Luckily nothing stayed a secret on her street. She'd have the full details by bedtime. For now she had to rely on the news. Her fingers shoved the remote further and further away until she was forced to get into a squat to retrieve it. She pointed into the air and pushed buttons until she heard the voice of the Channel 3 reporter on her lawn. Guilt tinged her heart the moment relief hit her. No one wanted to arrest her for swapping cakes. Thank heavens. She had a lot of nasty gossip to clear up already, she didn't need any more. This was her fresh start.

"We're here at a devastating scene in Montrose Hills this morning. Five are dead in an apparent bakery debacle."

Ruby sucked air hard into her lungs. Her eyes bulged and she turned quickly to the window. She crawled full speed, head down, until she hit the couch.

"Heavens," she breathed. Her lungs rose and fell at a runner's pace. Afraid now to see what was coming, she peered like a frightened child into a darkened closet, at the monstrous possibility before her.

One.

Two.

Three.

Four…Oh my.

EMTs rolled the linen covered stretchers one by one into the road.

"The five women gathered for a friendly game of Bridge," the reporter continued. "Friends since their stints in Woodland Rehabilitation following complications with their diabetes."

Nuts. It really *was* an exclusive club. *They were survivors.*

Well…they had been…at one time…

Before the fifth stretcher came forward, Ruby had crawled upstairs and was trying to disguise herself with a rain hat and coat. She'd torn frantically through her entire closet looking for something inconspicuous, but there were no decent disguises in her wardrobe. An old raincoat and hat would have to do. The television in her room showed the crowd pushed onto the sidewalks making an avenue for the line of ambulances. This was her chance.

Ruby inched downstairs and looked long into her pantry. She didn't want to leave. There was plenty of sustenance in there to outlast the commotion in the street, but she was compelled to flee. Fight or flight always ended in flight for Ruby. It took all the courage she could muster, but she forced herself away from the pantry and out her mudroom door.

Sneaking into the side yard wearing her Farrah Fawcett sunglasses, she planned to enter her minivan undetected. With the ambulances gone, she had a chance to slip away. "Excuse me!" called a voice too near for Ruby to pretend she didn't hear it. Ruby looked back at her house. It was also too late to make a run for her pantry.

She tried to look casual and turned to see the news reporter straightening her jacket. She was trailed by a man with a large camera at his side. It should have come as less of a surprise to her when she discovered the escape was foiled.

"Hi! I'm Emma Eaken with Channel 3." The woman stretched her hand out to Ruby.

Ruby's bottom lip sucked in over her teeth and her nearly invisible brows dove together for protection.

"Um," Ruby leaned against her van, wishing hard she'd hidden in her pantry when she'd had the chance. Cowering was her specialty. She hated herself for being brave enough to run. See where that had gotten her?

"Do you live here?" Emma asked somberly.

Ruby nodded too quickly, feeling like a portly bobble head in a raging wind.

"Did you know these ladies?" She snapped her fingers. The man shadowing her hoisted the camera onto his shoulder.

Ruby was frozen in its light. "No."

"Surely you knew Ms. Tanner," Emma pressed, glancing at the proximity. "Tell me about her."

"Uh."

"What's the matter?" Emma really looked at Ruby now, scrutinizing her strange ensemble. The sun was already warm, though it was early, and the forecast was for heat.

"Are you going to the hairdresser?"

"No." *That would be insensitive.* She shouldn't be getting her hair done in the midst of such tragedy.

"What's with the rain hat, then?" Emma's face contorted as if she might laugh.

Ruby grimaced at Emma's reaction. It was tasteless on her part, and showed her poor rearing. While sidetracked by the demise of American parenting, she noted Emma had a point. She did look silly.

Right.

"I'm not feeling well. I'm going to the pharmacy for some aspirin." The words came out brusque and hoity. It was none of the nosey reporter's business where Ruby went.

Emma's lips pulled hard to one side as she surveyed Ruby in her raincoat and plastic cap. After a long pause, she drew one well-manicured finger across her neck. The camera went down behind her. The duo strode away, and Ruby drove to Charlotte's home, breaking more traffic laws than she'd ever thought possible. Her behavior was shameful and she knew it. Someone could have been hurt.

Ding dong. Ding dong. Ding dong.

Thump, thump, thump.

"Good glory in the morning!" Charlotte's eyes squinted into the sunlight. "What on earth are you doing?" Charlotte looked at Ruby and then pulled her friend inside.

"What are you supposed to be dressed up for, anyway? You look like Maude." Charlotte pulled her satin robe tightly across her middle and secured it with the ties. "I suppose you want coffee?"

Ruby nodded.

"Hmph."

"Well, out with it then, are you going to tell me what brought you out of your house looking like that?"

Ruby collapsed into Charlotte's recliner. "Oh, Charlotte. I've done a very bad thing. I've made quite a mess…a real mess this time."

"Ruby, honey, it was an accident. How were you supposed to know he would die?" Clearly, Charlotte wasn't listening and she launched into her speech. "Losing a spouse is traumatic. It was bound to catch up with you emotionally. What you did wasn't anything more than what any other woman would've done in your shoes. You overreacted, and you were in shock, and you were drinking." Charlotte narrowed her eyes at Ruby, but Ruby was lost in thought staring at the ceiling. "The whole thing was a big misunderstanding really."

"Not that, Charlotte! Goodness sake."

With the coffee percolating behind her, Charlotte approached Ruby, who was still wearing her disguise. "Take off those stupid things and tell me what on earth is going on then." She tapped her foot and crossed her arms over her chest in her best no-nonsense pose.

"I went out this morning and switched Tillie's coffee cake." She pulled her sunglasses down to the tip of her nose and waited.

"What? Why?" Charlotte's eyebrows rose in obvious confusion. Her mouth twisted but she didn't speak again. It was evident she needed further explanation.

"I made her a new one with my mama's recipe. Her coffee cake is heaven on Earth." She sighed, flipping the glasses onto the coffee table as she considered the double entendre of her chosen words. "I swapped it for the one from Treeline that's delivered every Tuesday."

"What's this about? Is it because she complained you didn't order one for Kenneth's wake? Are you making some kind of point? Why the cape and hat?"

Poor Charlotte always misses the point. Ruby sighed.

"She's diabetic." Ruby watched the words sink in.

"Oh. Oh!" Charlotte's eyes bulged, and she sat in the chair nearest Ruby. "Is she alright? Did you forget?"

"She's dead, and no I didn't forget. For Pete's sake, Charlotte, keep up! How would I know that? All her flaunting and talk about a healthy diet and exercise. I assumed it was for the attention or so she could fit in her horrible clothes! I wanted to show her I am an incredible baker. Treeline would be lucky to have me. They would."

"What do you mean she's dead? How do you know?" Charlotte's cheeks flushed and she leaned back in the chair. She didn't look too good.

"It's on the news." Ruby groaned and then flipped the television on using the remote from the table. "They're all dead."

Charlotte's head shot up before her torso slumped over the arm of the chair in a faint.

"Charlotte. Charlotte." Ruby smacked at her friend's cheeks firmly. "Charlotte! Get up! I need you!"

Charlotte's lids struggled to open again. Without a word, she turned her full attention on the news before her.

"They were all diabetic," Ruby explained. "How was I to know? This isn't my fault. You need to eat more, by the way. You can't go around collapsing at every ounce of excitement."

"It most certainly is your fault! What were you thinking? Who cares if she didn't like your stupid coffee cake?"

"I do! And she might've liked it. I'll never know, but that wasn't the only thing. She was on to me about Kenneth, asking questions and being hoity."

"Hoity? That's a crime now? Punishable by death? For crying out loud, Ruby, you've killed six people this month!"

Ruby whirled to face her friend. "No, I have not! Kenneth had a heart attack, and those women weren't supposed to be diabetic. Those were accidents."

"They're dead! DEAD!"

"I think the news lady from Channel 3 is suspicious, too. I also didn't like the look the preacher was giving me at the funeral." Ruby chewed thoughtfully on her thumbnail as she stared off into space and considered her predicament.

"Ruby! Get a hold of yourself! Of course she seemed suspicious. She's an investigative reporter, and he's a minister!"

Now that point Ruby would have to dispute. "He's a Pentecostal," she argued. "He's hardly a minister."

Ruby rose to pour the coffee since it was clear Charlotte wasn't going to.

The kitchen was a shambles. Piles of ingredients covered Charlotte's counter. Bags of random sizes were strewn haphazardly atop a dozen mediocre cookbooks, and small appliances dotted the floor.

"What's this?" She spun on her heels. "You're, what, baking now?" The accusation was strong. Ruby was the baker. Charlotte was the helper. "No!" She settled back into the chair. "Well, yes, I had to agree. You know how Betty can be."

"Betty called you to bake?" The words barely escaped from behind clenched teeth.

"Yes, well, she said she couldn't count on you because the last time the cupcakes barely arrived in time for dessert, and she specifically asked they be there for setup." Charlotte's eyes stayed on the carpet. "I should have called you, but she gets me so flustered.

"Anyway, I guess I had to bake. You were busy committing a quadruple homicide, or whatever you call it. I don't even know the word for killing five people at once!"

"Hey!" Ruby's stumpy finger flew into the air. "Those cupcakes were late last time because my husband died that morning! I couldn't very well excuse myself from police questioning to deliver her stinking cupcakes!"

Her eyes stretched wide before they narrowed. "We're in this together, you." She glared at Charlotte for her dissention. "You knew full well what was happening and did nothing. That makes you a co-conspirator!"

"What?"

"That's right." Ruby's blond head bobbed frantically again. "Yep. That's right, sister. Turn me in or cover for me.

Those are your options. You'd make a terrible inmate."

Her voice softened on the final words. She was bullying poor Charlotte. She hated when people did that, and there she was doing the very same thing. "Here's your coffee." Ruby strode gracelessly across the floor and delivered the cup to her dearest friend. "I don't mean to yell." She resumed her position in the recliner.

Charlotte nodded slowly. "You've got to stop yelling at me. You're all wound up, and I can't think. This is quite a predicament, Ruby. We need to think, not argue. I told her the same thing. Betty, I mean, about the cupcakes. She was just bullying me. I'm a victim here." Charlotte's voice sounded small and insecure.

Ruby laid a hand on her friend's. "I know. I'm the same. I feel guilty all the time that I'm not better."

"Better at what?"

"Anything."

They exchanged a long look, forming an unspoken truce and recommitting themselves to a lifelong allegiance. Together, they would get through this.

"You're a great mom," Charlotte said. "Just look at Michael."

"You were a perfect wife," Ruby replied.

"You are a gifted baker, Ruby."

Their fight was over.

"You're my best friend," Ruby said.

"Alright then."

CHAPTER FOUR

Reverend Flynn arrived at Ruby's house that afternoon. Horrible timing. Ruby couldn't think of anyone she wanted to see less than she wanted to see him. Also, he wasn't invited. She could have been indecent or entertaining company. Neither of those had been true in a very long time, but surely the Reverend couldn't know that. His uninvited arrival was simply rude.

When Ruby heard the doorbell, she expected to find a salesman or some religious zealot. It turned out she was right on both counts. Reverend Flynn probably thought Catholics were a cult and had come to peddle his Church of Hope to her. Of course, he'd probably heard of her insurance money and wanted to add her to his list of tithers.

"Good afternoon, Mrs. Russell. I was wondering how you're doing and if there's anything the church might do for you in your time of loss."

Ruby swung the door open and motioned the reverend inside. She was all out of energy after the morning's tragedy and her argument with Charlotte. The reverend would assume it was widow's grief. She wasn't sure if she cared. If he wanted to be entertained fashionably, then he should have waited for an invitation.

"Sweet tea, Reverend?" Her voice reflected her fatigue and irritation.

"I'd love some." He removed his hat and seated himself on the sofa near the window. "You can call me Glenn."

Glenn Flynn.

Pentecostals.

"I'm getting on very well considering all things." Ruby smiled sweetly as she returned from the kitchen with their tea.

"It was odd, wasn't it?"

"What's that, Reverend, uh, Glenn?" She handed him a tall glass of iced sweet tea.

"The way he went." Reverend Flynn sipped the tea and nodded approvingly.

Ruby halted, then took her time placing her tea onto a new doily. She twisted the glass back and forth before looking at him. "It was a horrific embarrassment." The way Ken had looked on that stretcher, being taken to the ambulance, was actually horrifying. Nearly everyone on the block had seen it for themselves; Ken and his tiny teepee. There had even been a moment when she'd wondered if he'd fit in his casket that way.

"Horrific?" Reverend Flynn seemed puzzled somehow.

"Yes." Her voice was barely a whisper. "Glenn, of all the ways to go." She couldn't finish. She tried again. "If he wasn't dead, he would have died of embarrassment. My husband was a decent man."

That was what she was supposed to say, right? She doubted telling the reverend she really thought he went out the way he deserved, desperate to deposit something that no one living outside the city zoo wanted, was the correct response.

Silence stretched out between them, while Ruby's disgust for Ken was renewed. Reverend Flynn seemed to feel the same. He held the tea but didn't drink it. He watched Ruby unspeaking.

"More tea?"

"Ah, no thank you, Mrs. Russell." Reverend Flynn had a strange look on his face. "Have you spoken to his doctors?"

He was wearing a suit again despite the heat. It was confounding to her, the idea of door-to-door ministry. She eyed him top to bottom.

"No. Did you think I should have?" She hadn't expected an inquisition. Ruby wiped her brow. Heat crept over her cheeks and her tummy swam along with the room.

"Well, don't you want to know if they were each aware of the prescriptions?"

Ruby's face burned to her forehead. It occurred to her this man was setting up his own investigation of sorts. He shouldn't have had those details. She eyed him smugly then, with understanding.

Ah…Pentecostals. They were a nosey people.

"Mrs. Russell, we're each called home at our time. Only our Father," he motioned at her ceiling fan, "knows when and why."

"Reverend Flynn," she returned his tone. "I know why he died. I want to know why you're so interested. Did you know him?"

Reverend Flynn fell silent.

She reached for her tea. Sunlight streamed through the window and into the tall glass, sending sheaths of amber across the table. He was right. It was very good. When she felt her hands begin to vibrate, she replaced the tea and pulled them back into her lap at once. Glenn noticed.

"Is something the matter? Was it something I said?"

Reverend Glenn leaned towards her. His hands flitted without purpose in the air.

Ruby's eyes were heavy. She looked at the ceiling to steady herself. She had no idea how to get Reverend Flynn out of her house, but she wanted a lawyer.

"I hope I haven't upset you. It wasn't my intention. I stopped to express my condolences, to offer my services…"

A gasp ripped through her throat as she locked eyes with this person before her. "I think it's time you go, sir. I'm in no need of your services." She breathed the final word to imply a terrible scandal and he recoiled.

"Mrs. Russell. I didn't! I wouldn't." He stood and moved towards the door, shaking his head as he moved. "There's been a misunderstanding. I'm very sorry if I've offended you."

Ruby followed closely. Under the circumstances, Reverend Flynn continued moving away from her until he found himself on her front porch.

"You needn't return here, Reverend Flynn. You aren't welcome." Ruby closed the door in his face with a snap, leaving Glenn holding his tea in consternation.

She pressed her back against the door and saw his hat remained on her table. Grabbing it by the brim in one hand, she hiked up the front window with the other. Ruby called his name once before throwing the hat in his direction like a dilapidated Frisbee. It flipped in the air twice before landing in the shrubs just beyond the porch.

She slammed the window before him and drew the curtain. He left the tea on the front steps along with some church literature and a small New Testament like they gave away at the county fair. Ruby watched from between the slats on her mini blinds until he was gone. The tiny Bible was pink, probably to make her feel like it was meant for a woman. *Much too radical a gesture*. They needed to tighten the reins on those people.

How rude could one man be? Not only had he dropped in unannounced, but he spent his time there asking personal questions. Hopefully she'd seen the last of the good Reverend Flynn.

Bravely, she peeked at her lawn once more. The gray sedan was gone from her drive, along with the Frisbee in her bushes. His church paraphernalia remained on her steps. There was a $500 fine in Montrose Hills for littering. She idly considered turning him in. Ruby cracked open the door and looked for witnesses, then slid out into the sun.

She collected the things from her porch as soon as the coast was clear and carried the propaganda to the trash. *Good riddance.* Then, while placing the glass into her new cast iron under mount sink, the headline on the church bulletin caught her attention.

Reverend Glenn Flynn will speak at the Youth Awareness Rally next Thursday at noon. The rally will be held in the Montrose District Library. Proceeds will go to support the Girls and Boys Club of Montrose Hills.

That gave Ruby an idea.

She dug through boxes of books in the attic looking for her mother's old things. Mama had been an avid gardener and herbalist. Ruby hadn't allowed herself to think of her mother in a very long time. She'd loved to bake, and she helped support the family by selling her creations. Ruby always enjoyed watching her in their kitchen after school and helping in the family garden in the evenings. One book in particular would be of great use to Ruby, if she found it.

Dry, stifling heat burned her eyes and throat. Attics always made her claustrophobic. The exposed dusty rafters held the scent of a smoldering campfire and Ruby coughed. Tentatively, she perused the archives, stepping softly around crates full of memories, careful not to disturb them. With her senses assaulted, it was difficult to concentrate. Too many stimuli. Too much history.

There. She dusted off the cover of an old medical journal. Her mother had kept recipes for medicines in it, until Rose's death. Ruby's eyes stung with the memory and she pushed the thought aside. Mama had never really recovered from that, and Ruby had sworn she'd do what she could to take her mama's place in the family. She took up the cooking and cleaning and care of her mama. When her father left them, it had been a blessing to have one less mouth to feed. Ruby had been relieved and her mother had barely been any the wiser. It was sad, but the truth of the matter was that Ruby's mother had stopped living long before she had actually died.

She stood and tossed the remaining books back into the box and hurried out of the attic. Ruby tried to leave the past behind, all while bringing a portion along. The walls seemed to close in on her.

She didn't want to end up like her mother.

The doorbell was ringing as she locked the attic door behind her and tucked the key into her brassiere. "Good grief," Ruby muttered as she hastened along, smoothing her hair and drying her sweaty palms against her trousers.

Her heart was a flutter. She had so much to do and no time for distractions. She paused before the front door and took a deep breath. Her hands trembled slightly and the extreme heat of the attic made her chest itch. She hoped the hives didn't return. They were an astounding misery.

Ruby checked the driveway to find a small white car had replaced Reverend Flynn's gray one. Whoever had dropped in unannounced this time was welcome simply because they weren't Reverend Flynn. That one had better never return.

When the bell rang again, Ruby jumped. Her hand rested on the knob.

Claire Cummins stood on the opposite side, carrying a basket of mammoth muffins. The basket rested upon a navy blue book, presumably a photo album. She looked dazzling in the afternoon sun. Claire was young, thin, blonde and pleasant. She was one of Ruby's favorite people, hopelessly flawed and completely inappropriate for Michael.

That was important to Ruby. Had there ever been any suspicion of funny business between them, Claire would have landed on her backside somewhere near the curb. Michael didn't need any distractions.

That said, she was a refreshing sight.

"Claire, do come in. What have we here?" Ruby immediately recognized the chocolate zucchini muffins. It was one of the first recipes they'd made together. Always Claire's favorite, and one of Ruby's as well.

"I made our muffins."

Well, she is certainly thoughtful. Though Ruby thought it terrible manners to simply show up, she decided to forego the lecture. If Claire didn't understand basic etiquette by now, it'd be a fruitless endeavor on Ruby's part. Besides, the day had zapped her energy and Claire's muffins smelled like heaven.

"Whoa. Look at this kitchen!" Claire stood motionless in the doorway, trying to take in the scene before her.

"Do you like it?"

Claire was awestruck. Ruby's new kitchen was both magnificent and designed for use, a beautiful work of art and much more. She had conceived, nurtured and implemented every detail especially for her baking. Claire moved slowly around the perimeter of polished stone trailing her fingers behind her on the perfect bullnose counter.

"This is amazing. May I?" She tilted her head towards the cabinetry.

"Of course." Ruby sat at the island and watched. A smug little smile tugged at the corners of her mouth. Ruby was very proud of her kitchen, which she considered her second greatest accomplishment, the first being Michael.

Claire tipped the small door below the sink to reveal a hidden sponge rack. She pulled out the three bin trash drawer beside the dishwasher, and Ruby watched the proverbial light bulb flash on. Claire understood. She moved to the prep sink and tugged gently on the cabinet to its right. Another trash bin rolled out. Drawers with slide away compartments doubled as chopping boards, or second tier containment for frequently used items. Rollouts brought cookware to her hands. Ruby'd never have to crawl on her knees to reach the pan in the bottom of a low level cabinet again.

"Wow."

"Wow indeed." Ruby's chin lifted a fraction of an inch.

Ruby hefted a muffin to her lips and sighed. She'd set two steaming cups of coffee upon the counter. "These are fabulous." Ruby rubbed her fingertips against a linen napkin in her lap.

"They're all you. You know, at school, they encourage us to take our favorite recipes and add something unexpected. They call it zest. I've never found a single thing to improve this recipe. It's actually perfect."

Ruby's cheeks flushed and her lids slipped a bit, savoring the moment. The praise left her feeling generous.

"You're an exceptional young woman, Claire. Your mother must be very proud."

"She thinks I'm wasting my life baking. I was supposed to follow in her footsteps and become a CPA." Her expression made Ruby chuckle. She'd rolled her eyes reminding Ruby of a mirror two decades past. Claire was as much a surrogate to Ruby as Ruby had been to her.

"Well, we can't all please our parents," Ruby murmured softly against the steamy edge of her mug. Scents of French roast mingled nicely with the chocolate in the air.

"I can think of one."

Ruby knew immediately where Claire's thoughts were. "He was home for the funeral. He's very happy, doing well, and missing his mother, I hope."

"Oh." Claire traced the mug's handle with her thumb. "I'm truly sorry about Mr. Russell. I hated not being here for the funeral. I wanted to be there for you, but I didn't get word until it was all said and done."

"You didn't miss much."

Claire frowned, and Ruby knew she was being unseemly. She pushed her hair from her forehead and refilled their cups. She wouldn't apologize. "That Reverend Flynn officiated."

"From the Church of Hope?"

"Mmhmm." Ruby imagined him in a mousse mask.

"He's such a schmo," Claire complained.

"Yes. Precisely that." Ruby's eyes widened. She nodded and broke open another saucer sized muffin.

"How are you holding up?" Claire kept her voice gentle, a child comforting a mother.

"Just fine, dear. Don't you worry about me. I'm a tough cookie." Ruby winked.

"Okay. Well, I'm home now for a while, so we'll have more time to hang. Here, I brought an album to show you."

Ruby sighed. Hopefully Michael wasn't falling victim to the same vernacular at his school. It was a possibility. Before she could get lost on the tangent, Claire shoved an album under Ruby's hand.

"Feeling reminiscent, or are you going to show me all you've been up to in the big city?" *Heaven help her*.

Claire looked aghast and Ruby relaxed a bit. She'd seen what young women today would allow to be photographed. Intrigue crept in. *What has Claire chronicled and brought along?*

She made a raspberry sound and flipped open the cover. "This is a book of my creations and their recipes. It's just like the ones we used here after school."

"Excellent."

Together, the ladies settled into a comfortable afternoon of small talk and common interest. Claire clearly enjoyed the kinship she found in Ruby's company and never said a word about her evident distraction. Ruby, meanwhile, allowed her mind to wander frequently to other matters.

Claire's visit gave her plenty of food for thought.

*****

The following Friday morning, Reverend Flynn arrived to find a splendid display of baked goods in the church foyer. Everything looked delicious. The crowning jewel seemed to be a set of mammoth chocolate zucchini muffins. The card attached simply said, "Thank you for all your efforts at yesterday's youth rally. The event was a rousing success."

Another perk of being a minister. Though women didn't exactly beat down his door for a date, they did provide him with food. He rarely had to cook these days. Unfortunately, he hadn't had much of an appetite since Kenneth Russell's death.

Glenn meandered around his office. Something about the century-old parish warmed his heart. Even the furniture had been in place for the better part of that time. Placing his hat atop the coat tree, he headed for his chair before deciding where to begin. His inbox brimmed with duties awaiting his attention. Attending the rally on the previous afternoon had set him back more than he expected.

Stained glass reflected light majestically onto his planner. Beautiful sheaths of blue, green and gold twinkled over his desk and carpet. Nearly as beautiful as the sounds of laughter floating up the hallway from the kitchen. Many familiar voices, and a few new ones, drifted upward, hard at work within the parish. Leading such a motivated flock allowed him to focus on his work in the community. For this, he was ever thankful.

A young woman rushed past his door.

"Amy." He recognized her at once as the secretary's daughter. Amy came in on Friday mornings to clean the nursery before preparing sandwiches for the homeless shelter.

"Yes, Reverend Flynn."

"Take these with you today, won't you?" He gestured at the amazing array of baked goods. "It's not often we can do something more special than a few sandwiches."

Amy's smile showed pride and approval at his suggestion. "Right away." She left immediately with the basket of baked treats, and Reverend Flynn returned to his study.

Glenn wasn't sure why Kenneth Russell's death bothered him so much, but it did. In his opinion, the whole thing was amiss. First, Dave Douglas' daughter showed up with a man twice her age, then the man died in an unthinkable condition. Now, no one was asking the most obvious of questions, and that included Kenneth's wife. Glenn believed coincidences only occurred in books and on the big screen. In his experience, most things happened for a reason.

He remembered the first time Kenneth had attended

services with Daisy on Sunday morning. They'd arrived together, arms locked at the elbows. He had led her with muted authority. She allowed him. They sat near the back of the small worship center, both wearing warm autumn tones. Sunday attire had never particularly caught his attention, but those two had dressed for a formal event or a photo shoot, coordinating ensembles and drawing attention to their less than popular May-December relationship. Her strapless knee-length dress fit like a glove until the waist and then flounced. The color reminded him of fall leaves in the sun, somewhere between burnt orange and crimson. His dress shirt and tie coordinated, warm golden browns and sienna. Their shiny black shoes looked fresh from the boxes. The couple could have shared the cover of a JC Penny's catalogue. The way they were dressed made them stand out like sore thumbs. Most of Reverend Flynn's flock came in khakis and polos.

Reverend Flynn had hoped to find out the man was a friend of her father's, despite the duo's strange ensemble. When Daisy introduced him as her friend, it had given him the heebie-jeebies. He himself couldn't imagine having a relationship with a girl Daisy's age, and Kenneth was at least five years Glenn's senior.

"This is Kenneth, Reverend Flynn," she'd said while stroking Kenneth's forearm with her fingertips.

"It's very nice to meet you." Kenneth had extended his hand while Glenn had stammered. The moment embarrassed him even many months later. He was rarely rendered speechless, especially in church.

The usual line of parishioners had stood behind them, rushing the awkward moment. *Thank God.* A few weeks passed and the pair had become a regular Sunday morning staple. He'd grown accustomed to seeing them together. Kenneth seemed attentive and doting in regards to Daisy, so it became easy to accept their strange pairing.

Truth be told, Glenn assumed Kenneth was recently divorced and rebounding. He had been appalled to find out Kenneth was married. Of course, no one had mentioned that fact until it was too late. Daisy's father had called to say she was distraught over Kenneth's death and asked that Glenn speak with her, explaining the whole story in the process. Glenn's affection for Daisy and her family led him to offer to speak at Kenneth's funeral.

Contacting Mrs. Russell had terrified him. He had no idea if she knew everything that he knew, and he didn't know how to say he knew Kenneth. Miraculously, she hadn't asked until after the funeral. However, recalling that initial phone call still bothered him.

"Hello?" A sniffling voice answered on the first ring.

"Yes, I'm attempting to contact Ruby Russell," he said.

"This is Ruby."

"Mrs. Russell, I'm Reverend Flynn from the Church of Hope. I'm sorry to hear about the loss of your husband. I'd like to offer to perform the services for him, if you haven't already secured someone else."

Ruby had fallen silent. Her heavy breathing was audible, but she didn't speak.

"I'll do the service at no charge to you. I'd like to be useful to you and your family, if I can."

Glenn had been prepared to deliver some encouraging words and perhaps even try to sell the idea if she didn't accept, but instead of the continued silence he had anticipated, she agreed.

"Calling hours are Wednesday evening at five o'clock. The funeral will be Thursday at eleven. I'm having a wake at our home following the services at the Montrose Hills Cemetery."

"Thank you. Would you like to meet with me

beforehand to discuss…?" But she had cut him off.

"See you Wednesday. Good day."

The funeral had gone on in the same bizarre fashion. Those in attendance behaved in stereotypical suburban fashion, which was to say that they had mostly been catty and cruel. They gossiped and speculated about everything, teasing and taunting one another in ways that made Glenn quite uncomfortable. He could see a message directed from scripture alone would never do. He also noticed Daisy wasn't in attendance. He might have expected as much.

Mrs. Russell had puttered around the red casket looking more guilty than aggrieved. She wasn't what he'd expected. Not the typical grieving widow. She wore a sensible black suit with satin gloves and a hat with a tiny veil. She could have been out of a 1960s magazine. She fidgeted and jumped every time the door swung open. Whomever she expected had never arrived, and she had sat alone in the front row during the service.

Glenn had seen many reactions from women in these situations. One woman tried to wake her husband mid-service as a last ditch effort to uncover a sinister joke. There were wives who sat comatose and a few who had been in complete denial. Others broke into hysterics or blacked out. Reverend Flynn thought he'd seen everything, until he met Ruby.

Ruby Russell spoke only when spoken to, and she had never looked at the casket. Instead, she had fiddled idly with a thread on her bottom button and jostled her pearls against her breast. She had watched the clock as if a bomb were set to go off, and she had been the first one out the door at the close of the service. Ruby rode alone to the cemetery, and at the graveside she had looked almost bored. To call her detached was much more than an understatement.

Something else had seemed to be going on.

Reverend Flynn rocked heavily in his swivel chair, pondering it all. He rested each of his fingertips, one by one, against the other, trying to understand. The obvious hit him after a few long moments. He smiled, realizing that if it were a snake, as they say, it would have bitten him. If she had known about Daisy, he reasoned, that would explain her odd behavior. She probably looked for Daisy at the funeral and worried about the possible encounter. What woman would have mourned the loss of a husband who had planned to leave her? None he'd ever spoken to. He'd counseled many a heartbroken person in his career and they had mostly taken the opposite position.

Then came the newscast Tuesday morning, and it started him thinking he should check in on Mrs. Russell after the funeral. Five women died as strangely as Kenneth had right next door to the Russell's home. He nearly dropped his coffee that day. Five diabetics, playing Bridge, had consumed a three pound coffee cake and died. Glenn didn't feel unstable for questioning this. No, he felt quite the opposite, and he worried about Mrs. Russell.

He wondered if the citizens of Montrose Hills had all flipped their lids. How could so many people dismiss six deaths more fit for a horror film than reality? It didn't make any sense. Surely an investigator, a reporter, or someone would see this, too. He simply wasn't trained to get the answers he wanted. When he had tried, Mrs. Russell had interpreted his interest as a solicitation for sex and thrown him out.

No. He'd decided it best to leave investigating to the professionals. But he really would like to know what was going on.

As far as Ruby Russell's unusual behavior, he was certain she must have known about Daisy. It made perfect sense. He thought he might be cut out for some detective work. He had impressed himself with that little revelation. It fit perfectly. Nonetheless, Ruby's oddness intimidated him. She was edgy, grieving and angry. He promised not to call on her anymore.

Meanwhile, he listened to the women hard at work in the parish kitchen, and he began to write his Sunday morning sermon. A radio playing hymns in the distance set the backdrop. The acoustics were top notch. Reverend Flynn decided to speak on deception Sunday. There was too much of that going on all around their tiny community.

With the delicious aromas wafting down the hall, he struggled to concentrate. On Fridays when all of the ladies were in the kitchen, lunch had special appeal. Pride for his flock filled his chest. They had hearts for mankind, desired to serve and devoted hours to the betterment of their community. Being part of the task force assigned to inner city food banks ranked high on the list of most rewarding parts of his job. Reverend Flynn gave silent thanks for the devotion of his flock gave to their chosen missions and set himself to writing the best sermon he'd ever written.

*****

Across town, Emma Eaken sat at her desk bouncing a brightly-colored rubber band ball against the wall. She'd covered a myriad of strange stories in her time on air, several in the past week alone, but none like the coffee cake fiasco. She squeezed and released the orange ball trying to get the truth out of it, but found no answers. The tiny office was relatively tidy for a newsroom. Photos and news clips hung from her walls. Appointment cards and contact numbers hung pinned to a corkboard. The odor of stale burnt coffee glued it all together. Maybe it was an accident. Though, it didn't make sense none of those women knew the coffee cake contained sugar. The women were all about forty years too old to have made a suicide pact. With any luck, she might prove a packaging error. Now, that would be a story.

Emma looked at the spread before her. She'd researched similar situations, diabetes and local deaths, trying to find a tiny thread to pull. If only she could get a finger-hold on something, then she'd unravel the mystery and reveal the truth. This story could transform her career. Her tiny cube office would become a nice dressing room with her name on the door and a mirror on the wall. Checking her makeup in the tiny compact from her purse was degrading.

Emma dialed up her friend at crime scene investigations on a hunch, or out of hope.

"Tony, this is Emma. Can I come and take a look at the inventory on the coffee cake killing?"

"Killing? I hear it was some dietary fluke. Not a murder."

"Says you." Emma smiled into the receiver. "I have a hunch."

"Well, then, come on down. I'm here till nine."

Emma had no idea what to look for, but she needed to find something. The wackiest story she'd heard in a decade had to have some aspect she could blow up and play upon, until she gained notoriety. Everyone she'd graduated with had already established themselves as a household name in their community. She still covered graduations and blizzards. Whatever time or effort it might take to find her thread would be worth the trouble. She'd unravel the whole case singlehandedly and be rewarded for it with a bright future as an anchor woman.

Emma grabbed her things and headed out. She needed to think. The sun shone brightly and people peppered the streets. Emma headed to the coffee shop a few blocks over. With a giant bucket of iced latte in hand, she could really look at the facts. She needed to find an angle on this coffee cake story. If the angle on the cake fell apart, maybe another angle lay with one of the women or their relationships to one another. A betrayal or an affair would be her golden ticket to the anchor desk. Second to a scandal, a severe mental break would work. She sat for hours scribbling until she had a book full of theories and bunny trails. If none of them panned out, she reasoned she'd at least have the makings of a good who-done-it.

Lost in possibilities, Emma made it to the station at 8:45 p.m. *Better late than never.* She knew Tony wouldn't shove her out the door when the clock struck nine, so she went prepared to dig in. She thumbed through dozens of crime scene photographs. Everything seemed in order, aside from the five dead women slumped over their cards and cake. A bakery box in one of the photographs caught her attention. She had a lead. She'd hoped it had brand with a logo. Nailing Hostem's for five deaths related to mislabeling would have instantly made her career. Unfortunately, upon close inspection the plain white box didn't leave her much to go on. She'd have to take what she could get. Her next step would require a little finesse, but Emma was always up for a challenge.

She needed to get into the Tanner house and see the inventory inside the cupboards. If her hypothesis proved correct, then the food in the Tanner house would all be very appropriate for a diabetic diet. She'd already learned these women met during rehabilitation from complications to the disease several years back. They were comrades. This tragedy must be negligence on the part of the baker. She wanted that story. Now she needed to unearth the name of the negligent baker.

CHAPTER FIVE

Ruby sat in the sunroom with a plate of tea sandwiches and flipped on the television. The five o'clock news kept her apprised of community events in Montrose Hills, after the anchors finished expounding on the crime inside the city. Like every day, the anchors started by detailing the perils of city life.

"In Kensington City, seventeen people were confirmed dead and several more in serious condition following a meal at the Partridge Parish."

Ruby rolled her eyes and shoved a finger-full of side swept bangs over one ear. As she bit into a tiny cucumber square, the reporter brought her eyes back to the screen. The victims had been poisoned, but it was not the story that caught her attention. She was surprised those sorts of places didn't have more instances of sickness than they did. It was the perky young reporter that got to her.

Emma Eaken. The reporter who had badgered her after the untimely deaths of Tillie and her Bridge club, stood with a mic to her lips. Standing before a homeless shelter in

Kensington city, the busy metropolis bordering Montrose Hills, she detailed the atrocity. Emma posed on her pointy heels, flaunting her youth and perfection. The sight of her caused Ruby to drop a petit four on her lap. That girl was annoying in more ways than could be counted.

"Beans!" Ruby rubbed her blouse fast enough to cause friction. She headed to the sink for some cold water.

"Local churches are pulling together to support the Partridge Parish," Emma explained in keeping with her charade of care. "Hundreds of volunteers come here each week to provide the more than four thousand meals served every month."

Meals! Pish. Bean soup and franks hardly comprise a meal.

No use. The shirt would need to be laundered. Quite a shame. Ruby made plans to call Betty as soon as she changed and inform her of the opportunity to serve this mission. She needed to redeem herself for the tardy cupcakes situation. This was a good way to get herself back into Betty's good graces.

"Reverend Glenn Flynn of the Montrose Hills Church of Hope had a few words to say." Ruby flew into the sunroom, blouse undone, mouth open wide. That man shouldn't have been on the news. He should have been…well, he should have been in the closest bathroom to wherever he was when he enjoyed his fresh pastry basket. Ruby's hands trembled as she considered that he hadn't eaten from her basket. She had worked very hard on everything in that basket, and he was too good to even try it, any of it? Rude.

The scene behind him was chaos. It seemed the callous Ms. Eaken had barged in there, wielding a microphone and camera crew, before the EMTs could escape. Now the entire viewing area was subjected to the gruesome event. Stretchers and bodies flowed from the building in a deluge. Policemen fought against the crowds, and Ruby considered she might soon be witness to a riot. Reverend Flynn stood a few yards away looking morose and perturbing.

"Our congregation joins the thousands of lives who have been touched by this ministry in one way or another. We provide foods and services here on a weekly basis and are distraught and thoroughly disheartened by this travesty. We're opening our door this week to anyone who may desire counseling to deal with this senseless loss."

"Amy Anderson was here this afternoon from your church?" Emma asked the reverend.

"Yes, Amy brings sandwiches here every Friday. Our ladies ministry team prepares all week for our Friday donations. Then Amy delivers the meals, sandwiches mostly, and occasionally something special the church might receive such as a fruit basket or baked goods. Sometimes, we can offer more following a speaking engagement or rally."

Ruby clutched her chest. She fell into the wall and tried to remember the Lord's prayer. The serenity prayer was the best she could do, but she gave it with gusto. *How on earth can this keep going wrong?* It simply wasn't fair!

Ruby ran up the stairs to her room and changed her shirt. She hadn't want to kill Ken, and he had died. She had wanted to show off to Tillie and instead, she had killed the whole Bridge brigade. She tried to give Reverend Flynn a nasty case of diarrhea and instead she took out a whole colony of poor, helpless, homeless, hungry people.

"I can't get anything right!" Ruby raged like a spoiled schoolgirl and flung herself onto her bed, pulling a pillow over her face so she could scream into it. "I'm going to hell."

She pulled the pillow from her face with a huff. *All those poor people.* Her heart clenched recalling the parade of stretchers. A tear slid over one full cheek. How could this happen? All those lives…their families… A lump formed in her chest hard as a rock and cold as an ice cube. She was a killer. The other cheek felt damp. Her ribs squeezed tight against her lungs. The room shimmered at the edges and black dots interrupted her vision. Panic. She knew this feeling, this awful, disruptive feeling. If she let it, it would consume her again.

The best thing she could do now was get busy on the cleanup. Spending the rest of her lifetime in jail for an accident like this seemed a waste. She could, however, do what she could to make up for this travesty.

Ruby called Charlotte. Charlotte was cleanup.

The phone rang several times before she picked up. Ruby recognized a cacophony of sound, mostly loud crashing and familiar machinery, before she heard Charlotte's exasperated voice.

"Yeeeees?"

"Hello?" Ruby tapped her receiver against the dresser. "Hello! Charlotte? What the devil is going on over there?"

"I'm baking!" Charlotte sounded as if she were being held at gunpoint.

She'd given the short version. She was baking. The short version told Ruby a lot.

She rolled her wetted eyes and threw one forearm across her face.

*****

"Charlotte. Be serious."

"You have been too busy to help me, and you told me you would. Betty called today and…" Charlotte's voice quivered. Tears were imminent.

"Stop. Clean up, and come over." Something in Ruby's tone set the hairs on Charlotte's arms at attention.

"What?" It occurred to Charlotte there was a great injustice there. She was baking, surrounded by a horrific mess, yet Ruby expected her to drop everything and run. Hmmph. As she surveyed the scene before her, turning slowly enough to wrap her skinny jeans within the fifty foot spiral phone cord, the request suddenly seemed very reasonable. Ruby needed her. Ruby always needed her. Ruby never thought clearly, and she was lucky, really, to have a friend like Charlotte. And Ruby could bake. Charlotte could not.

"Fine. You have to help me bake then."

"Of course."

"Today, Ruby. You have to help me bake…today."

"Of course. What are we baking?" Ruby's defeated tone worried Charlotte. She let down her guard completely.

"Snickerdoodles."

"No."

Rude.

"Lady Fingers?" Her tone formed a question this time.

"Only if we have a proper recipe."

"Betty Crocker?"

An exaggerated sigh accosted Charlotte's ear as she worked to free her feet from the cord before she tumbled over.

"I have something. I'll check my books and pantry while you get here."

"Alright. I just have to straighten up."

"Mmmhmm."

Charlotte said a polite goodbye while Ruby remained in another world. The possibilities of what might have her so bothered troubled Charlotte a great deal, but there was no use in stressing over it until she knew what "it" was.

The process of cleaning her kitchen and then herself took longer than Charlotte had anticipated. The dropped flour had spread its fallout like a mushroom cloud. She had to, quite literally, wipe down her entire kitchen. Even the window above the sink had a thin white film. Her body looked the same. It took a shower and shampoo to erase the evidence of her kitchen catastrophe.

Charlotte worked hard to put away the contraptions she'd purchased for the endeavor and wondered if she might return them. They were open but misused, and hopefully, there'd never again be a need for such equipment in her home. Baking wasn't a good pastime for her.

As she tidied up, she wondered more about what had spawned Ruby's panic. Perpetual drama consumed Ruby. *Ruby Russell, coffee cake killer.* Considering her recent hobby of baking up death, the possibilities were endless. She lived like a daytime original movie. Charlotte hurried a bit to finish her chores.

The moment she'd returned everything back to its place, Charlotte headed outside to her car. She double checked her oversized bag to see she had what she needed: makeup, phone, money, identification, medication, keys...no keys. She headed back to the house only to find she was locked out without her keys. It wasn't the first time. Probably wouldn't be the last time, either.

Ruby told her years ago to hide a key under a rock or in a rock, or near a rock. It was years ago. Who could remember? She walked along the side of her house looking into the flower beds. There were at least a thousand rocks. Charlotte squatted for a more thorough investigation. She admired her crimson toenails while she was there. It was no good. There was no way to tell where the key hid. Charlotte was definitely stuck, and she hated to walk all the way to Ruby's, so she resigned to turn over all the stones in her garden until she located the key. Four ruined fingernails later, she was dirty again and still stranded at her house.

A warm breeze threw long locks against her cheek and she suddenly remembered. She had left a window open that morning. That should have been what she looked for first, not a rock. Charlotte climbed back onto her porch and looked around for busybodies. She didn't see any, so she mounted the railing and shimmied in through the cracked window. She made it, at the expense of her new blouse and carpet.

"Cripes!" A large potted fern toppled onto its side, spewing topsoil over her beige carpet. "Ugh." Charlotte looked back and forth between the plant and her door, knocking dirt from her pants. If she cleaned up the mess, she'd be even later and probably in need of another bath. So, she shut her eyes and reached for the keys on the hook beside her front door. With one hand over her face, she grabbed the keys and pawed at the door until she found the knob. *Good grief.* Everything was always so complicated.

On her way to Ruby's, she took the long route intentionally. She needed to think. Ruby had gotten herself into a real mess, and it wasn't the first time she'd called upon Charlotte to be the voice of reason. Normally, her troubles had been with Kenneth, though, or Betty, but this was multifaceted nuts.

Six people dead, and Ruby in the middle of every one. She needed to make it right, and she needed to execute some self-control for goodness' sake. Convincing Ruby she wasn't in control would be the first obstacle, but even before that, they needed to cover up any loose ends. Charlotte knew from all her mystery-novel reading that there were always loose ends.

Then she needed to convince Ruby she should leave the reverend and the news reporter alone. Ruby had definitely looked a little wild when she had mentioned those two. It made Charlotte shiver when she thought of that look. Nothing good would come of it. Maybe they could move away together. Ruby had money now, and Fiji was nice anytime of year. Of course, getting her that far from Michael would be impossible. Ruby grieved his absence daily. He shouldn't have gone so far away for college. They'd shared more than one pot of coffee on that topic. He certainly could have chosen a closer school, but it was easy to understand his motives, so long as you weren't Ruby.

Charlotte eased into the residential thirty-five mile per hour speed limit as she turned toward Montrose Hills Estates. When she pulled into Ruby's drive, the house was lit up like a Christmas tree. She found the door unlocked; not a safe way to behave considering the recent neighborhood tragedies. Charlotte walked in on high alert, ready for anything. She removed her silk Pucci scarf and tossed it over the back of Ruby's sofa. Ruby bustled around in the kitchen. Before she even laid eyes upon her, the devilish aroma reached out to tempt her.

*****

"Ruby?" Charlotte called to announce her presence.

"Here!" Ruby popped around the corner, carrying a mixing bowl in one arm, stirring wildly with the other. "Meringue!"

"You're baking?" The kitchen was immaculate.

"Yes. I told you I would. I've made Cream and Berries Cream Puffs, dipped five dozen chocolate strawberries, baked apples, rolled truffles, and I'm mixing this meringue for my tarts. Where have you been?"

"I had to clean up." That said it all and Ruby accepted it as explanation enough for the nearly three hours which had elapsed.

"Well, I'll get these finished, and you can help me box it all up. I've got satin in the drawer for bows." She threw her head toward the new lazy Susan.

"Thank you, Ruby, for doing all of this. All I managed to create was a certifiable mess."

"Certainly." Ruby's eyes darted.

"How was your day?" Charlotte spoke with care

probably trying not to imply anything which could set Ruby off. She must have known Ruby's general excitement wasn't over meringue. "I didn't even ask when you called. The baking had me discombobulated."

"How did that turn out?"

"I brought Snickerdoodles. The ones I didn't burn." She fished a plastic sandwich bag from her purse and held it high.

"That's nice. I'll put on the coffee." Ruby set the bowl on the counter and pulled a bottle of Irish Crème from the cupboard.

"I really have made a mess, haven't I, Charlotte?" Her words caught in her throat, and she turned away from her friend.

"Actually, I don't know how you do it. If it weren't for the heavenly aroma, there'd be no evidence."

"Oh. Thank you. I meant, you know, with the other things."

"Oh. Well, yes. I suppose you have, but we can clean it up if we think hard about what there is to clean."

"Okay." She squeezed her friend's hand gently across the island. She loved when they were on the same page. It saved so much time.

"What needs attended to first?"

"Well, that was one of the reasons I called on you this afternoon." She peeked over her friend's shoulder to see the sun had set. Night had finally arrived. Ruby had been cursing Daylight Saving Time all day.

"Have you seen the news today?"

"Yes. I had that on while I baked."

"Did you see Reverend Flynn on the news about the mission in the city?"

"Yes. I missed the story, but I got the gist. Sad, wasn't it? Those people going to the mission to get food, being hungry and then dying when they were given sustenance. I hope there weren't any children involved."

Ruby's legs went numb. She almost toppled over. She hadn't considered all of the children that ate at the mission. She needed to do something nice for children to make amends for the episode. Her insides twisted and pulled painfully beneath her skin. Living with what she'd done was far worse punishment than a court could ever impose. She pictured Michael's face as a child and choked on her tongue.

"Charlotte. I sent the reverend a basket this morning."

Charlotte waited.

"I was angry and wanted to punish him for hounding me and being insufferable. I used castor beans to give him a serious case of…" she grimaced and pointed to her tummy. "My mother used the beans for castor oil when I was a child. But…I think I didn't do what I thought I did."

Charlotte watched, clearly unwilling to speak until Ruby made her point.

"Don't worry. He didn't eat anything inside my basket. If he had, he wouldn't have been on the news." She blinked once and a tear slid from beneath her lashes and ran along her nose.

"What happened to the basket then?" Charlotte's voice came out firm and cautious, despite the fact that her face grew pale. Ruby fidgeted with a dishtowel and refused to look at Charlotte

"Ruby?" She nudged, cocking her head to the side. "What happened to the basket?"

"I can't be certain, you know," Ruby stalled.

"Ruby. You're being cagey."

Ruby leaned against her enormous custom fridge.

"I think he may have donated it to the mission, and I think I made ricin not castor oil." Charlotte's knees buckled.

"Oh Glory! Ruby! All those people!" She closed her eyes

and Ruby turned to hide her shame. "That's thirty people in three weeks!"

"Oh, Charlotte, let's not get carried away. There have only been twenty-three so far." Ruby struggled to keep her voice even and her expression dismissive. "It's not like I'm doing this on purpose! You know they were all accidents. I can't be expected to know the health afflictions of the entire world, or understand the complicated workings of pharmacology. I didn't even know *castor* beans made anything but *castor* oil until after I saw the news. And how on earth could I have known the ungrateful Reverend Glenn Flynn would *donate* his *gift* basket. What an egghead!"

"Glenn Flynn?" Charlotte smirked before her look turned pensive. "What do you mean, *so far*?"

"You know what I mean, Charlotte! I need to make this right. I want you to come with me to start fixing it. I can't do nice things to make up for the bad things if the bad things end me up in jail."

"Okay, but come where? I can't imagine what you're up to, and I'm guessing we aren't headed down to see officer O'Leary and make a confession."

"No. Over to Tillie's. It's not a murder investigation, so no one's been over to clean it up yet. Her family lives out of state and won't be in until the funeral this weekend to handle her estate."

Charlotte swallowed hard at the word funeral. "What will we do there?" Her eyes jumped towards the Tanner house.

"Well, I need to plant some evidence and see about removing something else." That reminded her of the evidence. Ruby ran to the cupboard and dug out a bag wrapped in tinfoil, wrapped in plastic wrap. It took a stepstool and the removal of several unopened boxes of cereal to reach the odd package.

"What's that?"

"Step one." She turned on the water at the sink in unison with her garbage disposal. Ruby began unwrapping the mystery item and shoved the coffee cake in pieces down the drain.

"Is that…?"

Ruby nodded as she worked. "Yes. I had to read up about it. I wasn't sure if they could remove evidence from my disposal. They can't. I was willing to drive it across state lines and throw it in a dumpster, but this is better."

"Why didn't you just eat it?"

"Please. It's a sugar free coffee cake! No thank you, plus think of the terrible circumstances surrounding the thing. I wouldn't want any part of that." She made a sickened face and shoved the last of the pastry into the sink. The loud gurgling of the disposal seemed fitting. It took a few minutes to finish it off and bleach out her sink, just in case. Then, it was time for their excursion.

A few minutes more and the daring duo was stalking in the rear yard. It was a fortunate twist of fate Tillie's home was situated on the cul-de-sac. A neighbor would have had to be out in their own yard to see them.

"Here." Ruby shined a pocket light onto a small rectangle in the door.

"The doggy door?"

"You can fit."

"I most certainly won't!" Charlotte protested.

"Try."

*****

Charlotte had heard that tone before. For all her nerves and anxiety, she'd often thought Ruby could command armies in that disposition. She had already lost that battle once. She wouldn't bother again.

Charlotte knelt before the small rectangle and scooted in,

until her hips stuck. She should've worn her skinny jeans.

"What are you doing?" Ruby whispered too loudly.

"Resting."

"What?" Her voice was muffled, separated by the door between them.

"Can you reach the lock from there?"

"No."

"Roll over."

Giggling ensued. Charlotte twisted in the tiny door, until she reached the lock.

"Excellent!" Ruby clapped quietly.

Charlotte rolled back onto her tummy and laid there. "I'm stuck."

"I know you're feeling degraded down there, but let's please act like a lady, not a sailor."

"I said I'm stuck!" This time her voice raised the ears of local canines and a collective barking began.

As she lay half in and half out of Tillie's house, Charlotte was alarmed to feel Ruby yanking at her pants.

"Wait! What are you doing?" Charlotte protested, suddenly in a most unseemly predicament.

"Removing your trousers. They should be burned. How ugly."

"They're cargo capris. I thought I might need the pockets."

"What for? What on earth did you think we'd be doing?"

Charlotte began to wriggle frantically in effort to save her pants, but in the end Ruby won. Her arms, already inside, made the efforts fruitless. Charlotte grabbed hold of a table leg, and pulled. Her body crashed onto the hard kitchen floor, bare legs and rear end revealed to the world. She pulled her feet inside and Ruby came straightway into the room as well.

She extended the capris in Charlotte's direction, careful not to look. Charlotte stood, bracing herself against the wall to get dressed. She pulled her belt tight around her middle, in case Ruby tried to accost her again. She switched the light on to manage the tiny buckle.

"No!" Ruby flew at her, knocking her into two tiny food bowls on the floor. Her newly covered bottom became stained with brown mush and water. The light was off when she righted herself once more.

"Have you lost your apple-baking mind?" Charlotte cursed into the dark.

"Have you? Are you trying to alert the neighbors you just broke into Tillie's home?"

"Me?" Charlotte barked. Even for Ruby that was harsh.

"If the doggie door fits." Ruby turned her back on Charlotte and got busy.

Charlotte dabbed at her pants with some damp paper towels and shoved them into her pocket. Heaven forbid she create more evidence. Meanwhile, Ruby went through Tillie's cupboards.

The kitchen was small for the size of the house. Tillie's cupboards were white, along with all of the woodwork and doors. The countertop and floors were blue, though it was difficult to tell much more in the dark. Charlotte hoped they wouldn't happen across Tillie's dog. He'd be mad to see she sat in his food.

Ruby moved methodically through the room. She removed a half a dozen items from Tillie's cabinets and replaced them with items of her own. She dumped a bag of snack-sized chocolate bars into a drawer and covered them with oven mitts. She emptied a box of sugar free drink mix packets and replaced them with the kiddie kind. The process went on for several minutes. No questions were in order. This appeared to be a well-thought-out plan, so Charlotte took a seat, rubbing uselessly at her pants.

"Hey," she whispered. "Is this the box?"

Without a word, Ruby replaced that, too, and then began to go through her trash.

Headlights illuminated the room briefly, scaring them both rigid. The ladies looked at one another and the sound of car doors sent them scrambling through the dark. Ruby shut off her flashlight and tripped over the trash can through which she'd rummaged.

"Toast!" She cursed. Trash slid everywhere.

"Come on!" Charlotte twisted the back door knob as the front door swung open. It was too late. The foyer light snapped on.

"Toast," Charlotte agreed.

Ruby grabbed her friend by the belt and tugged her away from the door, dragging her bag full of scene setters and evidence with her. It was a clear shot from the foyer. Charlotte had an idea. She pulled Ruby and her loot into a darkened door and left the door open by a crack to listen. Ruby was immediately sullen.

"I thought this door led to the basement," Charlotte lamented. "Tillie has a walkout basement."

"We're in the laundry room," Ruby whimpered. "Now what?"

"Here!" Excited, Charlotte motioned to the half window over the dryer.

"I can't fit out there." Ruby sat on the floor, kneading her hands and fighting back tears from the sound of it.

They would have no good explanation for this. None at all.

*****

"I can." Charlotte was gone, feet first, out the window. A muffled thump against the siding was the last she heard of her comrade. Nice to know who her true friends were.

"Someone's been here." A woman spoke in the next room. "I told you this was worth looking into."

"Right." A man's voice answered. He sounded less enthusiastic.

"This trash has been overturned. Someone was looking for something. Let's just hope they didn't find it and we can."

Ding Dong.

Where am I, Grand Central Station? How many people could come to this one house, on this one night, at the precise same time?

Ding Dong.

"Now you've done it. Some neighbor's going to report us for unlawful entry."

"I'll talk," the woman said pointedly. "Come on."

Ruby listened as the footsteps retreated and she took one deep breath.

*****

"There's no one here." Stuart called from the front lawn.

"What?" Emma's voice dropped an octave, suspicious and perturbed.

"There's no one. I looked up and down the street." He shrugged. "Let's get out of here. We can call the police station tomorrow and follow the proper channels."

"Sure." The word dripped with sarcasm. "Following the proper channels always helps." She turned and headed back to the kitchen. She knew firsthand one should never let a cop in on an investigation. He'd demand the evidence she had, use it to finish the job and then claim the glory for himself.

Emma couldn't find anything in the trash to serve her purpose. In fact, she did find a candy bar wrapper. That didn't support her theory so she threw it back. Inspection of Tillie Tanner's cupboards turned up the same. There were hidden chocolates and sugary drinks. It was all wrong. She would have had problems before if she really ate like that, wouldn't she?

Stuart strode in through the back door. "All clear."

Emma nearly fainted.

"How'd you get in there!" She held both her chest and her forehead. Her heart jumped in place. "You just scared the daylights out of me, Stuart."

"The door was open. I thought you did it."

"Why would I do that?" Emma's cheeks burned from embarrassment and anger. Composure under pressure identified a good reporter and she was a good reporter.

"Uh, to let me in?"

"You could have knocked." She straightened her shirt, concentrating on her heart rate.

"The door was open. Why would I knock?"

"Open?" Emma's brows rose up in unison.

"Open."

Emma raced out into the backyard, peering into the night.

"Now what are you doing?" Stuart lolled in the doorway.

"Did you see anything out there?" She asked from a few feet away.

"No. Nothing. Probably some kids playing ding dong ditch. Are you about finished? I'm hungry."

Emma stood like an antenna in the yard. That didn't seem like the type of game kids in Montrose Hills would play, especially since the entire town knew Tillie Tanner was dead. She turned slowly looking for something. Anything. There was only the night, a bouncing empty clothesline and Ruby Russell's bay window. A brunette sat staring back at her, sipping from a cup and munching casually on cookies. The interior light created the look of a stage, and Emma wondered if the brunette could see her as well.

She fought the urge to march right over and question the woman. Considering the whole of her predicament, she returned to Stuart instead. On their way out of the cul-de-sac, Emma wrote down the license plate number of the car in the Russell's driveway. She would locate this woman later and question her. Certainly she had seen something from her position in the window.

"Well, Did you get any new leads? Will you be trading your all weather gear for an anchor coat soon?" Stuart asked.

"No," she huffed. "I got nothing on the bakery. The box was unmarked and I can't even prove it had a coffee cake in it. It looked brand new. Something stinks, Stu."

"You shouldn't have been digging in week old dead-lady trash," he scolded.

Emma rolled her eyes and stared at the pad where she'd written the plate number. She knew not to underestimate the value of a lead, no matter how small it seemed at first.

*****

"Charlotte!" Ruby exclaimed, barreling through the mudroom door. "Charlotte!"

"Stay there, please. We have a spectator." Charlotte spoke cordially, her eyes glued to the window reflection.

"Who's out there?"

"Channel 3." Charlotte let her eyes roam to Ruby's. Ruby was bent over, hyperventilating near the back door.

Headlights flashed over the front door, pausing for a moment, and then crawling away.

"What did you do?" Ruby asked from a topsy turvy stance.

"I saved your derrière."

"I thought you abandoned me."

"When have I ever abandoned you, Ruby Russell?" Fury bubbled in the words.

"You leapt out a window!"

"And rang the doorbell to give you a way to escape."

Ruby's voice began to shake heavily with relief, and tears began to stream. "I knew it. I knew Emma Eaken was on to me. She probably saw me and is headed off to tell the police everything." Charlotte watched a month's worth of raw emotion flood from Ruby.

Ruby made her way to the spice cabinet and retrieved a small amber bottle.

It was no secret Ruby had been hospitalized after her son left for college several years back. It was more than she could take when he'd chosen a college that necessitated a plane ride instead of a simple commute. Ken, of course, had blown off her stay, claiming she had needed some time to herself anyway. Lots of stories circulated at first. The official story centered on a surgery and rehabilitation. However, in the six weeks Ruby spent at Heartland, she never saw anyone with an injury not self-inflicted.

When Ruby came home, Kenneth had emerged. A slow fade between personas, but it began while she stayed at Heartland. Who knew how he spent those weeks until she returned? He certainly hadn't spent his time with Ruby. In the end, she received a broken marriage, a counselor and a basket full of pills.

Ruby rarely needed the pills, and the remaining bottle had been unopened for a very long time. During an especially frustrating session with her counselor, Ruby swore off the medication, but she could never bring herself to toss it out. She shook the bottle hard into her palm and swallowed quickly. Then she looked at the label for a moment too long.

"What are you doing, Ruby?" Charlotte's growled.

"I need something for my nerves. You tell me to take them all the time."

"Yes." She nodded. "But what are you staring at?"

"What?"

"I saw you reading the label. Why would you do that?"

"Well!" Ruby threw the bottle back onto the shelf. "I didn't know there'd be a deposition. I simply wondered if they were outdated."

"Ruby, it's been a year. Of course they're outdated."

"Will they hurt me?"

"You?"

"Yes, Charlotte! Who do you think I mean?"

Charlotte's eyes landed on the window, and she moved to shut the curtain. "They can lose their potency over time, but they won't hurt you." Charlotte had worked as a nurse's aide in a local clinic a long time ago, before people needed a college degree to candy stripe. Ruby knew Charlotte couldn't resist an opportunity to show her smarts, and it changed the course of the conversation.

"If you're going to start taking them again," her eyes returned to study Ruby "then you should be in counseling. Call your doctor, won't you?"

"Alright." She heaved the box of wine onto her counter. "Would you like another drink?"

"I'll take some more of that Irish coffee." Charlotte smiled sweetly. "I don't condone the drinking, but it's been quite an evening."

"Excellent."

CHAPTER SIX

"Dr. Kessler, thank you so much for seeing me on such short notice." Ruby took the doctor's hand daintily in her own.

"Please." He motioned to an inviting armchair near the window. "Won't you have a seat?"

Ruby sat on the edge of the chair, both feet firmly on the ground, back poker straight. Being there with him again made her both comfortable and uncomfortable. Nothing had changed in the five years since she'd been there last. The muted green walls, the white woodwork still in need of a scrub, photos of his wife, and the exact placement of the furniture, all the same. The plants had grown. Nothing more.

"I heard about your husband. I'm very sorry for your loss." He scratched something into his small notebook.

Ruby didn't respond. She shifted her feet to cross them at the ankles and removed her small white gloves, taking special care with each motion.

"Ruby?" The doctor's voice drew her attention. "Ruby,

you requested our meeting. Is there something you'd like to talk about?"

"I've been under a lot of pressure, and you helped me so much last time."

"Last time?" Dr. Kessler ran his hands though his thick gray and black hair.

Ruby fussed with her gloves, continuing to give Dr. Kessler the silent treatment.

"Do you still see Charlotte?"

"Oh, yes. We're as thick as thieves."

"Partners in crime?"

Ruby's lips pulled down.

"Maybe I shouldn't have come." Her feet planted against the golden bamboo flooring, urging her body to stand.

"You did come. You called, scheduled an appointment and arrived here ten minutes early. There's something you'd like to tell me. Please, don't make me get out my crystal ball." He smiled a familiar lopsided smile. He reminded her of Michael when he did that. She softened.

"Ken's death came as quite a shock and a complete embarrassment. It wasn't enough he humiliated me in life, he had to do it in death as well." Ruby's tummy knotted.

"I heard about the unusual circumstances. What an odd thing, a fluke I hear."

"Yes." He had her attention now. She scooted around on the edge of her seat unable to leave, unwilling to stay. She'd found an old friend. He'd known her so well once before. He'd understand, so long as she could remain coy. There stood much to be lost if she slipped even a little.

"First Ken, then my neighbor and her friends. Then those hungry people at the shelter in the city..." Her head shook slowly in sadness. Tears stung her eyes. All those people from the shelter, how could it be true?

"Ruby, did you know any of those other people?"

"No. Just Tillie Tanner, my neighbor. I didn't know the rest."

"Ah, two deaths so close to home can be tough, and the media can bring awful things into our homes, but we can't fixate on them. What are you doing to stay focused? Are you still baking?"

Ruby cringed before she could speak. She had no intention of discussing her recent baking with this fellow. She simply wanted peace of mind and perhaps a little something for the anxiety. Her cheeks felt hot, but her hands were cold as ice.

"Ruby, you don't look well. Please don't be offended. You look lovely, but your eyes ... I can see you're burdened, and I can help you if you'll open up to me."

"I got to bed late last night." The attention and sympathy pleased her. Didn't she deserve both after all she'd been through?

"Are you not able to sleep?"

"I stayed awake boxing up all of Ken's things. I plan to take them to the mission after our appointment." Her first act of reparation.

"The mission from the news? Isn't that in the city?"

"Yes."

"You used to hate the city. Have you warmed to the opportunities?"

"They've suffered a devastating blow. I hoped I could help, and no, I have not warmed to the opportunity to be mugged or otherwise assailed."

"Are you bringing them anything else? Your baked treasures perhaps?"

"No." Ruby bit the inside of her cheeks and ignored the talk of bringing baked goods to the Partridge Parish. "I'm donating Ken's things. They can have it all, aside from his extensive collection of toiletries and golf paraphernalia." Golf had always seemed a drug to him. She detested the sport, its expense and Ken's obsession with all things related. "The toiletries went into the trash a month ago… and I plan to offer the golf equipment to Michael, but he has always had the good sense to stay away from the game."

"How is Michael? Was he home for the funeral?"

"Of course. Michael's a good boy. He looked wonderful, more cheerful and vibrant than I anticipated. An absolute joy to have home!"

"Was the funeral what you expected? Was it what Kenneth wanted? I know how difficult it can be to say good-bye publicly like that. It's tricky business, funerals."

"The funeral was further embarrassment but at least it's over." She raised her forehead, daring him to argue. "He chose a red casket, Dr. Kessler. Red. Some local Protestant spoke, that fellow from the television. People grouped up and whispered." Ruby moved her head, a slow, tiny movement.

"Reverend Flynn?" He scratched more into his notes.

Ruby could only huff and play with her shirt sleeves.

"He's a nice man. Mr. Flynn. I've met with him on many occasions. He often recommends me to folks from his parish after they experience a loss or tragedy of some kind."

"He's a boob." Her mouth pinched and she considered throwing her little gloves at him. "He spoke about Ken as if he knew him. Well, as if he didn't know him. He spoke about someone else completely, but with authority as if…" Ruby's muscles tensed. Her jaw clenched. "Can we please not talk about that imbecile? I'd rather I never saw him again, and I don't want to waste time discussing him further. Idiot." She added the final thought under her breathe slightly, but only slightly.

"Hmm," Dr. Kessler rubbed his chin and cheeks.

"Alright, Ruby."

A long beat of silence settled between them. Next stop, the corrupt city of Kensington. She needed to keep her phone within reach, in case of abduction. She patted her jacket pocket to be sure. Her fingers traced the small rectangular form right where she expected it to be, nestled in the pocket fabric, right beside her new pepper spray. The doctor interrupted her mental inventory, earning the stink eye before she got her pleasantries back in order.

"Vibrant?" A new, warmer expression played in the hilt of his brows. "You say Michael was vibrant?"

"Yes, especially so…but not at all in an inappropriate way. I raised him right, doctor."

Dr. Kessler nodded. "Vibrant. Is he in love?"

"With whom?" Ruby stuttered, unprepared for such an accusation. She'd completed her inventory and begun figuring up a way to run Reverend Flynn out of town. His seemingly random statement shattered her concentration.

"I shouldn't know, Ruby. I thought you might. When men start behaving "vibrantly," there's often a woman behind it." His easy smile assured his good nature.

Ruby hoped her smile showed hers as well. She'd always thought herself to be the woman behind her son's joy. "He didn't mention any girl."

"Well, just a thought. I'm sure being home, whatever the circumstance, was the reason. You'll let me know?"

Ruby nodded noncommittally, maintaining her pleasant facade

"Is there anything more you'd like to discuss today, Ruby? Our time is nearly up." She looked at her watch to confirm. The hour had ticked away into the ether. Dr. Kessler pulled his prescription pad from the drawer of his desk as he spoke.

"I'm a little concerned about your loss of sleep. Grief is a tough road and you'll need proper rest to get through the stages ahead. Would you like something to help with the anxiety?"

"Yes. I'd like that very much." Ruby craned her neck to watch as the doctor began to write upon the pad. She didn't try to deny it. They both knew she was as anxious as she was blond. "Is there something other than what I took the last time I could try? The last pills gave me a queasy feeling. I didn't like it."

Dr. Kessler looked up at Ruby before he began to write again. His expression remained blank as he processed her request. Ultimately, he complied. "Can I see you next week? I'd like to talk with you more about Michael."

"Certainly. He's such a good boy."

Ruby made an appointment with the receptionist and then proceeded to the pharmacy downstairs.

Outside she moved with purpose to her van. The city made her uncomfortable. She had no way to tell who might intend her harm and that was unsettling. Plus, a lot of funny business went on in the city, the kind not found in the suburbs. There should be some way to mark the dangerous ones, some manner of helping the innocent stay safe in the city. At their next visit, she'd suggest Dr. Kessler consider leasing office space in Montrose Hills.

Ruby locked her doors the moment she got inside and arranged her hair in the mirror. The doctor was right. She looked tired. If Ken hadn't had so much junk, she could have gotten a decent night's sleep before she saw Dr. Kessler that morning. Her pale skin and flushed cheeks probably frightened him. Her eyes were puffy too. She had returned to him after all those years looking a mess. Unfortunate, but she thought the meeting had gone well. She already looked forward to her return.

The drive to Partridge Parish passed without incident as it was only a few miles from the medical building. She avoided hooligans and panhandlers with ease. In the parish parking lot she pulled right up to the front doors, further avoiding any derelicts and degenerates who happened along. She didn't intend to walk farther than she had to considering the clientele. Ruby ran fresh gloss over her lips before stepping out of her van.

Around the back she opened the door and looked for help. Only a few homeless people sitting against the building in sight. None of them so much as glanced her way. Ruby pulled two heavy bags from the back, and then pulled the door shut. She carried the bags to the building and walked inside.

The empty halls vibrated with echoes. Someone should have been at the door. She wanted to make a delivery. Ruby followed the noise down a green tiled corridor with a plain cement floor and ugly fluorescent lights. "Hello?" The noises grew louder.

She heard a kitchen nearby and recognized the clatter. "Hello?" She smelled beans, the soup du jour, no doubt. The chef hadn't bothered to add any onion. Ruby wondered what the other meal options in the city might be. When she had more time, she'd help them with their menu.

"Mrs. Russell?"

"Reverend Flynn." She nodded.

"What are you doing here?" The shocked look on his face had her fingertips curling at her sides.

"I've brought some of my husband's things. I wanted to help. You seem surprised." Her voice held an accusation and so did his.

"Why don't you seem surprised to see me?"

"Don't you work here?" She asked innocently.

"No, Mrs. Russell. You know full well I work at the

Church of Hope in Montrose Hills."

"Oh, I don't recall any of that, but I did see you on the news here last week."

"Then you know what a tough time this mission is going through."

"That's why I'm here." She smiled, lifting her bags towards Reverend Flynn. "There's more in my van."

The reverend followed her outside and assisted in relieving her of the lot. "This is very generous of you." He looked her over. "Are you current with what went on here last week?"

"Food poisoning," she said glumly. "Just awful."

"Yes. We lost seventeen people that day."

"Maybe you could hire a new cook. That bean soup doesn't even have onions." She pulled her door shut and checked to see that it had latched. The reverend stared at her. His mouth open wide. He was obviously shocked by something, but for the life of her she didn't know what. She sifted back through their conversation for the cause.

"This is a mission, Mrs. Russell. We don't hire anyone. It takes hundreds of volunteers to keep this place running." Ruby smelled a lecture coming on and wished she could magically disappear to avoid it.

"We're hardly worried about onions!"

Yep, lecture. She'd said something wrong.

"We have thousands of meals to provide at the least expense possible. Certainly you understand as much?"

He spoke as if he addressed someone with a low I.Q. and she took offense. Her shoulders squared. She understood plenty. She understood Pentecostals and their lackeys were unappreciative, inappropriately rude and also poor cooks. She was trying to help him. Fury built behind her teeth.

"Maybe you should screen your help better, Reverend,

or maybe you should hire a food tester to control your casualties next time." The expression "if looks could kill" crossed her mind. "They're homeless, not animals! Good day," she spat and climbed into her "getaway van." Reverend Flynn stood unmoving in her rearview mirror, yoked with bags and holding a stack of boxes.

Creep.

*****

Charlotte was thrilled to hear the doorbell. She'd been hoping Ruby would stop by instead of call. They had no way to know if the phones were tapped. She threw open the door and stood speechless in the threshold.

"Mrs. Mason?" Emma Eaken asked with a come-hither smile.

"Yes." Charlotte backed away from the door.

"I'm Emma Eaken." She looked around the door casing before stepping inside. "May I come in?" She had already crossed the threshold and was, clearly already "in," leaving Charlotte trapped.

Charlotte turned her head to look at the sofa and Emma sat. "I work for Channel 3 news."

Charlotte knew exactly who she was and where she worked of course. She did have a television in her home. However, from her extensive mystery novel reading she also knew this was one of the pivotal moments where she needed to learn what she could while revealing nothing. So she went to her kitchen and put water on for tea without speaking a word.

The silence didn't even give Emma pause. "I wondered if you knew a woman named Tillie Tanner."

Charlotte's head turned left and right, eyes wide, lips parted. She was going for wide-eyed innocence. She hoped she wasn't missing the mark.

"Do you know Ruby Russell?"

Charlotte nodded.

"Mrs. Mason? Are you alright? I can come back another time."

The thought of a second visit from Emma Eaken sent a full force panic through Charlotte's frame. She leaned against her kitchen island. Of all the things she didn't want at that moment, another visit from Channel 3 topped the list. "Why'd you come?" She recovered from the initial shock, and realized her responses were critical.

"Well, to be honest, I saw you in the window at the Russell house last night. I was in the neighborhood investigating the deaths of Tillie Tanner and her Bridge club. I took the liberty of using your license plate to get your name and address. I'm hoping you might have seen something out of the ordinary last night."

Charlotte fumed at being tracked down like a criminal with license plates and such. But the admission did give her the ammo she needed.

"I saw you and a man in the Tanner backyard." She turned the tables on Ms. Eaken.

Emma blushed. "Yes. That was out of the ordinary, but before you saw me, did you see something else?"

"No, just you." Charlotte's head moved to corroborate her words. She should gamble more. She wished she could see herself in a mirror because she was certain her poker face was impressive.

"Hmm. That's odd. I wonder if Mrs. Russell saw anything. I should try her again." Emma gathered her bag and turned for the door.

"No." Charlotte blurted. "Ruby wasn't well last night. I went to keep her company until she felt better."

"Oh, is she feeling better now? What was the matter?"

"She's not well. She has a bug of sorts and you know those can be tough on us as we get older." Charlotte spoke with authority. "She'll rest for the next couple of days, I imagine."

"Then, you only saw me last night? No one else outside of the Tanner home?"

"You and that man." Charlotte's tone hinted at something.

"Stuart," Emma stated without inflection. "He's a friend who keeps me company when I'm looking into things."

"Did Stuart get the key for the Tanner home, or was it you?" Charlotte advanced on Emma, having recovered from her former disposition.

This time Emma back peddled her way out the front door.

"I can see this is a bad time. I'm sorry to have bothered you, Mrs. Mason. Forgive my intrusion."

Exactly the reaction Charlotte had been hoping for but the wily look in Emma's eyes hinted that she wasn't going to give up on her investigation. Charlotte needed to push a little harder. "Today's or last evenings'?"

"Have a nice day." Emma was out the door in a flash.

*****

Emma had spent her entire life in suburbia. She knew firsthand their community was more friendly and open than not, and when people acted like Mrs. Russell and Mrs. Mason, something was amiss. The reporter in her tensed with excitement. She couldn't wait to check in on Mrs. Russell. Time was essential. The bit about her being ill was over the top. Grown women didn't babysit one another when they were sick. As soon as she considered it, she pushed a little harder on the gas pedal. If there was something going on between them, Mrs. Mason had likely already put Mrs. Russell on alert, so she'd have to be swift.

Emma's tiny smile grew into elation when she turned onto the cul-de-sac. Mrs. Russell stood hunched in her driveway unloading the van. She appeared rather well for someone whose nurse expected her down for several days. Emma slid her car in at the curb and hopped out.

"Mrs. Russell!" She closed the space between them with haste. "Hello there! I'm not sure if you remember me or not. I'm Emma Eaken from Channel 3. We spoke earlier…" She threw her gaze in the direction of the Tanner home.

Ruby followed her gaze. A bag of groceries broke under its weight, and sauce sprayed up one leg of Ruby's pant suit. Cans cascaded toward the street.

"Berries," Ruby muttered.

Emma raced toward the drive in her three inch heels, scooping up renegade staples as she went. Ruby headed toward her door carrying what she could and towing the busted sack along behind.

"You know, you can have blue jeans hemmed if you're intent on wearing them." She looked the girl over.

"What do you mean?"

"Then you wouldn't have to wear such heels, or you could simply choose a smarter pant, or a proper skirt."

Emma nodded, smiling at Ruby's disposition. For a woman she'd met wearing raingear on a sunny day, she was pretty opinionated on the topic of fashion.

Ruby's lips drew together in a peculiar pucker.

"You, on the other hand, are looking rather dapper today, Mrs. Russell."

"Thank you. I rather enjoying the day until now."

"Until I arrived."

Ruby smiled sweetly. "Well your arrival unfortunately coincided with this mess, so…" Ruby let the statement hang as she fumbled to get the door open and held it with one hip for Emma, who carried in the rest of her groceries for her. Once Ruby made it to the kitchen, she dropped the sacks onto the counter. She put the busted one directly into her sink.

"Excuse me. I need to clean up."

Emma unloaded her arms from the family room side of the island. She wouldn't be dismissed so easily. The interior didn't impress. While tastefully done, the carpets were a pattern Berber, and the wood was whitewashed circa 1996. Mini blinds hung in the windows behind her curtains. However, the one thing she couldn't deny was the cleanliness of the place. It was utterly spotless. "Would you like any help with the other bags?"

"I'll manage," Ruby said, dismissing Emma Eaken from her presence. She hadn't told her to get out, but she may as well have been waving in Emma's face.

Emma didn't accept. She had questions. Her eyes lifted to the kitchen. She'd given the Russell home a visual once over and nearly missed the juxtaposition before her. Once Ruby stepped aside, the sight overwhelmed her. Everything else reeked of the 1990s, but the kitchen did not. The room before her was a magnificent specimen of today's finest accoutrements.

Easily the largest room on the first floor, mahogany cabinetry rose from floor to ceiling. Shiny nickel knobs twinkled in a shower of recessed lighting. Each cabinet had its own light, illuminating the glorious marble countertop beneath. Pendant lights hung in a row over the island, and a large bay window behind the sink invited natural light to warm the room. Several decorative glazed pots held herbs there.

The appliances sprouted larger than life from the wide wood planked floor. Red controls on the massive stove might as well have had price tags attached. The double door refrigerator hid beautifully behind panels matching the cabinets. As Emma struggled to take it all in, the ceiling caught her attention. Paneled in copper plates, each was stamped with an intricate pattern which enhanced the effect of stage lighting all around her.

She closed her mouth when she looked at Ruby who stood at an angle with her back to the very large farmhouse sink. She worked at her pants from the smaller, shiny prep sink beside a large butcher board section of countertop. The woman who seemed always two gasps away from a stroke fretted and scrubbed and leaned against the most impressive kitchen anywhere outside of a magazine cover. The kitchen of a great chef. Ruby seemed more like a bumbling busboy than a chef during the two encounters she'd had with her.

"Are you sure you feel up to it?" She watched the sweat rise up on Ruby's brow. It made Emma nervous. Perhaps she really wasn't well.

"Why wouldn't I feel up to it?" Ruby grouched.

"I'm sorry. Mrs. Mason said something like that."

Ruby froze. Emma didn't miss the change and decided that was her cue to make an exit.

"Now, you don't look so well," Emma called as she strode victoriously out the door, leaving Ruby alone. *These ladies may not want to talk now, but they will.* Emma's heart raced from the thrill. Something was going on.

*****

Ruby flew at the girl, who escaped by only a few pointy-heeled steps. She slammed the door shut and slid to the floor, resting her head on her knees. "Oh my," she whispered. "This is very bad. It's very bad, indeed." Several minutes passed before her vision steadied. Her shirt grew damp with perspiration. The phone rang. It took all the energy she had left to reach it. Getting off the floor was harder than she remembered.

"Ruby!" Charlotte shouted before Ruby could utter a proper "hello." "I've been calling you all day. I don't know what the sense is in carrying a mobile phone if you refuse to turn it on! Where have you been?"

"I met with Dr. Kessler. I told you." Ruby considered hanging up on the snitch. "I turned my phone off to meet with him. Then I stopped at Partridge Parish and the baking outlet." Resentment pricked her brow. She needn't account for her whereabouts to Charlotte. She didn't need a keeper, and she didn't need Charlotte reporting on her life.

"Are you alright?"

Ruby had about enough of that for one lifetime. Why did everyone assume she wasn't well? Was there a rumor going around? "Am I alright? Am I alright? Yes! I'm fine!" Ruby pressed one hot hand to a hotter cheek. Her stomach churned as she imagined Emma and Charlotte having tea and discussing her private matters. The betrayal burned her and she hoped not to vomit into her newly bleached sink.

"Well, that's great," Charlotte sounded dejected. "That news reporter came here. She's trouble Ruby." Charlotte's words tumbled out in a messy mix, confusing Ruby at first.

"She came here, too, and I agree. She's a nuisance. Haven't I said that? Do you see now? Do you see?"

"Yes. I do. She's awful."

"Well, she says you talked with her about me. You said I wasn't well." Ruby reported. "What was that supposed to mean anyway? You think I'm crazy? Is that why you sent me to see a shrink?" Adrenaline roused Ruby from her slump.

"No!" Charlotte yelled into her receiver. "Ruby, I told her you weren't well and you'd be in bed so she wouldn't go over and bother you today, or anytime soon. I bought us time. You were supposed to be in bed."

"Why on earth would I be in bed?" Ruby retorted. Charlotte's plan made zero sense.

"Because I told her you were sick!" Charlotte screamed each word. Did she believe Ruby hard of hearing or just not very bright? She didn't like either insinuation.

"How was I supposed to know what you told her?"

Bang. Bang. Bang.

It sounded as if Charlotte beat the phone against something hard, and Ruby pulled the receiver away from her ear. "You're supposed to turn your cell phone on if you leave the house," Charlotte yelled into the phone. "Why even take the phone with you if you won't turn it on?"

"I was at the doctor." Ruby screamed back at her. She struggled to regain control of her tone. "Listen, the next time you decide to lie about something, please leave me out of it. You've made quite a mess this time."

"Ack!" Charlotte hacked into the phone and Ruby disconnected.

CHAPTER SEVEN

No, Ruby's life wasn't a fairytale. The prince she married had turned out to be a frog. Her potions weren't what she hoped for either, but she'd stopped baking with ulterior motives. The population of her kingdom, had they know, would have thanked her. Still, there was much to do before she could truly enjoy the new-found solitude of her castle.

"What would you like to talk about this week?" Dr. Kessler asked.

"Well, I like to talk about Michael."

"Alright then, how is Michael?"

"He's wonderful." Ruby placed one hand over her heart. "He's so smart and kind and appropriate."

"Appropriate?"

"Oh, yes, always. He knows what's expected of him in every situation and he's respectful above all else. My boy is downright good to his core, salt of the earth. I raised him right." Her head bobbed in proud confirmation.

"Have you spoken to him since we last met? You mentioned he seemed very well at the funeral, all things considered, and I wondered if my hypothesis was far off."

Ruby's bottom lids twitched inwardly. She remembered his accusation perfectly well, and she'd rather hoped he wouldn't bring up that outrageous nonsense again. Her Michael wasn't involved romantically. She'd know. A mother knew these things. Michael stayed busy studying and working hard and making a nice niche for himself in society. Her young man had a bright future with no room for romance.

"Ruby, have you spoken with him?"

"No." The guilt flowed through her. Michael had tried to reach her many times in the past few weeks. She had a dozen of his messages saved on her machine, but finding a good time to return the call had proved impossible. By the time she settled in the evening, it was after ten o'clock and not a proper time for phone calls. She started baking for Betty most days much earlier than acceptable for a morning phone call. The timing gave her fits. She needed to put the call on her calendar. She needed to let him know not to worry.

"No? Hasn't he kept in touch? I assumed after your loss, he might take some time off from school to be with you." Dr. Kessler twirled his glasses by their stem between his thumb and first finger. His expression pensive.

"I'd never ask such a thing of him, doctor." But he had a valid point. *Why hadn't Michael at least offered to keep me company for a few days?* He had to know the difficulty she had with such a large and sudden loss. He should have stayed to take care of her. Ruby grew uncomfortable. She didn't like the niggling doubt Dr. Kessler tried to plant in her mind. Her boy was perfect. She needed to prove that to Dr. Kessler. She crossed her arms and pondered how to go about it.

"Well," Dr. Kessler, shifted, crossing one leg over the other and placing his glasses upon his nose again. "Let me know when you talk with him. I'm interested in his preoccupation. It could have a significant impact on you." He made a notation in his notebook.

Ruby said as little as possible for the remainder of their session.. The minute she got home, she'd call Michael and find out why he hadn't at least tried to stay with her. Ruby barely heard a word the good doctor said. She worked to keep her answers short and general, in the event she had to say anything at all.

Dr. Kessler excused her ten minutes early. She appreciated the gesture.

"See you next week, Ruby?"

Ruby nodded, smiled and left.

*****

Dr. Kessler had worked with Ruby's family before, and having her back in his office posed an emotional challenge for him. On one hand, Ruby clearly needed continued therapy, but on the other, he wished he'd retired last summer as his wife suggested.

He sat at his desk looking at his notes. Something seemed amiss with Ruby. She kept something she wanted to tell him hidden. He could find no other reason for her attending sessions while refusing to speak. He tapped a pen against his thin lips and pointed chin, contemplating the Russell family. An average upper-middle class family, for all intents and purposes. Working father, stay-at-home-mother, and one child off to college. But beyond those basics, the Russells were nowhere close to average.

His eyes drifted over the countless frames on his desk. His office brimmed with his wife's beautiful face. He counted his blessings for the peace and normalcy he had outside his office door.

Pulling a snapshot from the corner of a small frame, he smiled. Meredith was his first and only love. They'd met in college where she had perfected the term flower child. She studied minimalist perspective and philosophy. To this day she lived as a purist, a yoga fanatic and vegan extraordinaire. He had studied politics until he decided to cure insanity. He chuckled recalling his immature thoughts. They shared a carefree life then. Not much had changed. Meredith remained his perfect counterpart.

The phone rang, as it often did when he thought of her. A result of their cosmic connection in her mind. To him, a reflection of the amount of time he spent thinking of her.

"Hello, sweetheart," he cooed.

"Hello."

He imagined her blushing as they spoke.

"How's your day so far?"

"Well, I miss you as I always do, so I'm hoping you're free for lunch."

"Always, for you."

"Fabulous. I'll pack a basket. Will you meet me by the lake in the park?"

"Without a doubt, but I'll pick something up on my way," his voice teased, though he intended to do just that. In thirty years, he'd never managed to acquire a taste for vegan faire. Their differences aside, no one could ever say Dr. and Mrs. Kessler didn't make a lovely couple. They were perfect for each other.

*****

At home, another message from Michael waited on her answering machine. Ruby returned the call immediately. She tapped her fingers on the counter while she waited and tried in vain to keep from focusing on the doubts Dr. Kessler had forced into her mind. Her heart drooped. He hadn't made an effort to take care of her when she needed him.

"Mom!" His voice held a mixture of relief and joy. "I've been trying to reach you for forever. I've called every day.

Where have you been?" The excitement passed and his voice became cross. "I was ready to send the local authorities."

Any mention of "authorities" these days was an anathema to Ruby. She put up her guard. "Why?"

"To check on you. What do you think? Why haven't you returned any of my calls?"

"I've been busy and haven't had a chance. You know, you could have come in person. You needn't send strangers to check on me if you're concerned." Ruby let a little of her petulance leak into her voice.

"Mom, I'd have to miss work and school and pay for airfare to and from. All those preparations to find you too busy to let me know you aren't in a coma or something? Wait. Are you alright?"

Ruby had spent the better part of an hour preparing to scold him. Being asked yet again if she was alright sent her in search of some wine. She was fine.

"I wouldn't want to inconvenience you." Her voice betrayed her, pitiful, sad and tormented, irritating her further. No wonder everyone always asked if she were alright.

"Mom, I'd do anything for you, you know that. I've been trying hard to get you every day."

It was true, she couldn't deny that. But still…She lifted her chin an inch and waited for more.

"I would have come. I promise. If I thought something might be wrong, I'd have sent the authorities to be with you immediately while I crossed the world to get to you."

Silence.

"I would have rented a camel and crossed the desert."

She allowed a smirk to rise before squashing it.

"I would have hired a band of pirates to sail me through the seas."

The smirk returned. "Pirates are dangerous."

"I would have walked their plank into shark infested waters."

"And then what?"

"Fought the sharks with my bare hands before swimming the Atlantic to reach you."

"Fine."

"I love you, Mom."

"Alright then. What else did you want to tell me? You called to check on me, but what else?"

"You always see through me."

The pause grew uncomfortable for her. "Michael?" She shut her eyes tight, praying he'd prove Dr. Kessler wrong about another woman in his life. She'd had enough of sharing her men. The last time it hadn't ended too well.

"Well, I hoped I could come up and stay with you for your birthday."

"Oh, Michael!" She clapped her hands together. "It'd be the perfect gift!"

"Alright then. I have a surprise when I come."

"Excellent! I'll make up your old room and prepare all your favorite things."

Her mind flooded with all the ways she could impress her son when he arrived. It'd be ideal if he moved home as soon as he finished school. Even better if he changed schools and came now. She put it on her list of things to address. She'd get materials on all the local schools and have them on hand when he arrived.

Ruby twisted the phone cord around one plump finger. All things considered, perhaps she should look into making a move in his direction. Ruby played with the idea, but only for a moment. *Moving is such a hassle.* Easier for him than her. It'd be better for her to finish what she'd started in Montrose Hills and get back to normal, minus Ken.

However, this new development did mean some

changes to her plans. Ruby needed to get things cleaned up before Michael came to see her. She wanted to give him all her attention. She had too many distractions at the moment.

"Thanks, Mom. I'm so glad to come, and I think you'll be happy for me. Life is more incredible than I've ever imagined it could be. It's almost as nice as when I lived at home with you."

"Oh, someday maybe you'll have the chance again."

"Maybe." Michael left it at that. "I've got to get to class and I work tonight, so I'll call next week. We'll finalize our plans, and we'll be together soon. Your birthday is right around the corner. You're thirty this year, right?"

"Hush, you." She blushed. She had raised him right. All the doubts Dr. Kessler tried to plant in her withered away.

They exchanged a few kisses into the receivers and Ruby floated away from the phone, her chest inflating with pride as she went.

*****

Michael sat at his small table and sipped a soda reliving the strange conversation with Ruby. He knew his mother, and whomever he'd just spoken to on the telephone wasn't her. When she hadn't returned his calls, he'd imagined her sitting alone all day in his father's closet, maybe wearing one of his sweaters and crying. His mother would have tortured herself over the loss. She should have been comatose for at least another four months.

The picture of her at his graduation, hanging front and center on his refrigerator, was all he could think about. His high school graduation had been difficult for her. She swelled with pride despite the coming loss. He had no good way to explain his reasons for leaving town. College was his chance to decide for himself who he wanted to be. She was hurt and angry, but she smiled despite the visible perspiration. Above all else, she wanted him to be happy.

Ruby lived life on edge, in search of love and approval. Michael understood her and had made a point of being her hero since third grade when he realized he made a difference. His father never tried, and his mother needed a hero more than anyone he'd ever known. She needed to be loved.

Muffled voices and music filtered in through the walls of his small apartment. After his years of college life, returning home to Montrose Hills for any period of time worried him. He'd always known he couldn't live there forever. Going back made him feel like a fly heading into a beautiful web. Luckily, he didn't have to return alone.

Michael stood and tossed a soda can into the recycle bin. His mother had been too busy to return his call, though he called every single day. What kept her busy? She didn't seem depressed, didn't pout. She sounded alive. He drummed his fingers against the phone, considering another call. Mrs. Mason would know what his mother had been up to.

Michael tapped the phone against his forehead. Charlotte knew, but she'd never tell. He sighed and laid the phone down. It comforted him to know his mother had a friend in his absence, but Charlotte Mason was not who he'd have chosen. Of course, Charlotte had no one else, and his mother was alone now, too. His stomach tightened with guilt. He shouldn't have left her, but he didn't want to become her either. Making the decision to leave at eighteen still haunted him. He'd second guessed it every day for seven years.

"How'd it go?" asked a soft voice from behind him.

"I'm not sure."

Sophia Walsh stood against the far wall, allowing him space. Her smiled reminded him of cherubim. The soft cotton sundress hung from her shoulders and stopped just above her knees. A flimsy white sheath and nothing more. Sunlight danced against it, wreaking havoc on his concentration.

Michael crossed the room in three long strides and scooped her into his arms. He buried his face in her peach-scented hair. A tiny gasp from her sent goose bumps up his arms. He pressed his warm lips against hers and no longer feared for his mother, or anything else. He was home.

CHAPTER EIGHT

The last rays of an Indian summer sun warmed Ruby's shoulders. She knelt in her yard, pruning the plants and bushes. Her immaculate flower beds deserved trophies. Everyone always said so. Gardening soothed her much more than speaking with Dr. Kessler. Everyone should work the earth with their hands.

Ruby rocked back on her heels, adjusted her sun hat and wiped her brow. Fall flowers bloomed all around, their sweet aroma scented the air. Satisfaction filled her and she allowed herself a little smile. She didn't condone pride, but sometimes it couldn't be helped. Some things deserved a little pat on the back. Her beautiful garden served as a brilliant example.

Voices interrupted her reverie. Looking in the direction of her van, she found three cars lined up in Tillie's drive. The sun made it difficult to see faces, but she hoped Tillie's hillbilly family hadn't arrived. She had gotten a good look at that motley crew when they came to arrange her funeral, and she counted one look as fill for a lifetime.

The Tanners had made themselves at home for a week after the funeral, a vacation from whatever Appalachian rock they crawled out from under. The whole lot of them had sat on the front porch every evening drinking beer, of all things. They even pulled Tillie's grill around into her driveway instead of leaving it on the rear patio, where they all belonged. Ruby cringed, remembering the language, the obnoxious laughter and the way the men spat and the women flicked cigarette butts onto the driveway where children drove over them with dump trucks and bicycles.

Her heart hammered. Her peace shattered. She stood and made her way around front. Ruby surveyed her property line. Anyone observing her should see she merely critiqued her landscape. Using her peripheral vision she sized up the set of cars. They weren't the Tanner cars. *Praise God.* The fact they were all cars evidenced that. A sedan led the pack and parked nearest to Tillie's garage. Behind the first sat two new foreign models. Each far more sensible than Ken's, though equally expensive by the look of them.

Ruby inched back, packed up her gardening things and took off her dirty gloves. Then made her way to the side door where she entered casually. Upon closing the door, she sped upstairs to Michael's old room which faced the Tanner house. With the light already off, she only had to stay out of the sunlight and pay attention.

The trio inside Tillie's house moved past one window after another, up the staircase in single file, two men and one woman. Her hand flew to her chest. Heaven help them if they were up to what it looked like they were up to. The neighborhood didn't need those kinds of shenanigans, for pity sake. Decent people lived there.

Why didn't they have better acoustics? Their homes stood no more than fifteen feet apart. She should hear something, shouldn't she? Useless. She abandoned her post.

Back down the stairs she went. Her hands slid along the railing, and her knees wobbled beneath her. She barely made it out the front door before the last two cars pulled away. She missed her chance to learn anything about the little parade.

The sedan was still in the drive. The woman appeared on the front porch, locking up with an enormous set of keys. The sight of her said she belonged at any private club in town, but her beater car betrayed her. The car belonged outside of a thrift store. Only one reason a woman in a six hundred dollar suit drove a ten thousand dollar car and left an empty house. Tillie's family must have hired a realtor.

Ruby sighed. There was always one more thing in need of her attention. Something continually disturbed her peace. She found an ounce of relief knowing the three of them didn't plan to take up residence beside Ruby, but now she had the added stress of not knowing who would become her neighbor. The woman circled around her car and opened the trunk. Time to seize an opportunity, to make friends and get the inside scoop on who wanted the position. Ruby sighed. She really didn't like meeting new people, or interfering. People, in general, proved too judgmental and sometimes mean. She teetered for several moments before cowardice took over and she turned to run.

"Hi there! Hello!" The woman slammed the trunk of her clunker and called out to Ruby.

Ruby tugged at her filthy apron and played with the muddy gloves she toted. She hadn't thought this through. The realtor looked fabulous and she reeked of fertilizer and potting soil. How embarrassing. She chastised herself as she smiled at the woman. She normally made much better decisions.

"Hello." Ruby extended her fingers to the woman.

"Hello!" The over-perkiness didn't fit a woman of her

age. Ruby tsked her tongue. People had such a hard time being understated.

"I'm Kim Carson. I'm the realtor in charge of finding you a new neighbor."

She found a measure of comfort knowing this woman realized how much Ruby would be impacted by the new neighbor. It shouldn't be just about selling the house. The neighborhood needed to be considered. Ruby liked her better already.

"It's a lovely area. No one ever leaves unless they have to." True. Most of the neighbors had built their homes in the neighborhood when only a field and a giant stone entranceway had existed. Since then, Montrose Hills had become a local landmark.

"Did you know the previous owner?" Kim tried to draw Ruby into conversation.

A lovely area indeed. She couldn't leave, not even to live near Michael. She'd lived in Montrose Hills too long to leave, so she needed to tie up some loose ends. She rather hoped to be done with all of that mess for a while, but as they said about a woman's work…never done.

"Ma'am?" Kim's strangely fearful expression drew Ruby back to the situation at hand.

"Yes, the Tanners lived there many years, They were a," *cough, choke,* "excuse me," she rubbed her chest before she continued. "…nice people. Um, I think I need to go in and get a drink of water, excuse me."

"Wait!" Kim exclaimed. "Here you go then, a business card. In case you know anyone who might like to take a tour. It's a beautiful home, great price, awesome area."

Awesome. Ruby's tongue threatened to poke free of her tightly pressed lips.

She sighed and turned away after forcing her hand toward the card. "Awesome," almost made her leave it hanging there between them. But proper courtesy dictated one take what someone offered, within reason. Kim wouldn't sell many homes in the neighborhood talking like a valley girl. The thought refreshed Ruby. She hoped realty wasn't Kim's main source of income, though her car implied differently.

The next few weeks proved a terrible trial of Ruby's patience. Cars paraded past her home without a break and at all sorts of hours. Once she even found a couple with small children on the lawn after eight at night, as if the children didn't need sleep. Not the kind of people Ruby wanted living next door, but ever since Kim Carson hammered a for sale sign in front of Tillie's house, the traffic hadn't stopped. The whole point of living on a cul-de-sac was peace and quiet, but if the traffic continued that would be a completely moot point.

The thought of children living next door set Ruby's teeth on edge. Children were loud and messy and they always came in groups. She imagined every horrific scenario a hundred times. Tricycles in her driveway and balls in the flower beds. Some obnoxious playground equipment or clubhouse would ruin the view from her tea house out back. Erecting a ten foot fence would only make her yard look less spacious and more institutional. That wouldn't do at all. There had to be a way around the nightmare. Tillie Tanner's home shouldn't be on the market. She was ruining Ruby's life, even from the grave.

For once, Ruby looked forward to her appointment with Dr. Kessler. She had plenty to say and all of it was perfect fodder for counseling. Finally she'd get her dollar's worth. Surely others went to therapy to unload about their neighbors? Ruby couldn't wait.

She laid out the entire story for him at their next visit. She told him about the hours people kept and the headlights in her window. She mentioned the realtor and the children. By the time she finished, her hands dripped with anxiety and hives threatened her throat and face.

As always, Dr. Kessler tossed all the atrocities out the window and picked the smallest minutiae to fixate upon. "You don't like children?"

"Not particularly, no. You can't tell anyone about that though. It's privileged."

"Of course not. Also, it's not uncommon. Some women appreciate children more when theirs are grown, pining for their youth. Other women, like yourself perhaps, appreciate the experience but are happy with their new season of life."

"Well, that's me." Her pointer finger bobbed in the air. "The second one."

"Speaking of children, how's Michael doing?"

"Wonderful!" Ruby perked up at the mention of his name. "He's coming to stay with me for my birthday. We have it all planned out, and he's bringing a surprise." Her lips turned up in a smug smile, her pride far too much to contain, though she knew it wasn't polite to boast. Dr. Kessler was dead wrong about him. Michael was her savior since his childhood and she worshipped the ground he walked on. Her smile hitched wider. The difference between her and the other Catholics at Mass was she knew her savior. She didn't need to light a candle or kneel at an alter. "Have you asked if he's seeing anyone?"

"No. That's his business to tell me. I shouldn't need to pry it out of him. Anyway, he would have told me, and so he's not or I'd know." Ruby gave the doctor a warning look.

"Ah." He buffered, taunting her.

Ruby's eyes narrowed. She didn't like it when Dr. Kessler thought he knew all about her and from the sound of it Michael, too. She paid him to listen, not to be nosey and accusatory.

Ruby fought the urge to slap him. "I'm not sure how, but I need to find a proper family with grown children to buy the Tanner house." Unwilling to discuss Michael any further, she changed the subject.

Dr. Kessler laid his pen on his desk and stared at it a bit too long. "How are you planning to do that?"

"I haven't the foggiest, but there must be some way." Ruby did a have a few ideas. She'd witnessed enough awful families on her cul-de-sac of late to learn a little about herself. She learned she wasn't entirely opposed to arson.

"You've become very take-charge. Have you noticed the change?"

"A woman without a husband must take matters into her own hands. Would you prefer I sat home alone fretting over things?" She kept her words light, but her gaze didn't match the tone.

"It's such a significant change. I wondered if it were conscious or not. Sometimes we evolve without intent where circumstance makes the change necessary."

"I haven't evolved," she spoke the word with disgust. "I'm stepping up, nothing more." Stepping up seemed a solid description for her new life. His words, "taking charge," sounded as if a negative connotation hid beneath them. Stepping up sounded more…noble.

"It's nice to find something in life to control."

Ruby thought of Olympic champions. "Precisely."

"Hmm." He tapped the pen against his lips. "Control is nice, so long as one goes about it in a healthy and productive manner. What do you control now, Ruby, with Michael on his own and Ken gone?" His face shone with interest.

"Everything."

"I see." He leaned back in his chair, putting another few inches between them. "Everything." He repeated the word without intonation and she nodded.

"Do you care to expound on that?"

"How do you mean?" She knew exactly how to provoke him.

"Please, tell me more about your stepping up." It sounded less noble and more indecent when he said it.

"Well, I'm baking." Nothing new there. "Charlotte and I have more fun now, shopping excursions and tea." Ruby smiled.

"What else?"

"Gardening. I'm also getting things in order for Michael's visit. I have every day planned out."

"Are you still volunteering? You spent so many hours with your organizations before. Do you do that still?" It occurred to Ruby that Dr. Kessler seemed uncertain. He lacked his former confidence and looked a bit apprehensive. The idea that she might be the cause tickled her, but she didn't smile. Not yet.

Ruby shared her secrets with no one.

"Yes, a little. I've been busy." Ruby blushed. She knew she wasn't spending enough time on her volunteer work aside from baking daily for Betty's causes. She had more time with Ken out of the way, but she spent less time doing good deeds. She thought of the people at the homeless shelter once more. Could she ever make up for that? Her heart clenched and a bead of sweat wetted her temple. She lowered her eyes to seem coy, hoping the doctor wouldn't see her sweat. She knew that in the right light, her naturally black lashes cast shadows across her high cheekbones, accenting her large blue eyes. She kept many secrets there. Her mother had said eyes were the windows to the soul. But Ruby shared her secrets with no one.

"Busy?" Dr. Kessler pressed.

Ruby stared. He broached yet another closed topic. Rude.

"How about Ken? How are you doing, adjusting to an empty home, knowing he's gone? Sometimes it takes a while to sink in. Are you taking the medication? Is it helping?"

"Dr. Kessler," Ruby smirked. "You seem flustered. I normally admire your natural composure."

He smiled again.

"The grief, Ruby? I'm trying to discern your need, but every week when you leave, I feel I have no idea where the hour went. I'm not sure I'm helping you at all."

This time, Ruby gave Dr. Kessler a familiar look, pity.

*****

Traffic slowed in her neighborhood after Ruby ran copies of the paper from Tillie's untimely death. She made sure to keep them in the little Plexiglas box which contained information on the house, as well as wedged in the glass front door to the Tanner home. One thing about Montrose Hills was news traveled. Anyone who hadn't heard the tale of Tillie's house of multiple death knew now, and the rush to move in diminished.

Ruby snuggled into her favorite chair in the sunroom with some Earl Grey tea and the television. Her programs were starting soon and she couldn't wait to put her feet up without the annoyance of headlights streaming past all evening. The news anchors wrapped their final segment. Soon she could watch celebrities try their hand at dancing. Watching was always a stark reminder that an entire country existed out there in dire need of some culture. She knew millions watched with her, and witnessed the graceful art of dancing. It satisfied her to know they were exposed in some small part to an era where charm and social graces had been very important. Still, she doubted they took any of it to heart. She also wished the women would feel the need to cover themselves better, but they never did.

Preparations for Michael's arrival were set. Happiness

bubbled in her chest. Dr. Kessler continued to peeve her with his hints about Michael seeing a girl at school, but she shoved the thoughts aside, determined to enjoy a quiet evening. Dr. Kessler often pushed when he shouldn't and asked far too many questions. It bothered her that he couldn't simply be happy she came every week. When he wasn't pestering her about Michael, it was Charlotte or her baking, or her feelings about Ken's passing. His poor wife must count her blessings he worked so many hours. Therapist or not, his prodding felt intrusive to Ruby. Still, it didn't suit to be unhappy with Dr. Kessler. He couldn't help his nosey nature.

Ruby stirred her tea and set the cup on the table beside her. Her eyes ran over the clock and back to the television. With only a few minutes until her show began, the thrill of anticipation collapsed when, Emma Eaken's smug face appeared center screen. Emma stood in front of a strip mall waving her microphone around. Apparently a buy one get one free sale was enough to dispatch a camera crew these days. Ruby rolled her eyes and pumped up the volume with the remote, making a show of her irritation.

"…has had its share of problems in the past, but this is a case of killer confections. Emma Eaken, Channel 3 News." As the camera shot pulled wide, Treeline Bakery appeared as Emma's backdrop.

Oh my.

Ruby hoisted herself from the recliner and headed for the porch. She hadn't had time to look at the Daily Gazette. With any luck, the paper would provide something more to go by. What was Emma Eaken up to now? She opened the paper wide and ransacked the entire thing, page by page by page. The paper made no mention of Treeline Bakery or Tillie Tanner. Ruby relaxed. No need to go jumping to conclusions.

She cursed Emma Eaken for ruining her show for her. Ruby missed the opening credits. Then her mind wandered, causing her to miss even more. Bleary eyed, she waited for the recap during the eleven o'clock news, but she never made it past the weather.

In the morning, the phone woke her. The ringing played into her subconscious until she thought the fire alarm sounded. In her dream she made the most beautiful creation for Michael. White coconut cake adorned with extravagant white sugar crystals, each detail intricate and precise. The final portion burned. She smelled the acrid smoke and tugged at the jammed oven door to no avail. The fire alarm blared, but try as she might she couldn't reach it.

"Hello? Hello?" Terror filled Ruby's voice as she answered still half asleep. The dream played fresh in her mind and her heart pumped furiously.

"Good, you haven't left town. I think you may need some help, and I'm coming over unless you're on your way out somewhere." Charlotte's kind voice snapped her to attention. What did she mean?

"You woke me. I fell asleep in the armchair last night, and I had the worst dream."

"Honey, it's not a dream. I'll be there in half an hour." Charlotte hung up and Ruby wobbled against the wall, getting her bearings.

The clock revealed the length to which she overslept. Eight o'clock already. If Emma Eaken hadn't ruined her evening, she would have slept in her own bed and woken properly at six. Now she'd lost half the day, and it looked like company was coming. *Good Grief.*

Ruby dumped her coffee out. The timer had prepared it at six, then shut off after an hour. Her favorite French roast classified as both old and cold. She started over and waited impatiently, tugging at her clothing, wrinkled from sleep.

She gave her stove door a tug, too, just to make sure, then wandered through the living room to the front porch. The paper waited on top of her hedges.

Ruby tucked it under one arm and returned to the kitchen island. Coffee sizzled and snapped as it brewed and dripped into the pot on the counter. She poured the available drops into a large mug and began her morning routine. She removed the rubber band from the paper with a snap and stored it with the others. Paying for the news she watched the night before classified as foolish, so Ruby kept all the extras like rubber bands and plastic baggies when it rained. Inside the paper revealed everything she'd missed on the eleven o'clock news.

DEADLY DESSERT.

> Treeline Bakery is under investigation for their possible involvement in the deaths of five area women. Earlier this summer, the ladies, who were long-time friends, met for a weekly game of Bridge. Nancy Nelson, Patty Penland, Joyce Girard and Debbie Dexter arrived at the home of Tillie Tanner on a sunny Tuesday morning. An investigation of the morning's events turned up one small clue. The Bridge club never met without their favorite coffee cake, ordered and delivered by Treeline Bakery.
>
> Treeline has long boasted its award winning line of sugar free products. The coffee cake, their most requested item on the menu, is served in rehabilitation centers across the state. That's where the fatal five made their acquaintances. All were sufferers of Type 2 diabetes, which led them to Mill Creek Meadows where they vowed to change their lives. Afterwards, these women met regularly for encouragement and fellowship. Treeline's sugar free

coffee cake was a staple on the menu. Little did they know, the thing that brought them together would eventually keep them apart forever.

Ruby shut the paper. This required more coffee. The implications of this investigation could be promising. Tying the coffee cake to Treeline made for very good news. She filled her cup and went to change clothes. Charlotte needed to hear this.

*****

"What on earth?" Charlotte shut the door behind her.

"I'm working on something delicious." Ruby smiled wickedly at her friend.

"You'll weigh two hundred pounds if you eat all of that! Food is not the answer. Whatever it is, we can talk about it."

"Silly, Charlotte," Ruby scolded, still smiling. "I have a plan."

A plethora of white bakery boxes, along with their removed contents and golden labels covered the kitchen island and much of Ruby's countertops. Only the tiniest portions of smart gray marble peeked from underneath it all. Charlotte frowned. She'd never seen Ruby's kitchen in such disarray. For her to be so happy, despite the mayhem was inconceivable.

"What are you up to?" Charlotte glanced over her shoulder and out the nearest window once or twice.

"Emma Eaken has everyone looking at Treeline," she said in her most mysterious campfire voice. "They figured out Tillie ordered from Treeline every week and are investigating."

"Yes." Charlotte covered her mouth with her long fingers. "An investigation." That's exactly what she had called to discuss, but never dreamed how it would frenzy Ruby.

"Yep." Ruby licked a whisk from a large glass bowl. "This is our out. I'm wrapping things up."

Charlotte watched Ruby scrape the bowl. Thick yellow liquid oozed into a round aluminum pan. Ruby hummed some sort of melody. Her eyes stretched a little wider than Charlotte preferred.

"Ruby, you're baking."

"Mmmhmm."

"You have a kitchen full of pastries."

"Mmmhmm."

"I shall repeat my initial inquiry. What are you up to?"

"I'm sending Emma Eaken a cheesecake."

The words floated around a while before Charlotte questioned them. Making a cheesecake was beneath Ruby and she didn't like the reporter. If she intended the cheesecake as some sort of reward for looking at Treeline, then it was the opposite of helpful. In fact, it was incriminating. Unless…

"You wouldn't." Charlotte's heart jerked and sputtered.

"What an incredible opportunity! Surely even you see that? I can put all eyes on the bakery. Tomorrow morning, I'll be home free, and then I can get my new life in order. There's no sense having this miraculous kitchen if the only things I ever bake are poison. I have a near heart attack every time I drop anything off for Betty. It's killing me. Besides, Michael's on his way home, and I want to get this mess behind me."

Charlotte sat motionless in a chair near the wall. Her mouth parted and her eyes grew damp. The investigation wasn't good news. Investigations never were. Ruby should not be happy and know better than to get any further involved. She couldn't afford to be reckless. Charlotte stared at Ruby's new marble floor, listening to the progress.

Twenty minutes later Ruby announced, "Time to

destroy the evidence." She packed all the pastries from Treeline into her own bakery boxes and carried them to her van. Charlotte puttered along beside her. The Treeline boxes and golden seals were returned to their hiding spot in Ruby's new pantry. The goodies she prepared for a trip.

"Aren't you even going to ask where we're going?" Ruby said, her voice thick with disappointment.

Charlotte gazed out the passenger side window, not wanting to know. She still hoped to come up with a plan to stop the madness. She didn't come up with anything. She couldn't believe that Ruby plotted. Charlotte was supposed to be the planner.

Things were going from bad to worse, and she couldn't care much less than she already did about where they might end up. Every time she came to Ruby's aid lately, Ruby was off complicating things, without so much as a word to her.

"We're taking all of these things to the mission in the city where those people died. I want to help out, and it's almost dinnertime, or it will be by the time we arrive." Ruby's sounded confident.

The women rode in tense silence. Sounds of birds and traffic poured in through the open windows. Rushing wind beat Charlotte's hair against her cheeks and stung her eyes. Though she sat only two feet from her dearest friend, the woman beside her felt more like a stranger.

She nailed the timing. A crowd milled in the lot when the van pulled in.

Charlotte looked at the faces, imagining those who'd eaten Ruby's last deposit of sustenance. Her tummy roiled. The people had thin faces and limbs. They looked so sad and despondent. As if their roads weren't tough enough, they now had to come get food at a location where others had died doing the same.

*****

"Are you going to help me or sit there?" Ruby asked Charlotte as she moved to the back and unloaded boxes.

"Ruby Russell?" Reverend Flynn hustled to the van.

"Hello, Reverend." Ruby spoke with grace. "I've been baking and I wanted to offer some special treats to the mission. This place has been through so much this year."

"That's very kind, Mrs. Russell, very kind."

"Thank you." Ruby moved around him and made her way to the building.

Reverend Flynn followed, carrying another bundle behind her. "Mrs. Russell, I wanted to call you."

Ruby stopped in her tracks and waited, without turning toward him. He passed her and pulled the glass door open. She continued onward. "I'd like to come by and see you tomorrow, if you don't mind."

"Oh," she breathed again and hoped her perspiration would be attributed to the load and not to her nerves. Charlotte needed to come over tomorrow, now. "That would be lovely. Would you like to come for tea?" As she spoke the words, her mind turned them over, displeased to be forced into such a situation. What reason could possibly bring him back after their last visit?

"Tea will be fine. I appreciate your hospitality, ma'am."

Her spine stiffened. She'd forgotten how much younger he was than herself. Then he called her ma'am. With any luck, tomorrow would be his last visit. She needed a plan. Ruby hurried back to the van after all the sweets were delivered. Charlotte sat motionless, staring through the windshield at nothing.

"You have to stop by tomorrow afternoon. Reverend Flynn wants to come for tea."

"What for?"

Ruby was glad to hear her speak. The last time Charlotte

fell quiet like this it ended in a nervous breakdown.

"Tea, and I don't want to be alone with him. Who knows what he's up to."

Charlotte nodded. She made her excuses to leave the moment they pulled into Ruby's drive.

Ruby arranged her van in the driveway and waved good-bye to Charlotte.

She rummaged through her enormous bag looking for her house key until she reached the door. All of her lights burned bright inside the house and a strange car sat across the street.

She shoved the door open with one hand, and stopped cold.

"Mom? Where have you been?" Michael snaked his arms around her middle and spun her off her feet.

When did he get home?

CHAPTER NINE

"I was delivering some pastries to the local mission." The hint of a question peeked behind the statement.

Michael laughed and rubbed his stomach. "I hope you didn't have plans for that cheesecake in the fridge."

Ruby's heart stopped. "What!" Her blood ran cold and her face flamed with heat. She pushed past him and raced for her kitchen.

Michael followed. "It looks like heaven."

Ruby hefted the cheesecake from the fridge and inspected it from every angle.

"It took all my self-control not to rip into it, but I was too worried to eat."

"What's wrong?" Ruby dropped the weapon onto the counter, satisfied to find not so much as a finger-mark in the topping. Catastrophes seemed to encompass her.

"You!" he exclaimed joyfully. "I thought you'd be here waiting for me on the porch, or have dinner ready for a hundred guests. Instead, I find an empty house, doors locked and not even a note. You scared me, Mom."

Her birthday? She'd forgotten, and apparently so had Charlotte.

"I made reservations at La Petite Maison. Can you be ready in half an hour?"

Ruby threw her arms around her son and choked back the pride and tears. He was simply too much. No wonder she revered him. How could she not?

Ding dong.

Ruby turned toward the door and heard silverware jostling behind her. Michael pulled a server from the utensil drawer and prepared to help himself to the cheesecake.

Ding dong.

Squish.

"Mom!" Michael grabbed Ruby's arm and pried her from the countertop. She'd thrown herself onto the cake as if to protect him from a live grenade. She couldn't bear to look at him, and he slowly released her to answer the door.

Ding dong

"Coming." Michael's voice remained calm as he left her side. He glanced back at her ruefully.

Ruby continued to lay there, spread atop her counter, stuck by cream cheese and cherry syrup. She laid her cheek against the granite until she heard an unfamiliar voice.

"Is everything alright?" the voice asked. "Have you had a chance to talk with her? I could have come later. When did you get here?" The voice belonged to a woman, one whom Ruby had never met, but seemed to know her son well.

A round of whispering began. Tears welled up in Ruby's eyes. Her Michael could have been killed by her own poison-baking hands. The door clicked shut, and Michael's voice sounded again.

"I've been home almost two hours. I sat here alone. I think she forgot I was coming, and then," he hesitated, "she's not acting like herself. Give me a minute, would you?" Silence followed. His footfalls returned in a moment.

"Mom, I planned to talk to you earlier, but things aren't turning out right. Umm." He waited while Ruby disengaged her blouse from the sticky red mess. She looked as if she'd been knifed.

"Sophia is here and I hoped she could join us for dinner. I planned to discuss this with you when I arrived, but the afternoon came and went and here we are. I know you'll love her, Mom. I do." His prideful expression lit his features. It didn't take long for Ruby to realize what was happening. She grabbed a dish towel from the drawer and scraped the mess from her blouse.

"I'll get that, Mom. Really." Michael motioned to the mess on the countertop.

Ruby slipped around the corner towards the stairs. What must Michael think about seeing his mother dive onto a cherry cheesecake like that? She should have pretended to drop it on the floor, but hindsight was always twenty-twenty. Ruby pressed her back to the wall, pondering "Sophia."

She leaned against the stairs and listened.

"Should I go?" Sophia whispered.

"No. I want you two to be best friends, so the sooner we get started the better."

Ruby dragged herself up the stairs contemplating suicide, murder and what the worst birthday in history might hold.

As she crept back down the steps twenty minutes later, Ruby took in the young girl seated with her son. Sophia was unarguably the worst thing to ever walk through their front door. She dressed almost as neatly as Ruby. A grey pencil skirt of appropriate length covered her knees, black patent leather heels covered her crossed ankles and a matching belt cinched her tiny, size-nothing waist. She chose a matching grey silk blouse and headband to complete the very lady-like ensemble. One delicate strand of pearls rested across her collarbone. Her hands lay folded in her lap and her childlike eyes widened as she watched Michael move around the room. Ruby hated her immediately.

She eyed the spotless kitchen. The young couple had erased the entire mess, leaving no evidence there'd ever been one, aside from Ruby's soiled blouse and demeanor.

"Mother!" Michael jumped and ran to meet her. "Mother, this is Sophia Walsh. I met her at school in a culinary course we shared. She reminded me so much of you I struck up a conversation with her and we've been thick as thieves ever since."

"You bake?" Bile rose in Ruby's throat.

"No, ma'am. I'm afraid baking isn't my forte after all."

One point in Sophia's favor.

"Shall we go?" Michael waved his watch at his mother and locked elbows with Sophia. Then he reached his palm outward to Ruby, and she glared at the offering. In her experience, sharing didn't end well. Her eyes darted to the floor. Memories of Kenneth in his chocolate mousse mask flitted past.

Michael drove them in the rental car, although Sophia's car would have done the job just as well. As it was, Sophia rode in back while Ruby took the passenger seat. If Sophia had driven, Ruby and Michael could have talked in the back. He had a lot to answer for.

Tension zinged inside the car. Ruby's new blouse wasn't right for dinner at La Petite Maison, but Michael hadn't given her time to prepare the way she liked. She knew Sophia appeared to be twice the lady she was and Ruby's feathers ruffled further with every mile. Michael didn't sabotage Sophia. She'd probably spent the entire afternoon getting ready. He chose to ambush his mother on her birthday. Ruby sulked and stewed in the passenger seat the entire way to dinner, glancing at the strange man beside her from time to time. Where was her Michael? Her temper sparked whenever they spoke to her. She had nothing to say to either of them. They must know what they'd done and if they didn't, then Ruby would never be able to make them understand. An enormous sigh flew from her lips.

"So, did you say you delivered food to a mission?" Michael looked at his mom.

"Yes, the Partridge Parish. It's downtown."

"Oh," Sophia gasped. "Did you hear what happened there? Michael, did I tell you?"

"No. What happened?"

"All these people went there to eat and they died. They got some kind of food poisoning. They're still looking into the details. My mother and father have donated their time to the ministry since they heard."

Michael gave Ruby a satisfied smile. Ruby turned her face towards the window.

"What did you take them?"

"Everything," she answered. "Mostly desserts."

"My mother's a fabulous baker." Michael beamed into the rearview mirror.

"So I've heard."

"What was going on with that cheesecake?" Michael asked.

"What?"

Michael gave her the stink eye. "You worried I'd eaten it, as if it was a special treasure for someone. Then you crushed it as if no one should have eaten it."

Sophia sat silent.

"You're speeding." The speedometer showed thirty-seven in a thirty-five zone. He nudged the brake and rolled his eyes. She wouldn't answer those questions tonight. He showed his intelligence when he dropped the subject and concentrated on his speed the rest of the drive to the restaurant.

La Petite Maison wasn't an easy place to get a reservation and Ruby began to understand why Michael had gone to such lengths. It certainly wasn't to celebrate his old mother's birthday. Worse yet, he must have made the reservation a month ago when he first told her he was coming. That meant he'd been seeing Sophia for at least as long and had kept it from her. In fact, she tossed the idea around further; they were serious enough a month ago to plan to bring her home to meet his mother. That meant they'd been dating far longer. Ruby held onto her stomach, certain the contents would soon make an embarrassing reappearance.

The valet took the car, and Michael led the women into the restaurant. Cool evening air fluttered Ruby's bangs against her face. Even Indian summer ended sooner or later, and the proof chilled her cheeks. Their five o'clock reservation meant an opportunity to watch the sunset from their position on the lake. La Petite Maison boasted one of the only places anywhere near Montrose Hills where that was possible. It would have been Ruby's idea of a perfect evening, if only they hadn't had a third wheel.

In the foyer, soft music played while they waited to begin the not-so-casual dinner. The atmosphere impressed as always. Ruby could count on one hand the number of times Ken had brought her there. Reservations at La Petit Maison were saved for special occasions. No doubt the reason Michael had chosen the spot for his shenanigans. He wanted to make the night special. Ruby rolled her eyes. Michael pulled her close.

The maître de led them to a small round table near the back of the restaurant. Candles flickered alongside fresh flowers in the center of a crimson cloth. Ruby planned to seat herself between her son and the girl, but the table made it impossible. Instead she busied herself with finding a good reason for Michael to leave Sophia in the dust.

"Sophia, what do you do for a living?"

"Right now, I'm a teaching assistant at a local elementary school, but as soon as I finish my degree, I'll find a position as a teacher, locally, I hope." The glance in Michael's direction didn't go unnoticed. Ruby pressed on.

"You aren't studying for your graduate degree?"

"No." Sophia blushed. "I'm finishing my bachelor's degree this spring. I'm a little younger than Michael."

"How much?"

"I'm twenty-two." Her eyes darted as she waited for Ruby to think that over.

"You're just three years younger. That's not so bad."

Ruby planned to point out the shortcomings of dating younger women to Michael after they returned home.

"Three years separated you and Dad, right?"

Ruby cringed. Three years and a plethora of other things like class and good sense.

"Where are you from?" She said she wanted a local job. Local to Timbuktu sounded perfect.

"I'm from Ashland." *Muffins.* Ashland was a neighboring community not twenty miles from Montrose Hills, and arguably nicer. The homes were exquisite, as were the schools, and the affluence rivaled Montrose Hills in every way. The Russells had moved to Montrose before Ashland had made a name for itself. So much for Timbuktu.

Ruby sighed and tried again. "Do you attend church, dear?" She knew the unlikelihood of Sophia or any other full-time college student making time for traditions like church. She herself hadn't been to St. Peters in eons.

"Absolutely! My family and I attend St. Luke's

Cathedral in Ashland. At school, I attend a small Catholic chapel near the university. Religion is a major deal breaker for me in dating." She sounded her age. "I was ecstatic to hear Michael is Catholic!"

"He rarely attends mass." Ruby shoved a forkful of lettuce into her mouth as her salad arrived. Throwing Michael under the bus was for the best.

Michael glared as the waitress placed his salad before him and left.

"Well, that was the case when I found him, but Michael attends mass with me. For over six months now we've gone together on Sundays, Wednesdays and Saturdays. He even helps out with the altar boys on Sunday evenings."

Ruby watched as Michael stroked Sophia's hand. She fought to keep her lettuce down. Over six months. Michael had no idea what terrible timing he had. Bringing a girl home right now was unimaginable. It wouldn't do. Sophia looked like something Ruby would have, if she were in the market, ordered from a designer daughter-in-law catalogue, but she most certainly was not in the market.

"You'll have to excuse me. I'm not feeling well. Would you mind taking me home?"

"You've only had one bite of…" Michael stopped short. Ruby knew her look said to not embarrass her. She knew he never would. "No. I don't mind, Mom."

Michael and Sophia exchanged looks and stood in unison. The threesome headed home to Montrose Heights, the once fancy but still prominent subdivision in Montrose Hills, and then the young pair continued on to Ashland in Sophia's sedan.

Ruby watched the taillights disappear and immediately began to bake. She pulled her hidden bottle of wine from behind her bread maker and drank as she worked. She deserved a release after the night's nonsense. A few glasses of Chardonnay later, she felt much better. The buzzer on her stove sounded. Ruby skipped into the kitchen, potholders in hand, anticipation on her lips. One soft click from the opening oven door sent a shiver across her chest.

*****

Michael pondered the change he saw in his mother. Ruby's behavior was peculiar, even for her. She had a whole new persona. Perhaps his father's death had done more damage than he'd originally seen. He was somewhat thankful not to continue the odd evening.

"You're mother hates me."

Michael's anger quelled at the sight of Sophia. His beloved sat no more than a foot away in the passenger seat, heartbroken. She had prepared all day for dinner as if they were dining with the Queen of England, and Ruby had behaved insufferably. Flames of heat ran up from his back as they made their way towards the Walsh home. The odd mix of frustration, anger, embarrassment and now heartache was enough to rouse tears.

"She doesn't hate you." He looked at her sideways to see a great puff of air lift her bangs, and he smiled.

"Who could hate you?" It was a sincere question, designed to soothe, but genuine all the way through. Michael had no idea who could not love her immediately as he had.

Sophia twisted a loop of thread back and forth around her finger. Her eyes cast down. Her bottom lip pressed outward.

"Sophia," Michael coaxed. "My mother's more than just odd. She has, problems, dealing with things. I'm a little worried about her."

"You were bound to find love sometime."

"Yes. I know, and I assume she did, too, but I'm sure she would have preferred I waited until she died." A little crooked smile appeared. Sophia sat speechless.

"When I left for college, she went away too, for a while. She needed time to process the change, to understand I didn't leave her just because I left town. She was never the same. After that, all her oddities amplified. Dad walked around on eggshells, trying not to upset her. I think he avoided her as much as he could. It became a vicious cycle. His pulling away made her more desperate to please him. It was a mess. Now he's gone, and she's alone." Michael released a long and deep sigh.

"We could move back here together. You could look after her. My parents would be ecstatic, and I can finish school here."

Michael grimaced.

"What? She needs you. So do I."

With one hand, Michael caressed Sophia's fingers, interrupting the busy thread. Sincerity thickened his voice, like molasses over warm toast. "I won't make excuses for her." It was a solemn promise on his part. "There's no excuse for her behavior tonight. There's no excuse for that behavior, ever, and I'll talk with her. I love you, Sophia." He kissed the back of her hand gently. "She'll love and respect you as I do, or we'll simply part ways."

Sophia opened her mouth to protest, but the tears began to stream and she was silent. This wasn't the evening Michael had envisioned. Sophia shouldn't be crying and his mother shouldn't be so odd. He expected her to be a little strange after they'd had a chance to talk, but Ruby was weird on a whole new level. She was strange when they spoke on the phone and flat out over the top all night, diving on cakes, and abandoning her birthday dinner. "Sophia, I'll fix this. It'll be fine, and Mother will be mortified at her own behavior as soon as she's thinking clearly. I only said what I said to assure you of my allegiances. You're number one from here on out. You are my future."

Sophia smiled and gave him a childlike look. Sophia needed him now.

"Genesis," he confirmed, clearly reading her amusement. "The man shall leave his mother and his father and he shall cleave unto his wife." He clearly heard the breath which caught in her throat. Yes. That was precisely what he was saying.

*****

The cheesecake set in less than two hours. It was against her personal standards to bake from a box, but thanks to the tragedy which had befallen its predecessor; a box cake would have to do. She packed the treat into one of the Treeline boxes she had hidden securely in a flour dispenser inside her pantry, and she sealed it with a Treeline seal. Then she printed out a small thank you card and stuck it right on top.

Ruby smiled at her creativity. She made great plans.

That morning, outside of Treeline, she paid a boy to go inside and purchase more than a dozen baked items. He had. At home, she unpacked them and placed them in her own white boxes from Cutie's. Then she saved the Treeline boxes to do business with. The homeless shelter had the great displeasure of consuming all of the Treeline pastries, but what did they know? They'd never tasted anything from Ruby's kitchen for comparison. Well, none who were still there anyway.

With the clean white box tucked securely under one arm, and the newly concocted cheesecake inside, Ruby marched to her van, where she placed the box on the front passenger seat. She had hoped to do this much later in the night, but she hadn't planned to have to work around Michael's dating schedule. She hadn't accounted for his involvement at all, or having to make a new cake. Ruby was miffed. Either the cake was going to be delivered right then or not at all.

She drove under cover of night to the Channel 3 News Station and parked in the shadows. It was a tricky business. The lot had a night patrol and cameras, both on a loop. A security guard walked casually past the front door a few moments after she arrived. Ruby rolled onto the lot in stealth mode, lights already off. The giant oak where she stopped gave her a clear view of the front door to the station and offered cover for her van. Once the guard was out of sight, she waited while the single security camera made its slow sweep of the lot. Then it was time. Ruby crept from the van and carried the box across the lot. She moved with all the silence of a freight train, landing on every fallen leaf or branch, kicking loose stones and cursing a random barn swallow that flitted too near.

At the front of the station, she gawked at the long flight of cement stairs. With her back against the railing, she forced her feet upward to the peak. She took care to leave the cake where it wouldn't be missed, and then she raced back to her van, looking like a woman in need of cardio training. Mission accomplished. Ruby drove home to wait up for her son.

*****

Only a few minutes after Ruby pulled away, the night watchman making rounds noticed the box on the steps.

"Emma Eaken," he read aloud and snorted. "Those reporters get all the fuss." He tore the thank you note from the top and tossed it in the trash can near the door. Then he pressed his walkie-talkie. "Hey, y'all, we got some dessert coming!"

*****

Emma arrived before dawn the next day. She still pressed the Treeline story, but nothing stuck. Treeline had all sorts of problems in the past, but nothing like she suspected. A quick Google search showed illegal immigrants hired to make deliveries. An internal money scandal made headline before the immigrant drivers, and Treeline once claimed to have a hundred calorie cream puff, which turned out to be an ordinary creampuff with a yellow tint. The local bakery made a few headlines, but nothing sinister. She needed something more substantial to land her a spot on the anchor desk.

"Please," she spoke into the sky, hands clasped before her. "Please let me find some small scrap I can use to break this story and start my career." Her arms thumped back to her sides. She'd hit an investigative dead end.

Emma climbed the station's stairs slowly. The door was locked. She dug in her bag for her keycard, but couldn't find it. The sun wouldn't be in a position to give her the light she needed for another few minutes. Aggrieved, she buzzed the bell like a visitor and prepared to show her badge to get in. Waiting to enter was as infuriating as knowing she'd be covering area deaths and weddings for years to come.

Until the day shift arrived, the main doors remained locked. Employees came and went by way of keycard. Unfortunately, Emma's new bag swallowed all items smaller than a bread box. If she'd arrived an hour sooner, she could have walked in with the morning news team. Their day started the night before. Hair, makeup and wardrobe alone took more than an hour. Emma showed up too late for them and too early for the administrative staff which wouldn't arrive for another hour. She was many things, but patient wasn't one of those. She began to pound on the door, and she screamed into the security camera. "HELLO!"

Soon an intern showed up, probably trying to make a good impression, and let her in. Emma was too embarrassed and aggravated to give him a proper thank you. She barreled into her office and flipped on her computer. Time to work on her story and find the angle she kept missing.

Emma flipped through her Treeline file. She was missing something huge, but what? It was an elephant in the room invisible to her. She thought back over the path she'd started on in June. Treeline was the common thread.

She remembered the horrific scene inside the Tanner home. Big band played in the background, while sirens whirled around the cul-de-sac and EMTs called orders to policemen and bystanders. It was quite the juxtaposition. One minute all those women enjoyed the music, the camaraderie, and then cake. The next minute, BOOM. POW. Dead.

Breaking into the Tanner home was supposed to have been helpful to her case. It wasn't. The Tanner home had held none of the things she expected. All the stowed-away sugar ruined her theory of the women in the home. She wondered if they ordered the sugar free at all. They had. Treeline confirmed the standing order. Everything about the home only raised more questions, and answered none.

Emma smiled. She knew one woman on the street she wasn't wrong about. Ruby Russell. That lady was a fruitcake. Everyone on the street said so. The wholesome-looking neighborhood bustled with loquacious liquored up ladies in need of an outlet. Emma heard stories ranging from dull to absurd on the Russell front. Unfortunately, none of those shed one iota of light on Emma's enigma.

Ruby was probably crazy. The only person Emma had ever met who was anywhere near as odd was Ruby's friend Charlotte. Unstable described them both to a tee, but they didn't make a story. Emma chuckled, remembering Ruby's rain gear and then the comments she made about wearing jeans, as if jeans were somehow inappropriate.

"Anna," Emma called out of her office, unsure if Anna

was the newest intern's name. She needed to check her messages.

"Yes?" A girl appeared.

"Can you make a stop at the front desk and check my messages? I was out most of the day yesterday, and there aren't any notes on my desk." Normally, the watchman dropped off visitor slips before he left in the morning. Her eyes ran to her watch. After seven and no messages. The night shift ended at six.

"I just came from there. There weren't any messages. I got fresh coffee." She shrugged.

Emma spun her chair in a huff and headed toward the front doors. She had passed an empty desk before. This time a smile greeted her.

"Good morning, Miss Eaken," a man behind the desk called. Emma hadn't taken the time to remember his name. Turnover at the front desk was astounding.

"Are there any messages for me?" Emma leaned in heavy on her palms, looking over the tall wooden structure.

"No. Messages were all delivered when I got in," he reported brightly. "Phone's been quiet since." He looked at his watch. "It won't last."

"Probably not," Emma tapped her fingers against the desk. No messages. If it were true, then it was a first.

"What did the night shift say?" Emma looked at the desk in case he somehow missed the slips of paper. "Were the phones down or something?"

"I don't know. I didn't see Sam to ask about it. I figured he called off or shot out early."

"Why?"

"Sometimes he does."

"Sometimes Sam leaves early?" Emma guffawed at the thought. She needed her messages.

"Sure, a few minutes, I guess. It's not like there's much

work for him on midnight shift. No guests, no deliveries, next to zero phone calls. Very few calls come through the front desk. Everyone has a mobile." He waved a finger in Emma's direction. "You get your mail and messages directly, don't you?"

"He's supposed to be a night watchman. Answering phones is only a part of his job. It's not like he's the receptionist." She succumbed to the aggravation. Of course she got her mail directly, but not the paper kind. The front desk was supposed to answer and take messages when someone stopped in or called her office.

Before she lost her temper with the man at the desk, she made a mental note to report Sam for his early departure. Then she decided to make her own trip to the mailroom Maybe she had something in the mail to keep her career alive until she made headway on the Treeline case.

The mailroom door stood open, propped wide by a rubber stopper, and the radio blared from beyond. Aside from a morning talk show host, she heard nothing; no voices, no gentle swish of the automatic postage machine, no thrumming of the sorter or copier or fax. Emma clenched her fingers into fists at her side, prepared to storm the mailroom. Perhaps the entire office staff had blown off their duties like the night watchmen. Maybe they had all gone out back for a smoke break, or called it an early weekend with Sam.

Emma snapped the radio off and looked for people. She had a mouthful to say to someone. It took only seconds to see the problem. The night shift hadn't cut out early. They'd never left. A pile of people lay on the opposite side of a long table used to sort the mail. Chairs speckled the floor around them. A spray of playing cards spread over them and on the table above. Beyond the cards sat a white pastry box filled with crumbs and four plastic forks. They'd enjoyed a cheesecake by the smell of it.

An hour later, the last of the ambulances carried the final body to the morgue for autopsy, but Emma didn't have to wait for a coroner's report. She knew what happened. She looked towards the ceiling and frowned. One security guard and three maintenance men was more of a lead than she'd wanted to find. She regretted having such a profoundly answered prayer. Emma gave her statement to the familiar policeman and left to interview the management at Treeline again. She hoped to catch them early before anyone else got word of the attack. Emma would get this scoop exclusively.

*****

Ruby heard Michael come in. "Out late, honey?" She rubbed her palms against the counter as she watched the morning news.

"Wow." He no longer crept. "I completely forgot how early you get up. I guess some things never change." His smile startled her, much too bright for the hour. Michael never got along with mornings.

"Where were you?" Ruby leveled her voice with disapproval, but her eyes stayed glued to the screen. How long could it take the inept reporters to break a story in their own building? Then again, someone like Emma Eaken might not come rolling in until lunch, for all Ruby knew. She slunk from the counter and decided to lay into Michael for his indiscretion.

"I took Sophia home. You know that." Michael lounged against the wall, still smiling.

"You should be ashamed. It's one thing to be out all night with other boys, but this is wrong, Michael. You've tarnished her reputation, if she even has one to be tarnished." She added the finale in a whisper.

"Oh." He turned his brilliant smile on his mother. "I don't think I did that."

Ruby eyed his crazy expression, fearful of what it meant.

"The Walshes are coming for lunch."

"What!"

"I invited them last night when I took her home and they agreed to come. It doesn't need to be anything complicated, and I'll help."

"What have you done?" Ruby spoke in a low tenor, using all the control she could muster.

"Mom, I wanted to talk to you at dinner, but you gave poor Sophia an interrogation and then you got sick and came home. Plus, you weren't home all afternoon yesterday. I didn't have a chance to talk with you and this is our only time home before Sophia and I both need to get back to school."

Ruby lifted her chin and shuffled in her house shoes to her son. She squinted her eyes to look up into his face. His blush showed all she needed to know. It was only a matter of words then.

"What did you do?" Each word sprang forth separate and feral. One brow rose defiantly.

"I proposed!" Michael threw his hands up, and his words flew. "I love her, Mom. She's amazing, smart, funny and absolutely phenomenal! There's no one like her in all the world, and I would have been a fool not to secure her hand before she had a chance to realize she could do so much better than me!"

Michael took his mother's hand and danced with her. Ruby snapped her wrist free.

"Get a hold of yourself. Are you insane? How will you support her? Is she pregnant?" Her eyebrows rose high on her forehead. "You've barely dated, Michael."

He held a solitary finger to his lips. "I love her, Mother. I will marry her and you will be a gracious hostess today for lunch. If you trust my judgment, the judgment you taught me, you'll see she's my perfect counterpart and you'll love her for that." He took her hand again and drew her close. "You need to know her family, so get ready."

Michael turned and took the stairs two at a time. Ruby leaned against the wall and looked at her cupboards. What would she prepare to impress the future in-laws in less than six hours?

"Holy smokes!" Michael yelled from his old room upstairs. "Mom, turn on the news."

Ruby slammed the cupboard door and skulked to the television. Her mood improved when she saw the Channel 3 station. She pulled up a stool and waited on pins and needles to hear about the young reporter's mysterious death following an investigation into the local bakery.

"Emma Eaken here, reporting live from another horrific scene."

Ruby's blood pressure took a dive while her body temperature sky-rocketed. Her palms burned like white hot coals below her wrists.

"I went to school with Em Eaken!" Michael called down the steps, sounding enthused. "How long has she been a reporter?"

Ruby couldn't speak. She focused all her energy on the girl's voice. Ruby still harbored the hope she was reporting from the beyond. Could she get nothing right? Knowing all those people died accidentally at her hand broke her heart every day. Now the ONE she needed to get rid of had survived. How could she make up for what she'd done if Emma insisted on pressing the investigation?

Tears blurred her vision. Realization crept in. No. No. She was lucky her efforts had failed. There had to be a more civilized way to fix this. She never should've tried to hurt anyone the way she did. Guilt crushed her chest. What was she thinking?

"Another case of deadly delicacies rocks Montrose Hills

this morning. Four are confirmed dead after consuming a little corporate cheesecake together at the Channel 3 News station." The cameras pulled back, revealing the chaos surrounding Emma. "One security guard and three maintenance men, with a combined seniority of nearly forty-four years, were found dead in the mailroom this hour. The scene included four cups of cold coffee and a Treeline cheesecake."

Ruby snapped off the television. *Four more. Oh my stars in heaven. What's the total now? Fifty? Why had someone eaten the cheesecake?*

Ring. Ring. The phone began and ended promptly.

"Mama, it's Charlotte," Michael called.

"I'm – I'll have to call her back." Ruby groaned, guarding her eyes against the day. There was no time for fretting. She had just over five hours to prepare a luncheon for complete strangers, the Walshes. And it needed to be one they wouldn't soon forget.

Ruby pulled every recipe from her index, searching for her biggest hits. She'd hosted her share of baby showers back in the day. Finger sandwiches and petite fours would be the right angle, if she could manage to find the perfect recipes, and if she had all she needed to prepare them.

Raspberry and orange teas, sconces with preserves and strawberry butter, cucumber sandwiches and smoked salmon with cream cheese sandwiches, the list began to compose itself as she worked. She topped the menu off with gourmet cupcakes, her specialty. She couldn't resist the opportunity to make her chocolate zucchini muffins. They were to die for. She even added her signature chocolate swirl on their tops and sprinkled them lightly with sugar crystals.

Decisively, she created a list of missing ingredients and called for Michael. He could shop while she got started.

"Yeah?" Michael appeared a moment later, rubbing a

towel over wet hair.

"I need you to run to Cutie's and pick up these things. I'll take care of the sunroom and begin on what I can in the kitchen while you're away. Don't dally."

Michael smiled.

"Get moving!"

"Yes, ma'am."

*****

Outside of Cutie's, Michael balked. The idea of entering a baking outlet seemed emasculating. Fairly certain everything on his list could be purchased at the local grocery, he considered leaving. But Ruby loved Cuties and she held the power over lunch, so he forced himself to stay. No need to rock the boat. Everything that entered her kitchen had to come there by way of Cutie's. This luncheon would be no different.

He parked half a mile away in the gigantic, always packed parking lot and tucked the list into his pocket. Nearing the doors, he waited for a series of tour buses to load up and pull away. People traveled from far and wide to visit Cutie's, though why, he couldn't say.

He passed a gaggle of women in plastic rain bonnets and weaved between rows of heavily decorated carts before entering the monstrous sphere. The ceilings inside Cutie's were high enough to house planes, and the occasional sparrow darted among the steel rafters. He hoped not to become subject to their target practice.

Ruby's list called for a myriad of things he had no idea how to find. Some of which he wasn't even sure he could identify in a lineup. He needed a GPS to navigate the store. He resolved to travel aisle by aisle, starting at the bakery. It seemed the logical starting point.

Michael sighed deeply before lifting an obnoxious pink basket onto his arm. The only choice more humiliating was to push one of Cutie's painted cupcake carts. If only he'd worn cargo pants to carry the merchandise instead.

Several minutes in, he fought the nausea growing from the sickly sweet scents. Holding his breath didn't help. He needed air again. With each breath he was overcome anew by the massive intake of air-born sugar. He remembered reading in Physiology 101, that after a few minutes, his brain should stop registering the smell. He hoped that was true.

Everything went black.

"Guess who! Guess who! Guess who!" Claire's voice was music to his ears. Michael grabbed her wrists and whirled around.

"Eclaire!" He kissed her cheek and lifted her easily. "Oh, I missed you."

"Me, too."

"Look at you." Michael raised her arms out to the sides like an airplane and turned her slowly before him. A soft pat on her bottom put color in her cheeks.

"When did you get home?"

"A couple of days ago. Don't tell Mom." He winked and she frowned. "What?"

"Is she alright?"

"Sure. I guess. She's been through a lot." His head tilted as he judged her tone.

"I don't know. I don't think she is. I went over to visit when I first came home and she was really off, not her usual things either. She was different. I think something's wrong."

"She's fine. There's been a lot for her to adjust to lately." He had a crooked smile.

Claire shook her head. "No."

"What do you mean, precisely?" Michael lifted his chin. "Be specific."

"Well, she's abrupt, even rude. Her passive aggressive attacks were nowhere to be found. She was pointed. Then her mind was in the ozone the whole time I visited. She used to be so thankful for companionship, especially in the kitchen. This time, she behaved like a pod person. Did you see her kitchen?"

"That kitchen is all her."

"No, it's not. Ruby is, was frugal. She came in here with coupons once a month. Now she's a regular and pays cash. Her new kitchen had to cost a hundred grand."

"Dad had insurance."

Again, Claire shook her head.

"Hey, I'm getting married." He laid his arms wide, waiting for a squeal which didn't come.

Claire's eyes widened. "To whom?"

"Sophia Walsh." Michael's smile dampened a bit at her reaction. Hadn't he just told her the greatest news of his life? Claire had always acted as his personal cheerleader.

"I have to get back. It was nice seeing you."

Claire disappeared into the bakery. Michael stood alone again regretting that he hadn't thought to open with a question or two about the contents of his list. Claire was too much like his mother to worry about. Who knew what went on inside their heads?

CHAPTER TEN

In just under four hours the sunroom was transformed and Ruby headed to the shower. She hated to leave her perfect setting, but she needed a shower and absolutely everything that went with it. The sunroom looked magical. She had outdone herself.

When the doorbell rang one and a half hours later, Ruby was ready.

"Hello," Ruby greeted the Walshes with Michael at her side. "Won't you please come in?"

Michael took Sophia by the hand and kissed her knuckles gently. Her mother swooned and her father's chest puffed full. Ruby regretted the entire event. Then she caught sight of the diamond on Sophia's hand and remembered Michael's heart. The luncheon was too important to Michael for her to act up. So, she inhaled through her nose, counted to three and led them to the sunroom.

"Oh, Mrs. Russell, everything looks exquisite!" Mrs. Walsh clapped once. "How did you manage on such short notice? We were barely able to reschedule our commitments in order to get here on time."

"Ruby," she corrected. "Please, if we're to be family, let's be comfortable. Come, sit." She avoided the topic of schedules.

"Thank you. Please, call me Bunny and this is Hugh."

"Of course." Well, at least her luncheon would impress them, even if she now had name inferiority on top of being outdone in faith and status. That was not to mention the way Bunny's husband gushed over her. Ruby didn't think she stood a chance.

"Let me help." Michael ushered the Walshes into the sunroom and joined his mother in the kitchen to bring in the tea and settings.

"You and Bunny have a lot in common, you know." Michael balanced three cups and matching saucers in one hand.

"I'm not sure how. So far we seem very different to me," Ruby said, a bit sullen. "Maybe she enjoys cooking more than her daughter?" That was a field she could play on.

"I'm not sure if she cooks." He turned the corner. "Mother Walsh, do you cook?"

Mother? Ruby almost dropped the tea. Certainly they hadn't become so familiar in one night's time. Her hands began their familiar tremor as her memory flickered. The look of pride on Hugh's face made more sense. He seemed to feel as though he had a hand in the situation. Perhaps he had. Michael had been keeping more than Sophia from Ruby. He had a whole family stashed away. Ruby shook her hands out one by one, transferring the kettle as she went. Apparently, Ken wasn't the only traitor in the family.

"Absolutely not. I confess I haven't had the opportunity to cook in years. Besides, I could never do the art any service. I've truly seen heaven on a plate and I could never compete with that."

Ruby brought the platters from the kitchen and served

her guests without a word. Pondering how a second betrayal had occurred beneath her very nose, made it difficult to concentrate on the conversation. When she finished, she sat, between Michael and Bunny.

"So, what is it you do, Bunny?" Ruby imagined her a pediatric neurosurgeon or some other career-oriented savior which would put her own homemaking lifestyle in a tiny brown paper bag.

"I eat." She smiled as she bit into a tiny sandwich.

A round of giggles began and Sophia spoke to clarify their little inside joke. "Mother's a critic."

"How interesting." Ruby hadn't seen that coming.

"She's writes for *Food Flair Magazine,"* Michael said as Bunny took another dainty bite.

Ruby relaxed against the back of her chair. Her stomach fell and her countenance joined the sentiment. *Of course she does.*

"This is divine." Bunny shut her eyes and let her lashes flutter.

Ruby looked on. Hugh discussed his golf game with Michael. They had played together. She didn't know when, considering Michael hadn't been home in so long. Sophia smiled adoringly and rubbed Michael's arm with both hands.

It was disgusting.

Bunny, still cherishing the tiny fare, interrupted Ruby's seething. "I must know where you trained." Her eyes were wide with curiosity.

When Ruby didn't answer, Bunny turned her eyes on Michael. "Shame on you, Mister. You shouldn't keep a secret like this. You're mother's a treasure!" Bunny lifted her glass with one hand. The other formed the universal "OK" sign and her lips kissed the air.

"Nonsense, Mother." Sophia leaned against Michael.

"He's always said what a fabulous cook his mother is." She turned her face to look into Michael's eyes. Michael stared back at her.

Ruby went to pour a glass of wine. "Excuse me." In the kitchen, she uncorked the nearest bottle and looked for a glass. It was early to be drinking and Michael wasn't privy to her new proclivities, so she worked quietly in the corner.

"Ma'am."

Ruby jumped several inches.

"Is there anything I can do to help you, Mrs. Russell?" Sophia stood a few inches away.

Ruby did her best to grip the bottle top and glass stem together in one hand, before she turned to her guest. The task proved difficult, but with a little help from her cabinet, she held both behind her back as she spoke to Sophia.

"Oh, no thank you. Just checking on things in here. Please, sit. I'll be right in."

Sophia stood there.

"Is there something else?" Ruby's voice became less gracious when she saw it hadn't worked.

"Mrs. Russell," Sophia struggled for words and Ruby fought back the forming perspiration. She needed a dry solid for her temples and forehead. That would be something useful. Someone should invent that immediately.

"I'm afraid you don't like me," Sophia continued in a small voice. "Michael adores you and I need you and I to be friends."

Ruby huffed and brought the wine from behind her back. Sophia continued to smile. She poured a glass and took one sip. "Sophia. Sophia." Ruby tossed the remaining wine back like an oversized Jell-O-shot. She held up a finger and refilled the glass.

Sophia glanced behind her toward the room where her family sat.

"Michael's my son." She wanted to articulate her feelings on the subject of their marriage, but this child wouldn't understand. The effort would be wasted. "I want him to be happy."

"I can make him happy."

Ruby contemplated her next words. *Mine, Mine. Mine* seemed inappropriate. She lifted the bottle again and saw Sophia make a little judgy face. Ruby turned to restore the bottle to the cabinet and considered how she might hurt Sophia without hurting Michael. But she couldn't. Her head hung in defeat.

"Is everything alright?" Bunny called. A chair scraped against the floor in the sunroom.

"We're fine, Mother." Sophia looked nervously at Ruby who worked to rearrange her expression.

"Sophia." *Butter.* No matter what she said, it'd make no difference.

"Sophia?" Michael called. Sophia turned and left.

Ruby downed another glass of wine. Then, feeling much better, she walked back into the lions' den. "How's everything?"

Only Sophia seemed ill at ease, her eyes glued to the table, no longer attached to Michael.

"I was telling Mother Bunny how you learned your way around the kitchen from your mother." Michael appeared proud.

"Self-trained." Bunny shook her head, obviously in awe. "Have you ever considered opening your own restaurant or bakery? It seems a shame to keep your talent in a bottle. Everyone should try this." She stabbed her fork towards her plate several times.

"No."

Michael and Hugh fell back into their golf talk and Sophia behaved like a wounded bird. Ruby wanted to scream.

"Do you still have the cheesecake Michael told us about? He mentioned you made a special cheesecake. I can only imagine what was in there!" Bunny looked like she might go looking for it.

Ruby's throat thickened. She shook her head. Her eyebrows cowered together. Anger became anguish. She had another mess to clean up. This one would be the toughest yet. She needed a plan, needed to think. She needed these guests to go home.

"Where did the cheesecake go, Mom?" Michael waited for an answer. "I planned to have it for breakfast."

"I dropped it." Ruby looked at him meaningfully. He'd seen her dive on it.

Michael smiled. "Yes, but I also saw the trash this morning. You baked while you waited for me last night. Sorry I didn't call, by the way. I lost track of time." He looked down at Sophia and patted her arm. She didn't look up.

Michael shot an accusing look at Ruby.

"I-I…" Ruby's face was numb. She wished for the stroke she once feared.

Ding dong.

Ruby almost knocked her chair over getting away from the table. "Excuse me." She was already outside the room. She hastened to the door, fighting tears, thanking heaven for the escape. She planned to buy whatever they peddled and thank them profusely for the interruption. The door swung wide with one strong pull and then she stuttered back a full four steps.

"Mrs. Russell, are you alright?" Reverend Flynn walked right in and took Ruby by her elbow. "Are we early?"

Ruby couldn't breathe. She looked around helplessly for a paper bag to puff in. She allowed the reverend to help her to the sofa. He sat with her and spoke with care, but she heard nothing other than her heart beating between her ears. She'd completely forgotten about his visit. Now here he was and she had a sunroom full of problems to attend to.

"I-I'm sorry." She breathed the words. "I'm not feeling very well."

"We can come back." This time the "we" stuck.

Ruby's eyes travelled around the room to find another guest. Still in the door frame, reluctant to come inside, stood a tall, thin, young beauty with dark hair and a familiar face. Ruby wished for death to take her. She absolutely needed to die. Die!

"Mrs. Russell, this is Daisy Douglas." Reverend Flynn motioned to the girl and she came to join them on the small sofa.

Visions of brutal acts flickered in Ruby's mind. She imagined hurting the girl in a multitude of ways and grew stronger as she indulged the thoughts.

"Daisy and her family have attended my church for years. Recently, I had reason to speak with her and she and I have had many, many lengthy discussions. Daisy has come to the opinion she needs to make amends for something she has done and is in search of repentance. She comes here out of love, Mrs. Russell."

The young girl quivered beside him. Her dark brown eyes stared at her uncovered knees, and her fingers scraped and fiddled with the deep crimson polish left on her fingernails. Her head bent forward, and from the angle, Ruby noted the makings of an Indian ink tattoo on her neck, partially hidden beneath her flowing dark locks.

A knock came upon the open door and Charlotte walked inside. "Am I late?" Ruby remembered her call this morning. If only she'd taken that call.

Charlotte's expression froze as she examined the girl

beside the reverend. Ruby had shown her those photos. Charlotte would know exactly who she was. She opened her mouth to speak but excused herself at once to the kitchen.

"Mrs. Russell," the girl spoke with trepidation. "I was a friend of your husband's." Her eyes shot up then to look at Ruby. "I didn't know he was your husband." Her head rocked back and forth. Her eyes revealed something Ruby understood on a deeper emotional level. This girl, too, had been betrayed.

Ruby didn't speak. "He told me his wife died. He said a few years ago, when your son went away to college, you went crazy and sent poisonous food to the staff at the university, trying to scare your boy into staying with you." The girl twisted and played with a large turquoise ring on her left thumb. Only a child would wear jewelry on her thumb.

Reverend Flynn twisted in his seat, and Ruby choked back a sob.

"I never would have…" Daisy burst into tears and Ruby's compassion wavered. She might share her pain, but she was also a cog in the machine trying to take Ruby down.

How many lies had Kenneth told about her? She could only imagine what else he'd said and to whom. A parade of faces played before her. Montrose Hills was a small enough community for everyone to have heard some form of his lies. The heat in her chest and neck made her woozy and she slunk back against the couch.

Revered Flynn's eyes locked onto hers and he seemed painfully uncomfortable considering he was the one to bring this embarrassment into her living room.

"He said you were in a mental health facility for months and faced criminal charges. He said you never really recovered and that you," she paused to whisper, "killed yourself."

"Mother?" Michael's voice stopped her heart. Her humiliation couldn't be aired this way. "Oh, I'm sorry. I didn't realize anyone else was here. I only saw Miss Charlotte come by."

Always the host, trained by the supreme hostess herself, Michael lifted the nearest tray and carried it to the living area where his mother sat with her guests. "Muffin?"

Ruby's heart clenched. *The muffins.*

Reverend Flynn looked at Ruby, then at the basket, and then at Ruby. His eyes made the circuit again and again until he shot upright and motioned for Daisy to join him. "I'm sorry, Mrs. Russell, obviously you weren't expecting us, for some reason, and you have your hands full. We'll be on our way. I hope you understand the reason we stopped by." He buttoned his jacket and reached for Daisy's arm.

Daisy wiped her tears and watched Ruby from the corner of her eye.

"Daisy Douglas!" Sophia's voice speared the silence.

"Sophia?"

Dear Lord.

The two girls embraced and began to bounce from the thrill of their reunion. "Oh my gosh, it's been four years!" Sophia gushed.

"You two know each other?" Michael sounded pleased.

"Daisy and I went to Francine Francis Academy together for, well, our entire lives."

Reverend Flynn's eyes drilled holes into the pile of muffins on the coffee table. Ruby didn't need an explanation for what he saw there. He had treated her terribly from the beginning, always nosey, in her business, and now the ultimate betrayal. Imagine, bringing that girl to her home. A colossal slap in the face. Now she supposed he'd find some fault with Ruby.

Preposterous! He seemed to have forgiven Daisy for her

disgusting relationship with a married man, who had been twice her age and obviously an unrepentant liar. Yet he'd condemn Ruby for her reaction to such behavior. It sickened her.

Time stood still. Ruby watched Reverend Flynn through lowered lids. She glared at him, like a bull ready to charge against the clown wearing a red hanky. He, in turn, pretended not to notice. His gazed jumped hyperactively around the room.

Ruby watched Reverend Flynn examine Michael, the muffins and the girls. When Hugh and Bunny exchanged a laugh in the sunroom, his eyes darted in that direction as well. No telling what he was up to. Every few beats he looked at Ruby again. She stopped bothering to look anyway other than irritated. This time she'd like to toss him out the window, and he could save his little pink Bible for Daisy. She needed it.

Reverend Flynn tugged on Daisy's elbow once more and nodded towards the door. "Daisy, I think we'd better get going. Mrs. Russell has a full house already."

He rubbed his palms against his slacks and tried to avert his eyes from the muffins. The girls continued to chat as if they weren't visiting the home one of them had wrecked.

"Daisy." He touched her shoulder.

The girls exchanged a few hurried words as the reverend pressed on about their exit. Then Flynn and Daisy were gone.

Sophia rejoined Michael hand in hand.

"Can you imagine? Me seeing someone from the academy at your mom's house. What are the odds of that?"

Michael snuggled Sophia under his arm and they meandered back into the sunroom together.

Ruby went to find solace with Charlotte. But Charlotte was nowhere to be found.

CHAPTER ELEVEN

Emma Eaken pulled into the Treeline Bakery parking lot in time to catch the manager on his way inside. The bakers had clocked in before five.

"No comment, Ms. Eaken." He waved her away.

"No comment on the fact you killed another four people today? This time they weren't diabetic. This time it was murder. Let's not mince words."

"First of all," he stiffened his back for battle, "I didn't do anything of the sort and neither did anyone in my bakery. Second, you'd better knock off the accusations before I bring a libel lawsuit against your station and end your pathetic little career post haste!" He pulled the door shut behind him and locked it.

Emma motioned her cameraman to set up and began her performance in front of the large green Treeline sign. "I'm standing here at the site of much speculation this morning. The quiet Montrose community has taken quite a shaking lately, and all crumbs lead back to Treeline Bakery."

Other reporters arrived right on her heels, and several

local police cruisers appeared soon after. The policemen worked on crowd control as local neighbors and families showed up to protest. Treeline's team of attorneys arrived within minutes.

"We have a court order," a large man in a blue shirt and grey trousers announced. "You must cease and desist immediately, Ms. Eaken. Your accusations are reckless and potentially damaging."

"You call it accusations. I call it compelling evidence."

"Your accusations are based on circumstantial evidence at best, and considering the witch hunt you've been on lately, it's no surprise."

Emma glared at the portly lawyer in the cheap grey suit and then motioned for the camera to stop rolling. She'd noticed over the man's shoulder a certain officer milling around the perimeter not far from her. She thought there might be another opportunity available.

"Meet me at the van." She dismissed her one-man crew and headed to the officer of interest.

"Lex," Emma called, smiling as she approached.

"Emma." He looped his thumbs into the brown leather belt holding his pants to his thin frame. "How have you been?"

"Better. There's something going on here. Nine deaths from food poisoning on two separate occasions? Both incidents included goods from this bakery. This is more than a coincidence." She bobbed the hand mic in front of him.

"I always said you should have been an investigator." He smiled.

"You never said that," she snarled.

He had often taunted her for her passion and the time she spent trying to get a seat at the glorious anchor desk in the nice comfortable studio.

"Give this a rest. No one from this bakery was anywhere

near your studio this morning. All morning bakers were here and accounted for. We have them both on video and by statement of the other morning staff." He shook his head, mocking.

Emma didn't share his sentiment. "Someone else could have delivered the cheesecake. The keys to those vans aren't locked in a vault, for crying out loud." She stomped her foot and crossed her arms over her chest, wanting to rap him over the head with her microphone.

"It's 2012 Emma." His voice dripped condescension and she stifled a shriek. "Even little community bakery trucks have GPS. They've all been right here since yesterday's deliveries." This time, he walked away from her.

"Emma." The Channel 3 truck pulled up just outside the flimsy police barrier. Stuart waved wildly from the driver's seat. "We've got to go," he called without stopping.

Emma broke into a run. An instant rush of adrenaline propelled her forward. Stuart wasn't prone to fits of animation, so whatever he had was good. Treeline would wait.

Emma pulled off her shiny pumps and leapt into the van. Stuart was kind enough to throw the door open for her. He stopped at the edge of the lot before pulling into traffic.

"What is it?" Emma trilled.

"You're never going to believe this one." Stuart jammed his foot onto the pedal and the van swung out onto the road.

Emma grabbed onto the little handle in the ceiling and pressed against the dash with her feet. "What's happening?" She straightened and put on her seat belt.

Stuart twisted his cell phone in the space between them. "I just got a call from the Church of Hope."

Across town they pulled in behind a row of fire trucks, ambulances and policemen. Emma launched herself from the moving vehicle, shoes in hand. The crowd surrounded Reverend Flynn's parish.

Stuart met a small knot of people in the street. Someone he knew came to clean the nurseries and made the discovery. Occasionally, Stuart was quite handy.

"What's going on here?" Emma asked the first person she saw.

"Reverend Flynn is dead, and there was someone with him. I don't know who else might have been in the building." The woman sobbed as she spoke.

No flipping way.

She didn't know if the woman was a member of the church, the community or just a rubbernecker. It really didn't matter because she had no facts and no further speculation.

Emma pressed through the crowd to the front stairs where the crime scene tape flopped in the wind, warning her not to pass. Stuart stayed close behind. Emma slipped first into her patent leather pumps and then into reporter mode.

"We're here at the scene of a terrible loss." Emma had to wing it if she wanted to break the story. There wasn't much to work with. "This tiny parish has been a landmark in the local community for over a hundred years, celebrating their centennial last summer with a week of services and activities for local families. The event coordinators thanked the leadership of Reverend Glenn Flynn for their success. But rumor has it this parish and community will need a new leader."

*****

Ruby collapsed.

Her luggage lay across her bed. Michael slept like a baby down the hall. Tickets to Fiji waited at the airport and she'd called Charlotte to let her know. The news played on her tiny bedroom television out of habit. After her horrendous encounter with Reverend Flynn the day before, she'd set things in motion for her disappearance. She couldn't be a penitentiary pastry chef. She had to get away.

Charlotte's phone rang and rang. She didn't answer her cellular, either. *Why own a cell phone if she won't turn it on?* Ruby growled. Charlotte had abandoned her when the reverend and his little Twinkie barged in. She'd been incognito ever since. If she didn't reach her soon, Ruby vowed never to speak with her again.

All sorts of potential dialogue swirled inside Ruby's head. She had so much she wanted to say to Charlotte that she felt like a kettle preparing to boil over.

By the time Ruby refocused, Emma Eaken was babbling away.

"Reports of a carbon monoxide leak are coming in. The coroner confirmed what was only a rumor moments ago. Reverend Flynn is in fact one of the deceased."

Ruby froze.

"He's been taken in for autopsy, which will provide more details to this gruesome event. I've also learned, he wasn't alone." Emma tossed windblown hair over her shoulder, away from her face. The growing wind ruined her perfect act.

Ruby's mouth hung open until her tongue stuck to the roof of her mouth. She needed a glass of wine.

"A young woman, who remains unnamed, is believed to have been in his office with him at his time of death." Ruby's breathing hitched.

Holy cannelloni.

"Speculation has it the two may possibly have been involved in an affair."

Ruby covered her mouth with one hand. The other pressed firmly over her chest.

"Condoms and a plain Ziploc baggie like this," she held

up a plastic bag as evidence, "were found inside the reverend's car with a loose amount of Viagra inside. Street drugs are dispensed this way. The unmarried reverend would have had a tough time getting a prescription filled discreetly around here."

Ruby scooted against the closest wall and decided she'd better remain seated. Her head swam. Questions multiplied. A stretcher rolled behind Emma, out the front door and down the cement steps into the parking lot. Emma's crew zoomed in callously. The Church of Hope might consider a name change. Ruby hated to look, but when she did, a thin tan wrist fell from the white sheet. A large turquoise ring centered the shot.

Ruby bounced in place, biting her lips until she thought she might explode. She didn't have to leave home now. Michael would wake soon. In a matter of minutes, she'd completely unpacked her life's possessions and returned her American Traveler to the closet. It was a miracle. She smiled upwards and raised her arms in victory.

Downstairs, she lit a fire on her stove beneath a large omelet pan. Joy filled the room and her swollen feet twisted left and right under heavy ankles. She didn't know what was going on in her community lately. There'd been more deaths since June than in all the years she lived there combined. But these last two meant she was free. She could stay!

When Michael arrived in the kitchen, Ruby hummed the Candy Man song.

"You look happy this morning. That's a switch."

Ruby had gone to bed early the night before, brooding. She only partially feigned a headache and sat up deciding how she could avoid prison for twenty-seven murders. She'd searched online for countries where the weather suited and the dollar held a good exchange. Also the country couldn't have an extradition policy with the United States. None of those were places she wanted to live. She had decided on Fiji and started calling Charlotte, who refused to pick up.

"You blindsided me with the tea for your new family. Then the reverend showed up, and your Mother Bunny is a food critic." Ruby tsked at Michael as she shoved eggs around the large pan. "I'm just thankful for today and all the goodness that came with it." Ruby was on top of the world for the first time in many years.

"Well, I'm glad you're in such good spirits today because we've decided to get married next month while the weather is still cooperative. We want to have the reception here, under your management." Michael widened his arms behind him and leaned his palms onto the kitchen island.

"Next month! Is your brain made of fruit, Michael?" Ruby waved a metal spatula in front of her face and then used it to roughly scrape breakfast onto a plate. She shoved the plate hard in his direction.

"I thought you'd be happy for me, Mother. Why wait when we're ready now? We have the perfect mothers to pull the whole thing off. I need you to work your magic." His crooked smile returned, and she couldn't possibly say no to that. Still, he deserved rebuke for his haste.

"Next month. Is she *in trouble*?"

"Mother, enough with that. Be serious."

"I don't know her." She pointed at him, then dropped her arms into her pathetic defeat mode.

"You know me." He threw it back at her, sounding sad. "Or at least I thought you did."

"Wait." She grasped at his arm as he tried to leave. Without Charlotte, she was alone, and Ruby didn't want to be all alone. "My magic?"

"Yes, we hoped you'd agree to oversee the whole event.

That includes the food, the cake, the decorations, linens, tableware, drinks and music. We'd hire a staff to assist you, of course."

The phone interrupted their negotiation. *A staff.*

"You'd have the opportunity to get to know Sophia and Bunny while you plan."

Ruby answered the phone, though she didn't recognize the number.

"Hello?"

"Ruby?" Charlotte's hushed voice came in a burst.

"Charlotte? Where are you and whose number is this?"

"I'm around the corner." She kept whispering. "This is my new number. I picked up one of those disposable phones last night. CSI calls them burner phones. Write the number down and then don't give it to anyone."

Ruby rolled her eyes and shot an apologetic look in Michael's direction. He didn't notice. His attention had shifted as he enjoyed his picture perfect breakfast. Ruby shook off the notion that she had lost.

"I need to see you. Can you come out?"

"Come out? It's the crack of dawn. Come over. I'll make fresh coffee."

"Is Michael there?"

"Yes." Stating the obvious ruffled Ruby's feathers.

"Come out then, please."

"I'm in my curlers? Can't this wait?" Ruby kept her eyes on Michael. She didn't want him to take off while Charlotte held her on the phone.

"No. It can't wait," she screamed into the phone. "Get your ass out here now."

Ruby pulled the phone from her ear and glared at it before slamming it down. Michael watched.

"Miss Charlotte?"

Ruby's eyes widened "How did you know?"

"You said it when you answered." Michael lifted himself from the stool and headed to the sink with his plate.

"Where are you going?" She glanced between her son and the front door, torn.

"Probably to the gym. We can talk about the reception later. Lay out some plans and I'll make dinner tonight." He winked. "Then we can sit together and talk." He kissed her lightly on her cheek before taking the stairs two at a time.

Ruby jerked curlers from her hair by the handful and made her way to the front door. Charlotte was parked on the curb in a strange car. She slumped behind the wheel peering up at Ruby's house. Her giant glasses looked funny on her small face and she gnawed on her fingernails like an animal when Ruby opened the passenger door.

"What is your problem, Charlotte Mason?" Ruby used her most terse whisper, hoping to scold without drawing attention.

"Get in." Charlotte shifted into drive.

For a moment, Ruby considered refusing, but curiosity was her mistress. "Whose car is this?" She climbed inside and admired the spotless interior.

"I rented it." Charlotte rubbed her cheeks and looked sweaty.

"Why?" Ruby hoped she wouldn't be expected to pull information from a woman who'd insulted her in order to get her out of her own house.

"I'm being inconspicuous." Charlotte turned her head back and forth in disgust and then took a wild left.

Ruby grabbed the dashboard to steady herself. "Where are we going?"

"The airport." Charlotte jerked the car onto the upcoming onramp.

"What!" Ruby gasped

"We've got to get out of here. I've been up all night

trying to figure it out."

"I'm sorry. I still have no idea what you're talking about."

Ten minutes later Charlotte pulled the car to a stop on the side of the highway and removed her glasses. She looked wild and Ruby became more than a little concerned for their safety. "You heard the reverend. You heard that child. He *saw*, Ruby. He saw the muffins. You had to kill those hungry people with your signature recipe." Her tone turned accusatory. "Why would you send homeless people chocolate zucchini muffins?" Charlotte gagged and pulled her forearm across her eyes.

"I didn't send them to the homeless people," Ruby yelled, exasperated at the accusation. "I sent them to the reverend in a thank you basket. It was supposed to look gourmet. *He* sent them to the shelter. *He* killed those people."

"Yeah, well he sent them and then Michael offered them to him at the very moment that girl was spilling your secrets." Charlotte's eyes bulged.

"Hey, you leave Michael out of this. He was being cordial."

"Oh, right, of course he was."

"Sarcasm isn't very becoming of you. It's for people who simply can't say what they mean."

"I meant, you shouldn't have made me do this!" The scream caused Ruby's head to sing. She covered her ears in defense.

The women shared a long moment of silence. Ruby recovered first.

"We don't need to worry about it, you know. We can just forget anything ever happened." Ruby hoped she'd diffused the situation. Charlotte needed to tone herself down a notch because Ruby had delicious news.

"No, Ruby, we can't." Charlotte spat through tight lips. "Murder's not something people get away with." Charlotte pulled back out into traffic, still moving towards the airport.

"They do when the only people who suspected them are dead." Ruby smiled with renewed zeal. Her news was certain to help Charlotte recover from whatever psychosis ailed her.

"Ruby, it's only a matter of time before they find me. They always find some random thread or tire print or other arbitrary piece of nothing that leads them all the way back to the killer."

"Charlotte, he's dead." *She isn't listening*. "I saw it on the news this morning. I'm safe." Ruby rubbed Charlotte's shoulder.

"I know he's dead. I was in your kitchen when the whole thing unfolded. I saw the look on the reverend's face. I saw how he tried to get out of there as fast as he could once he put it together. I went to your closet and took some things from Ken's box. I put some of his pills in a baggie and I grabbed some of those other things." Ruby knew Charlotte meant condoms and was thankful she hadn't said it out loud. "Then I went to his car while he was trying to drag Daisy away. I put them in the armrest."

Airport signs sped past them.

"I followed them, trying to think of how I could talk him out of telling anyone what he suspected. I tried to think of some way to introduce myself and start the conversation, maybe dissuade him. I planned to talk with him after he dropped the girl off, but he didn't drop her off. They went back to the Church of Hope and holed up in his office for twenty minutes while I lurked around trying to come up with some kind of plan. I hoped to discredit him in case I couldn't stop him from telling about the muffins."

Charlotte's knuckles whitened under her grip on the

steering wheel. She veered onto the exit ramp for the airport. Ruby tried to see where the story was going, but wondered instead how well Charlotte had prepared for an escape. She didn't see any luggage, unless she'd put it in the trunk. Even still, what about Ruby's? She didn't have any luggage. Not even a purse. She only agreed to walk out her front door for goodness sakes.

"Finally, I saw a man taking out the trash. He left the back door open. I went in and carried a knife around a while, but I'm not a killer. I couldn't do it. Then the man came back and I hid. I ended up in the basement. Ironic, right? At Tillie's we wanted the basement so we could escape, but we ended up in the laundry room. At the church, I wanted to escape and I ended up trapped in the basement."

"Charlotte, will you please try to focus. I still have no idea what you're talking about."

"I was stuck in the basement," she yelled. "It didn't have a walkout. I didn't know what to do, but I knew the whole ball of yarn was unraveling. I had to do something and there were no weapons in the basement. I dug through boxes of craft materials and puzzles and playground balls. It was useless. Then I saw the furnace."

Ruby slipped a thumbnail between her front teeth and waited on pins and needles for the rest. She knew the ending, but this was turning out to be a thrilling firsthand account. Charlotte pulled into the long-term parking area outside the west side of the airport and shifted into park. They both released their seat belts and twisted in their seats to look closely at one another.

"It was all I could think of." Charlotte sobbed. "I had nothing else and I couldn't see you going to jail. Plus, I'd be going, too. Michael's already lost his father. It wasn't fair." She wiped her nose along the sleeve of her shirt and turned to lay her head on the wheel. "I blew out the little blue flame and waited."

"Waited?"

"Yes. I waited. Then I heard keys and a door shutting and knew there was a way for me to leave. I climbed the steps and, sure enough, the man from the kitchen had left. He'd locked up and was pulling away when I looked out the window. I was saved. I left right away and never looked back. I couldn't call you until I had a plan, so I rented this car and bought this phone." She chucked the tiny plastic cell onto the dash.

"Oh, Charlotte!" The women embraced and cried and laughed until the emotional waves settled.

"We're going to be alright. You're too good to me, but I can't leave right now. Michael's getting married next month. I have to be there. I'm in charge of the reception. I'm management!"

"He's getting married?" Charlotte's gaze shifted back and forth between Ruby's eyes. "Alright then, but after the wedding, we go."

Ruby nodded and the women locked pinky fingers in a solemn pledge.

CHAPTER TWELVE

Mark and Meredith Kessler ate Thai noodles on their patio. Together they watched the birds and smiled. Their efforts to expand the landscape complexity had worked. In the past month alone, quite a few more local species had stopped to partake. The expansion was a complicated and lengthy undertaking. The Kesslers hoped they were only beginning to see the fruits of their labor. Meredith called it a labor of love. Mark enjoyed the challenge and the pleasure it gave Meredith.

"You've outdone yourself this time." He anchored the thin noodles to his wooden spears.

"Thank you." She nodded her head and snapped her own chopsticks together for show.

"I don't think I'll ever be as adept at this." He pushed the noodles into his mouth. "I mean, it has been thirty years."

Meredith rubbed his arm on the table between them and kissed his cheek with great affection. "It's good to see you relax. You've been tense far too long. Tell me what's going on at work? Let's talk." Her voice firmed.

They had agreed back in college that doctor patient privilege became invalid if it began to uproot their marriage. In all the years since, he'd only chosen to talk with her twice. Each time, under the same circumstances.

"Ken Russell died a little while back." He took another awkward bite. Meredith's forehead wrinkled trying to place the name, but she wouldn't, not without its counterpart.

"Ruby's been coming to see me since then."

Meredith wiped her mouth with a pristine organic bamboo napkin and laid her chopsticks beside her plate. She took a long drink of water and leaned heavily into her chair.

"I know how you feel about her. All I could think about was what she might be capable of under the stress mourning brings. I wanted to listen and gauge her mental state. The fact she contacted me told me she needed someone." His eyes pleaded for her to understand and forgive him.

"You promised."

"I did."

Meredith rubbed her thin face and sighed deeply. "Let's have it. How's she grieving?"

"That's one part of my troubles. I don't think she's grieving at all, unless she handles the process differently than every other human on planet earth, but I doubt that. She's an extremist in chef's clothing. She should be bringing me baked goods every week as evidence of her compulsive attempt to keep the hurt at bay. As far as I can tell, she's doing nothing extreme at all."

"That's good. Isn't that why you accepted her appointment? You wanted to be sure she wouldn't do anything like before?"

"Ah." He shook his head and pinched the bridge of his nose between his fingers. "I don't know. I'm missing something. What's worse is our history doesn't make me the best counselor for her. It probably makes me the worst. I'm skeptical and hyper sensitive, maybe looking for a problem where there isn't one." He looked at his wife in desperation. "She's not mourning. She lost her husband. Her son is away at college, and she's alone. This sort of thing should have wrecked her. She wasn't on her meds when it happened. She barely speaks to me when we do meet. It's not right."

"You said she's not mourning the loss."

He swung a large finger in the air. His eyes flashed to hers and back to his uneaten dinner. "I think the reason she's not mourning might be because she had something to do with his death."

A gasp burst through Meredith's full pink lips. Her hand fluttered uselessly in the air and then landed back where it began. "You need to tell someone and you need to stop seeing her."

"I can't call the police with my feelings. I have no evidence. I just, I need to get her to say something I can grab onto, but she's resistant. She comes and sits for an hour a week."

"She can use you to testify if she gets caught, you know. You'll have to say she came to you after Ken's death and continued to see you every week. She never gave you reason to believe she was involved."

Mark leaned his head over the back of his chair and asked the starry night for advice. He'd gotten himself in quite a predicament with no easy way out. He needed a plan, a tape recorder and a stomach pump.

"Give me a few more weeks?"

"She's dangerous." Meredith pushed her chair away from the table, placed her napkin upon her plate and walked away.

The morning paper awaited him with a fresh pot of organic roasted coffee. Meredith didn't approve of his caffeine addiction, but she'd managed a compromise by finding locally grown beans, untreated with pesticides. It was a give on both parts. The taste compared to rotted floorboards, but taken with a half cup of vanilla soy, it was consumable.

His morning paper waited on the counter, neatly folded to the local section. Mark smiled. Meredith's college dance troupe often made the paper when they came to town. He waved the paper at Meredith through the oversized window. She sat cross legged meditating in the yard with the local wildlife.

He slid into his chair at the breakfast table, and flipped through the articles. No theater announcements. Only page after page of local engagements and anniversaries. It puzzled him Meredith found this important somehow. Everyone they knew had been married for years. Mark looked again at his wife. Meredith sat motionless in the grass on her yoga mat. With no way to tell how long she'd be like that, he left for work without an answer. Ruby had scheduled an early appointment he didn't want to miss. Mark tucked the morning paper under one arm and took his coffee along with him.

Thirty minutes later, in the slow creep of traffic, he nearly caused a ten-car pileup. His eyes moved to the seat where the paper lay. Meredith had folded the paper back. She wanted to tell him something and he desperately wanted to know what. His curiosity, easily his most extreme characteristic, was how he landed his current role as psychiatrist. Staring at the creased paper, something clicked. He pressed the wrong pedal, gassing forward instead of slowing further and clutched the wheel. Luckily, he was at an intersection, which afforded him a few feet and stopped his transformation to a metal hybrid pancake.

Michael Russell was getting married.

Oh, a complicated matter indeed. His heart raced. There must be some reason Ruby had kept this information out of their meetings. Maybe she hadn't accepted it yet. Denial was common enough. Though he couldn't help but wonder if the reason had nothing to do with mere denial. Another possibility existed. What if she wasn't worried about the engagement because she didn't believe the wedding would come to pass? Now, that option had thorns. If Ruby simply denied what would happen, then Mark would call her on it and work with her. However, if Ruby plotted an effort to thwart Michael's plans, the result could be very bad. As complicated as Ruby seemed, one thing never wavered. Her reality centered around herself or Michael.

Mark Kessler cracked the top off the coffee he'd picked up on his way into the building and discarded the organic stuff. He opened the paper wide and stifled a laugh looking at Reverend Flynn's face on the front page. That would be the icing on Michael's wedding cake. Hopefully he didn't ask him to officiate.

Coffee spilled, scalding his fingers and chin. *Oh no.* Reverend Flynn wasn't on the front page this time because of some local event he'd attended, but because he died. The newspaper claimed carbon monoxide poisoning. He read the article at warp speed looking for baked goods and finding none. Carbon monoxide. A chill ran over his arms. What were the odds? The building was clear of staff, only the reverend and an unnamed woman perished. Police had sufficient evidence to link the two romantically. The information bred more questions. He read the article again.

> Two die in fluke furnace fiasco. Reverend Glenn Flynn and a member of his flock were found in his

office early this morning. When cleaning crews arrived, the bodies were discovered and 9-1-1 was called. Authorities determined the cause of death to be the result of a faulty furnace. Carbon monoxide poisoned the two as they visited.

Reverend Flynn took great pride in his operation of the oldest parish in the county. Perhaps someone should have suggested a new furnace.

Dr. Kessler's face heated through and he twisted and tugged on his wedding band until he resolved to cancel his morning appointment with Ruby Russell. He was in no mood to counsel and he needed to settle down before he saw her again.

Entering his office through his private door, he rang his receptionist. "Debra, would you please contact my first appointment. I need to reschedule, I'm afraid. See what I have available next week."

"Dr. Kessler," a low cautious voice returned. "That's not going to be possible this morning. Ruby Russell is here to see you."

Flabbergasted, the good doctor rubbed his face with one hot hand. He clutched the telephone with the other. "Send her in," he whispered.

*****

Emma Eaken poured over her notes for the one millionth time, begging for wisdom. There had to be something she missed. Too many big stories were right under her nose. If she ever had a chance at the anchor desk, it had to be in these notes. She just needed to put her finger on it.

Deaths. Most of the big stories were deaths. Five ladies playing Bridge. Seventeen at a soup kitchen in the city. Four men at her station. All food poisoning. Then Reverend Flynn and a young girl died of carbon monoxide poisoning. Twenty-nine deaths put the county at its highest murder rate in more than a decade. If only she could prove they were murders. She tapped her pen against her clipboard.

Twenty-nine people dead. Twenty-seven food poisoned. Emma could tie two instances to Treeline Bakery. The attack at the Partridge Parrish involved baked goods, but not from Treeline. The most recent was a furnace issue, but a poisoning nonetheless.

Emma had copied a few pages on each case while at the precinct, and she read them again and again, until they were worn along the bottoms. She huffed into the air and thumbed through the pile before her. Then something caught her eye. The investigation into the deaths at the mission had narrowed the food in question to some muffins. The contents of their stomachs were all basically the same and all included evidence they'd eaten muffins, gourmet muffins. Specifically, chocolate zucchini.

The muffins weren't unusual. Baked goods, especially day olds, were delivered all the time. The chocolate zucchini pairing, however, was notable. Who'd donate gourmet muffins to a homeless shelter? She propped her feet onto her desk and began to read from the beginning. Gourmet muffins sounded like a bakery to Emma. Her feet hit the floor when something else caught her eye. Those muffins had come from the Church of Hope, Reverend Flynn's parish. Finally, she had a thread to pull on.

"Gina!" She called for the nearest intern, who appeared instantly. "Get me the number for this woman, Amy. She works at The Church of Hope with Reverend Flynn. I think she may be extremely helpful to me."

"Right away." The girl disappeared.

A few minutes later, Emma and Amy discussed the tragic loss of a great man.

"I'm very sorry," Emma said solemnly. "I know this is a difficult time for you and your church. I'm calling to give my condolences, but I also have a question or two, if you don't mind."

"I don't think I'd be much help. I rarely had any time with him. I don't, I mean I didn't know him personally."

"That's quite alright. First, can you tell me about the young woman found with him?"

"Daisy?"

"Yes. Did you know Daisy?" Emma wrote the name on her notepad. They hadn't released that name yet. She wondered if they had been able to notify her family.

"Yes. I knew her. She came with her father sometimes. Her dad was nice. I heard rumors about him though. The women told me to steer clear."

"What did they say about Daisy?" She was on pins and needles. This call was a reporter's jackpot. Murder or not, dirt on the girl found with Reverend Flynn was an excellent story.

"She had a lot of suitors. They were mostly older than her."

"Like the reverend?"

The silence answered for Amy. She had enough suspicion to be prepared to not answer. "Amy, one more thing. Can you tell me about the chocolate zucchini muffins you took to the mission the day those people died?"

"Yes." She sounded relieved not be pressed to betray her former pastor. "Reverend Flynn received them that day. We nearly ate them on our way to the parish. They were so fancy, but we knew we were supposed to take them to the mission." Her voice cracked. "My mom and I almost died that day."

"Did the reverend buy them?" Emma hoped they were from Treeline.

"No. They were in a basket. It was a gift basket. It didn't have a card when I got them."

"Do you have access to the reverend's planner? What could he have been thanked for? Was it a birthday gift? Who could have sent it, and was it for him or the church in general?"

"He handled his own calendar, but I know he spoke at a youth rally held at the Montrose Public Library and maybe at the Kensington Women's Society. I don't know about his birthday. Uh, I'll be at the church this afternoon if you want to come and visit. You can speak with Mrs. Morris. She's handling the donations, and she comes in at two."

"Alright. I'd like to send flowers. Are the services set yet?"

"They're still coordinating. I'll ask again."

"See you soon."

Easy enough. Emma called the church and asked for Mrs. Morris' home number, then dialed her up.

"Mrs. Morris, I'd like to send flowers to the memorial service for Reverend Flynn and Daisy. I'd actually like to send Daisy's family a card, but I can't remember her last name.

"Douglas. You can send flowers to the church between now and Thursday."

"Do you recall the reverend's commitments the week before the accident at Partridge Parish, by chance?"

"Certainly. The youth rally was all he had worked on for weeks. He has a real heart for our youth." She sobbed once. "Had." Emma listened to her breathe a moment before she continued. "The rally was the only major event on his calendar that week. As always, it went off without a hitch, a phenomenal success, bless his soul."

"Thank you." Emma hung up and began looking through the phone book and calling every Douglas in order.

She made a side note to contact the Boys and Girls Club of Montrose Hills to see if they were happy enough to send a basket.

Finally, she nailed it. The woman hung up on her, but it was the right place. Emma tore the page from the book and headed to her car. She arrived less than twenty minutes later.

Opening her door, she removed her sunglasses to double check the address. The dilapidated row of houses stood on the fault line between the good and bad side of the tracks. This area was once part of the former, but in the last decade, that had changed.

Emma's shoes struck up dust as she walked across the front yard. The yard was not a lawn so much as a sand lot. The ground beneath her feet looked withered and brown from neglect and random trash. The porch railing shimmied when Emma touched it. The mini blinds inside the door hung at an angle, and it took some courage to ring the bell.

"I paid ya already!" a rough voice called from inside. "I paid ya. I don't want none. Go away!" The crashing sound of a broken glass came hard against the door.

"Mrs. Douglas?" Emma's voice shook. "Mrs. Douglas, my name is Emma Eaken. I work for Channel 3." The door swung open and a thin woman leaned against the frame for support.

"I know who you are, and I ain't talking unless there's a payday in it for me." She tapped a large glass bottle against the screen.

"I can't pay you." Emma turned on her charm. "I can get to the bottom of your daughter's death. Maybe if we had someone to blame." She let that float a minute.

"Why didn't you say so?"

The woman opened the door wide and stepped aside. "Make yourself at home. Excuse the mess." She tossed a pile of clothing off a worn green couch and onto the floor. Empty bottles and ashtrays full to capacity formed the cornerstone of her décor.

"Can you tell me why your daughter met with Reverend Flynn the day of their accident?"

"I suppose she was sleeping with him. That's what the papers said." The woman took a long drink and lit a cigarette.

"Do you believe that?" Something told Emma it wasn't true.

Tears came to the woman's eyes. "She always got on my case, you know? She'd tell me I shouldn't have so many boyfriends. She hated it when anyone slept over. I saw her using her boyfriends to get things I couldn't give her. She had men buying her things and driving her around. I'm sure her Pastor Flint was no different. He was a man, right? She probably used him, too."

"So, she often dated older men?" Intrigue tickled her fancy. Could some angry wife have killed this girl? Perhaps Flynn was the unfortunate casualty of another woman scorned.

"She always dated someone closer to my age than hers. Of course, turnabout is fair play." Her mother dashed a pile of dirt in the ashtray and continued puffing. "Oprah says she's trying to fill her daddy's absence or some psycho babble like that."

"I thought her father went to church with her."

"Yeah, when he was wanting something, forgiveness, or money, or sex."

Emma had never considered church to be a place to find the latter, but she hadn't been there in a while.

"Do you know any of the names of the older men your daughter dated? Maybe I could ask around and see if any of them might know something?"

"I thought you were going to help me find someone to sue. Like the church or the company who made that furnace. People don't have money, honey. Companies have money."

"I've got to start somewhere." Emma smiled.

After a minute, Mrs. Douglas crushed one cigarette into a volcano of ashes. She promptly lit another. Emma tried not to look around, make direct eye contact or think about the couch where she sat.

"Well, there was a dentist over in Monroe. Dick something. She used to see her high school counselor. No way she made the grades to stay in her yuppie private school on my income." She looked around. "That Richards man, uh, what was his name? He was the latest, unless that's true about the reverend. Keith Richards? Kenneth Richards."

"Okay. That helps." Emma stood to leave. She exhausted that avenue. "I'm heading to the church soon. I'll stay in touch, Mrs. Douglas." Emma offered a business card but the woman just stared.

"I'll let myself out." Emma pulled antibacterial wipes from her purse before she made it back to her car. That was one woman she never planned to call again, ever.

CHAPTER THIRTEEN

"Good morning, Ruby." Dr. Kessler's even voice grated her already frayed nerves. "I'm glad to see you today. We have plenty to talk about, don't we?"

Ruby had plenty she wanted to talk about, but none of that was possible. She had to stick to simple conversation. Sweat gathered on her brow threatening her composure.

She mashed her hands together. "Is there anything in particular?"

"Well," he tapped his hands on the morning paper. "I saw some things in the paper that may be of interest to you. Maybe we could start there?"

She had already made it clear she wasn't a fan of Reverend Flynn. That left the other thing she didn't want to talk about.

"Michael's getting married."

She waited.

"How do you feel about that?"

"I don't know, honestly. It's still fresh. He's too young, of course, and doesn't have a proper home or career." Ruby looked out the closest window to avoid Dr. Kessler's judgmental gaze.

"Have you met her?"

"Yes, and her parents." There, that was normal. Ruby had the entire family over for lunch. Dr. Kessler must approve of that.

"Are they nice? What do you think of them?"

"They're fine. She's fine. I have no points of objection, other than Michael isn't ready for marriage in any way. He has no idea what he's getting into. He can't possibly know who she is because he doesn't even know who he is yet."

"So, are you protesting or supporting the marriage?"

"Supporting, of course." Ruby eyed the doctor. She'd said nothing to make him think she'd protest. "I'm managing the reception."

"Ah." He wrote in his notepad and tapped on the paper.

"I'm supporting Michael. I'll be happy for him. The girl is acceptable and so is her family. I'm thankful to take such a large role in the planning. Most girls would have pushed the mother-in-law aside and planned it all with their own mother and friends. It's nice to be included." Saying the words out loud was refreshing. The truth warmed her, and Ruby ruminated on the warmth for a while. Perhaps it wouldn't be so awful to have family in town, or in the next town to be more specific. They would be close enough to visit and far enough not to. Michael and Sophia could buy the Tanner house.

"Who'll perform the ceremony?"

Ruby squinted at the doctor.

"Her family belongs to a nice Catholic church. Her priest will perform the ceremony."

"Hmm. That's nice. You were once Catholic, weren't you?"

"I *am* Catholic." She clutched her pocketbook, unhappy

with his new line of questioning. Dr. Kessler walked a very slippery path.

"Was Ken?"

"Yes, of course," she said.

"Then, why did Reverend Flynn officiate Ken's funeral? Why not a Catholic Priest? Someone from St. Michaels?"

Ruby bit hard into her cheek. No way to avoid this now. He had completely disregarded her explicit request to never discuss Reverend Flynn again.

"I don't pretend to know, Dr. Kessler. Reverend Flynn called and offered. I was terribly upset and accepted the offer. Now, before you continue on, I suggest you recall our previous discussion on this topic. I'll not talk about that man." Ruby coughed into a tight fist. Dr. Kessler wasn't much help lately and she needed help. Perhaps coming to see him was a waste of time.

"Yes. Of course." Dr. Kessler pulled back in his chair. "How's your kitchen renovation coming?"

"The renovation has been complete for some time and it's lovely."

The remainder of the hour filled with awkward conversation and long pauses. Ruby left planning a truce. No need to burn bridges.

The following week, she regretted the effort.

Upon entering Dr. Kessler's office, she found his desk in utter disarray and he didn't look like himself. Ruby sat in her usual seat and studied the scene before her. Dr. Kessler's hair had no gel. He wore a cotton shirt with a collar instead of the dress shirt and tie she'd come to respect. His eyes drooped and puffed with fatigue. Ruby understood. Marital problems. *He is at the time in life when adults realize they've wasted their lives.* The Kesslers didn't even have the reward of a child to show for their decades of bondage. *Sad.*

Ruby removed her gloves, one finger at a time, deciding what to say first. She eyed the ridiculous mess spilling from his desk. On the cusp of offering to clean the desk for him, something beneath the pile of strewn papers caught her eye. A small book lay all but invisible beneath the stacks of files. The binding angled away, but as she reached for one dropped glove, her heart stuttered and stopped. *BEAN POISONING – COOKING KILLERS*.

Dr. Kessler positioned his glasses on his face and dug for a clean pad of paper. Ruby considered the implications of such a book. She knew Dr. Kessler's wife was a vegan. The book could belong to her. A much more concerning option was Dr. Kessler becoming suspicious of Ruby. That would never do.

A smirk built upon Ruby's face as she realized the irony unfolding. If the latter of her theories was true, then Dr. Kessler could be having his own heart problems soon. She could make sure of it. She moved her face away from the doctor as he made his way around the desk to shake her hand and begin their session. She struggled to look at him without revealing her humor. Either he was an imbecile who missed absolutely everything she let slip each week, or a nosey ninny. Nose ninnies needed a lesson sometimes. Both provided good fun for Ruby.

"You're in good spirits, Ruby. How are things at home?"

"Very well, thank you." Her smile widened.

"The wedding plans?"

"I'm meeting with Sophia and her mother this afternoon. I'll have a chance to go over all the work I've done so far and get their feedback. I'm looking forward to it. I've got everything in order for when I get home. I only have to pack it up. The wedding will come together very nicely. I'm certain."

"What will you be serving?" An innocent question on

the surface, but Ruby thought he meant something more.

"Tea sandwiches, of course. We'll be meeting for tea."

Dr. Kessler nodded. "What all have you been working on to share with them?"

"I've put together three acceptable menus for the shower. I'll run those by them as well as ideas about the location and décor. I'll do the same for the rehearsal dinner and the reception."

"That sounds wonderful. It's nice to see you put all of your culinary talent to use. You're a blessing to this pair, no doubt about that."

Ruby's chest puffed a little. She straightened her back a bit and lifted her chin.

"How's Charlotte?"

Ruby's tiny slump returned. Her eyes darted to the floor. She cleared her throat and opened her mouth more than once before she could muster words. Anything she said would be call for crucifixion. Her cheeks flamed as she realized he knew more than he let on. He'd been playing with her like a cat with a mouse. His flowery words were meant to soften her up so she'd turn on her best friend.

When her eyes met his at last, his face was unreadable. Ruby imagined his lips twitched and a smile played at his eyes.

"I won't talk about her." The best way to avoid this conversation would be to fabricate an argument between them. Then it would be reasonable.

"Oh come now, Ruby, you two are like sisters. You've been like that since you met, right?" His fingers laced around one another.

She found it difficult to say awful things about Charlotte. She loved her so, and wouldn't talk about her. Ruby took a deep breath. "Charlotte's bossy, nosey and meddlesome. I think she's envious of all the new things going on in my life since Ken passed. My life was doldrums before because I stayed at home to make a life for my family, like she does. Since he died, though, I've been out doing things, and now I'm planning a wedding." Ruby rocked on the edge of the chair.

Dr. Kessler wrote in his notepad. Ruby searched his office for more books on food poisoning, but found none. The office looked to be in better shape than his desk, but not as neat as it had been. Dr. Kessler's eyes ran to the clock many times before he called the session's end a bit early. Ruby breathed easier. She'd pinched her skin between her thumb and first finger for forty-five minutes to control her urge to leave.

"Next week?" Ruby asked through gritted teeth. Her voice threatened to give her away.

"Certainly, yes. Speak with the receptionist and keep up the good work on that wedding." Dr. Kessler was up to something. Time to unsettle him a bit.

"I hope you find whatever it is that you're looking for."

"What do you mean?"

"Well, your office looks as if you've turned it upside down, unless you've had an office invasion and failed to tidy up. I hope you find whatever it is you misplaced." Ruby let her gaze run over the doctor from head to toe. He shifted his weight away from her slightly.

*****

Though he rarely lied to Meredith, Mark had one more task before he could keep his promise to her. She had asked him to stop seeing Ruby Russell, but he needed to look into something else first. Dr. Kessler stood to the left of his office window and watched as Ruby exited the building and drove south in her van. He waited there, absolutely still, for several minutes just in case she circled back for any reason.

Then he grabbed his jacket and hastened to the lot.

"I'll be back in time for my next appointment." He blew through the empty waiting room.

In the car, he made a call to his wife. Meredith normally had several women over for a group yoga session and luncheon on Tuesdays. The visit always ended in sangria and gossip. She wouldn't notice if he didn't stop in for lunch.

Voice mail picked up and Mark left a message before steering his vehicle onto the northbound highway. He had an appointment with Dr. Shrieve at Heartland Behavioral Health, a place Ruby had once called home.

The drive was excruciating. He used every minute to review his notes lying on the seat next to him. He thought about Ruby's demeanor and nuances. The facts stacked up like hotcakes. Her husband died a very unusual death, and then her closest neighbor. If the first was foul play, could the neighbor have been witness to something condemning?

Mark Kessler thought of the reverend who she wouldn't speak of and his sudden death. Then the mission where his church played a major role had suffered a great loss as well. Partridge Parish was a staple in the city's community. However, he had to consider the reverend hadn't been poisoned and frankly, he was involved in most of the local charities, not just with Partridge Parish. Regardless, all these unfortunate souls were tied to Ruby Russell. She was the axis of evil.

By the time the large estate came into view, the doctor's mind reeled with possibilities. He'd probably find he'd wasted his time traveling to see Dr. Shrieve, but he knew he'd go insane wondering if he skipped their meeting. Besides, he could drop Ruby as a patient as soon as he got to the bottom of this. Mark took a small amber cylinder from his glove box before he opened the door of his car. Anxiety afflicted him of late.

From the outside, Heartland Behavioral Health might have been a wealthy land owner's plantation set somewhere a hundred years back in time. The facility was immaculate. The grounds had teams of landscapers to care for them. It took a familiar eye to see the high grade security in place everywhere. Patients at Heartland were little more than inmates in fancy cells. They weren't there to recover from an illness. They were there for observation after a dangerous behavior, or series of them. Heartland served as a stop between jail and home for some, and a stop before formal incarceration for others, like Ruby.

Dr. Shrieve met Dr. Kessler at the door. The lockdown facility allowed guests with accompaniment.

"Dr. Shrieve, thank you for meeting with me like this." Dr. Kessler shook his hand and stepped through the glass door.

"Sam, please," Dr. Shrieve spoke in a neutral and friendly voice.

"Mark, thank you."

They made their way along a corridor with multiple glass doors and buzzers. It seemed every few feet a check point of one sort or another stopped their progress. Inside Sam's office, Mark breathed easier. He'd been in private practice too long. He was out of touch with those on the frontline, and becoming a snob.

Shrieve's office resembled his own, though Sam's glass was probably shatter resistant, and he noticed no breakable items in the line of fire. Framed art lined the walls. Mark suspected they were nailed there and the mirror to his left acted as a window to viewers somewhere beyond. Otherwise, a typical setting for counseling.

"So, you're working with Ruby Russell." Sam pulled a large manila file from his drawer. "I've also had the pleasure." The file he held was enormous. Mark's fingers twitched for it. Ruby was an onion whose layers increased with each one peeled. Mark's file on Ruby grew at breakneck speed as well.

"Was she here long?" He nodded at the file.

"Six months, but I had a lot to write about." The doctor smiled.

"I wish I could smile." Mark confided his own condition to this comrade of sorts. This man, of all men, understood what he was going through.

"Well, I had the security of knowing she was locked up when I left at night. You have the uncertainty of not knowing where she goes when she leaves your office. She's a wolf in sheep's clothing." He spoke without inflection. "An impulsive danger in an apron and pumps."

Dr. Kessler hadn't considered she might harm him. Until that moment, his concern had been focused solely on the community at large. How dense. If he were too pushy, if he rubbed her the wrong way, what would stop her from finding him? Nothing. Mark and Meredith had shared the same address and phone number for twenty years. He was a sitting duck. His thoughts ran to Meredith and her unsuspecting vegan clan. She literally couldn't hurt a fly. She'd refused to own a fly swatter.

"So, as you know, Ruby Russell spent some time here after she poisoned a few members of the faculty at a university out of state. She hoped to scare her son into going somewhere closer to home, or scare the college board into not accepting him. Either way, she was acquitted on all counts for lack of motive. She never uttered anything incriminating on the stand. Her husband spent a small fortune on legal counsel, and she agreed, off the record, to stay here for a stint, officially citing a nervous breakdown."

Sam opened the file and handed a group of pages to Mark. "Ruby was a shell when she arrived here. She looked like a child taken from her home. Weeks passed before she opened up to the idea of being here. She's smart. Once she came around enough to pay attention, she understood the rules. She wasn't going home until she completed the program and that meant participation."

"Did she?" Mark asked the question as if he didn't already know the answer.

"Yes. One day the orderly went to bring her breakfast and found her up and dressed. She even had her makeup on, as well as possible without a mirror. She asked him when she could see me. I knew then. She watched and listened all the time. She's a fox." His eyes widened and so did his smile. His head tipped back and forth. "A wolf."

"And after that day?"

"She played the game." Dr. Shrieve rocked back in his chair, looking pensive and pleased. "She came to every session. She took up kitchen responsibilities. She helped others, made friends, and read. She became a model patient. It was such an intense change we considered a secondary personality, but it was the same personality from before her admittance. She simply bounced back." Sam rubbed his chin appreciatively. "That was about the time she met Charlotte Mason."

Mark's spine stiffened. "Charlotte," he whispered.

"Yes. Charlotte Mason was here for a *very* long time. Ruby helped her. Those two had a sisterhood. I can't say who led and who followed. They were both nervous and self-destructive. Both prone to impulsivity and were overly-emotional as well as suspicious. They grew extremely close, attending sessions together and whispering in their rooms. They arranged to be together every moment they could. It was adolescent and, considering all things, a little unnerving."

"They're still very close, only Ruby claims they've had a

fight." Mark didn't believe her, but he didn't know why she'd lie about it.

"Thick as thieves," Mark breathed.

"What?"

"That's what Ruby calls them, thick as thieves."

"Really? Intriguing. Hmm, well, I'm not sure what to make of the fight. They needed one another while they were here. They worked together like crutches. One just isn't very useful. Two can get the job done."

"Can you tell me about Charlotte?" Mark knew he asked too much. Charlotte wasn't now, nor had she ever been, in his care. The line was gray. Though, she was a cog in his patient's life. He had no other tie. Luckily, Sam was feeling chatty.

"Well, Charlotte's a southern belle who moved north with her love. They made a home nearby. He passed on many years back. She struggled adjusting to life without him. Until he died, she'd been a nurse. In those days a lady could be a nurse without a degree. She worked in clinics mostly. I suppose her title was something like nurses' aide, but she worked at it for years. There's much to be said for experience." He swiveled in his chair and appeared to choose his words with care.

"Before she came here, she worked at a drug and alcohol rehabilitation clinic in the city. Hospitals no longer employed nurses' aides, but clinics, well they'll always need help. The clinic where Charlotte worked took in addicts from the street. The Haven of Rest offered food and encouragement. Most individuals who went were regulars. It was a terribly frustrating and disturbing place to Charlotte. Her husband had been taken from her, though he had lived a healthy life. He had no warnings. Then, everyday she went to work and watched people given a second chance, promise a new beginning only to return a few days later strung out and hungry or beaten. She snapped."

Mark struggled to process the information. The fact that Charlotte was as dangerous as Ruby made it difficult to breath or swallow. He'd always imagined their breakdowns bonded them, nothing more and nothing sinister. He contemplated a cross-country move or perhaps entirely overseas.

Dr. Shrieve spoke less clinically. "She was in charge of administering methadone to users suffering from severe withdrawal symptoms."

"No."

Sam nodded. "Charlotte said she gave them what they wanted. Apparently they wanted to torture and kill themselves, so she cut to the chase. Why continue to help them kill themselves slowly? She concluded it a waste of her time and taxpayer dollars, and started giving lethal doses to the returning addicts who she felt weren't trying to stay clean."

"She killed them, intentionally." Mark tried to compose himself, but he felt like a child at a campfire.

"Yes." Dr. Shrieve nodded, smiling. "She cited taxpayer justice." He turned his chair back to face Mark. "She was a real mess when she came in, grieving her husband and lack of family. She'd seen enough turmoil at the clinic to suffer a degree of post traumatic stress disorder. She spent a month in solitary confinement by choice. She wanted to die, I think. Then one morning, about six months in, she came reluctantly to breakfast, found Ruby serving fancy pastries and lattes and," he looked soberly at Mark. "Well, you know the rest. We released Ruby first. She was fully rehabilitated by our standards. Charlotte followed about a year later. Ruby visited her faithfully until then. Charlotte's still required to check in monthly, but that's the extent of her remaining punishment. Our legal system has quite a ways to go."

Mark's mouth hung open wide. He was poised to ask more questions but he was interrupted. His phone vibrated in his pocket. He held up a finger and nodded. "Excuse me one minute, would you?"

"Hello?" He found it difficult to speak. Emotion wrapped his head like a blanket.

"I love you." Meredith was apparently enjoying the sangria.

"Thank you." It was his way of telling her he wasn't alone.

"Okay, well, I only wanted to say I love you for being so thoughtful. You're the envy of all my friends, you know."

The words were sweet and welcomed but nonsensical at the moment.

"We love the bean dip. It goes fabulously with the sangria, corn chips, guacamole, and…"

"What. Bean. Dip?" Each word stood alone on his tongue. Beans were bad. He'd read more about beans in the past week than any other topic in the last two years. Beans were poisonous.

"Yes. Everyone wants the recipe. The jars were so cute wrapped in the little cloths. I found them on the doorstep when I came in from the market. Sorry I missed you at lunch. I hadn't expected you today."

"Meredith, I wouldn't have left food on the doorstep."

Sam sat up in his chair.

"What? If you didn't…There are a dozen ladies in our yard enjoying drinks and lunch. What do I do? Are you saying Ruby Russell may have…Should I call the police or the paramedics? Oh, no."

"Meredith?" Mark's voice leapt an octave when he heard the loud thump. "Meredith?"

Mark drove home fast enough to earn a ticket, but no one stopped him. He tried frantically to reach his wife a dozen times on his way. He was dialing the police as flashing lights came into view. He turned into his neighborhood. Parking two blocks away, by reason of necessity, he ran to his home. He passed knots of bystanders and police cars, fire trucks and ambulances. Tears blurred his vision until he had to slow in order to face what lay ahead.

On his front step, Meredith sat with her face in her hands. She didn't move when he approached. Her friends made their ways to their cars in the driveway whispering to one another as they went. When Meredith looked up, her eyes were red.

"I'm so sorry." He embraced her.

"I called 911. I nearly scared my friends to death, and I couldn't tell them why. You weren't supposed to have told me about Ruby." She dabbed at her nose with a wadded tissue. Mark offered her his handkerchief and she accepted. "Everyone's fine, and I look like a lunatic."

CHAPTER FOURTEEN

"Ruby," Dr. Kessler sat in the chair behind his desk, trying to look as stern as he felt. "Did you send a package to our home last week?"

After a week of discussion and critical thought, he was still as angry as the day he had arrived home to find his wife crying on their steps. Day by day he teetered between who was crazier, Ruby Russell or himself. He assumed she'd tried to hurt his family, but why would she do that? He'd done nothing to provoke her. He was wrong to make assumptions. People changed. It was unfair to hold her to a stereotype created out of a desperate act years ago.

However, his protective instinct warned him to keep Ruby at bay. He had no way to truly understand the disturbed mind. Maybe she didn't need to be provoked to react. She might be homicidal without provocation. Back and forth his mind went all week long. He barely heard a word any other patient said. He had spent days consumed with the enigma of her before, and Meredith fumed at the repeat performance.

"Why, yes!" Ruby's eyes lit up. "Did you enjoy it?" The innocence in her tone stood in stark contrast to the look in her eyes.

"Ruby, why did you do that?" He asked carefully, slowly, recalling his training for lie detection. He wished he'd taken more refresher courses instead of resting on his laurels. He remembered only key points. If she lied, she'd fidget. She always fidgeted. Perhaps she always lied. He ran his hands through his thick salt and pepper hair.

"I knew your wife was vegan." She seemed confused. "You told me. When I told you how I loved to bake, you told me your wife is vegan. We spoke about it at length. I remember because I spent some time at the library looking up vegan recipes. They aren't very interesting."

"It was," he searched for the word, "inappropriate." He'd chosen one of her favorites. She'd have to understand. "It was inappropriate to send a gift to me. We cannot have a friendship outside this office. It's against the rules of ethical conduct."

"Whose rules of ethical conduct?"

"Mine." He allowed a kind smile.

Ruby crossed her arms over her bosom and frowned. "Well, I'll keep that in mind, but I made the bean dip for your wife. I finally found a vegan recipe with a little zip and I thought of her. She's the only one of those people I've ever heard of." She leaned towards the doctor then, as if to share a secret. "I don't think it's natural."

"Why mail it? Why not bring it with you here?"

"I dropped it off, but no one was home. I wanted to give it to her personally, and I didn't bring it here because it wasn't for you. I added a nice card."

"There was no card. Meredith thought I'd left it."

"Why in the world would you leave food on your own

doorstep? Now that would be silly. You could have put it on the counter. You never told me you cooked." Her voice became accusatory.

"I don't cook. You haven't told me why you sent the dip."

"Yes, I did." Her head tilted over one shoulder. Her eyes narrowed. Dr. Kessler squirmed against the desk. He feared for what might happen if she discovered what he'd done.

Dr. Kessler had blurted out the whole story to the police at the scene. The only thing he kept to himself was Ruby's name, but anyone with any skill would be able to put two and two together if they wanted to. He'd had the dip taken in for testing by poison control. He'd insisted each of the women see a doctor. He'd made a colossal deal out of a little chip dip. He'd behaved like a complete lunatic, unable to stop until he knew Meredith would be alright. She had called him on it, but her safety trumped his pride. In the end, the tests discovered nothing but beans, salsa and seasoning.

"Are you feeling alright? You looked piqued."

Dr. Kessler continued to glare until Ruby spoke again.

"I'm working out menu scenarios for the wedding like I already told you." She made a slight huff for drama. "I have to come up with menus for a number of wedding related events, and I want Sophia to have some viable choices. You can't serve rubbish, Doctor, it presents poorly."

He continued to stare. His mind spun and his hands heated through.

"I searched through a thousand recipes for appetizers and dips and spreads and that one caught my attention. It was wholesome and without any animal byproduct."

"And you thought of my wife?" His voice seethed with sarcasm.

"I told you, she's the only one of those people I've ever heard of, so yes. Believe me, I'm certainly sorry I did." Ruby turned her face from him, probably to emphasize her own pique.

*****

Ruby used one glove to dab perspiration from her chest and throat. Anger and embarrassment coursed through her. Dr. Kessler was being very unkind. She fought the creases in her forehead. Tears worked their way up from behind her lids. A full twenty minutes remained in her session, but she walked out anyway. Dr. Kessler could be sure he'd only receive payment for the two-thirds of an hour and not a penny more. In fact, she didn't consider what went on in his office therapy at all. Perhaps she'd refuse to pay.

Inside her van the windshield shimmered and tears fell in a salty deluge. With great difficulty, she made it home. Horns blared, and people shouted. Her nerves frayed and her mind wandered to the bottle of wine in her cupboard, but she stayed on the road and in her lane. If anyone knew what she'd been through, they'd have given her a personal escort. She had no option but to drive home in her condition. She couldn't sit out front of the building having a breakdown. What would he think? Since when did a little mischief give the recipient rights to be so hateful?

Seeing her porch come into view was like laying eyes on heaven. Charlotte sat on her porch swing, head back, hands folded. She was the picture of solitude. Ruby's van lodged itself in the driveway and she hustled to Charlotte. She dragged her purse behind her, snagged it on a bush and then snagged her pantyhose when she tried to retrieve her purse. She lost a lipstick in the process. Charlotte met her at the steps.

Charlotte threw the bag over one shoulder and wrapped her free arm around Ruby's slumping shoulders. "What happened to you?" Her kind voice replete with indignation. Ruby knew that voice well. She'd often thought Charlotte could command armies when she was in that disposition. The fierceness of the tone made Ruby feel safe. Unfortunately for Charlotte, the security overwhelmed her and the tears ran anew.

She dug into Ruby's purse for her keys and let them inside. Charlotte went to the kitchen while Ruby lay down on the couch. In a minute, Charlotte returned with some pills and a cool, wet cloth.

"Take your time." She headed back to the kitchen. "I'll get the coffee going."

"No." Ruby waved one arm from under the cold white cloth. She'd managed to spread it over her face like a mask and held it in place with the other hand. "Wine, please. I'd like wine. It's in the cupboard."

"Fine, but I don't condone it."

Ruby heard the cupboard door click shut.

"Ruby Russell!" Charlotte exclaimed. Ruby jumped three inches.

"Ohhh." She groaned. She listened to Charlotte's footsteps moving heavily toward her.

"What is this?"

Ruby pulled a corner of the cloth back to see what she was being accused of. Charlotte held a freezer bag full of pills in front of her. "Oh." She recovered her face and motioned Charlotte back to get her wine. "Those are my pills from Dr. Kessler."

"Does he deal on the street now? No need for a pharmacy? You just hold out your hands or an empty sack and he pours them in? Don't you lie to me, Ruby Russell!" She slammed the bag hard against the coffee table.

"Hey!" Ruby shouted. "You're the one who told me if I was going to take medication I should see the doctor. Well, I do and he gives me prescriptions and I don't take them. After thirty days, I dump them in there and get my refill."

Charlotte looked like she'd been goosed. Her eyes sought answers from the giant bag of pills. She pushed the bag aside and sat on the little table with them. "Once more please."

Ruby huffed and sat upright. The act took more energy than she'd planned to expend before enjoying a glass of wine. She eyed Charlotte. There would be no wine without clarification.

"Dr. Kessler wants to see me every week." She spoke to Charlotte as if she were six years old or perhaps in possession of a very low I.Q. "He wants me to tell him I'm taking my medication and I'm doing well on it. So, I do. It's part of the charade." Ruby rolled her eyes and Charlotte visibly relaxed.

"Why not actually take the medication?"

"Because I. Am. Fine." Ruby shot up onto her feet and marched into the kitchen to pour her own wine.

"Why keep them? Street value?" Charlotte followed close behind Ruby into the kitchen.

"Street value?" Ruby yanked a glass from the drying rack. "Do I look like a pimp to you?" Ruby poured a glass of wine and rolled it against her forehead under her neatly sculpted blond bangs. Her cream blouse and pearl buttons perfectly aligned with her brown pencil skirt.

"No. You don't look like a pimp." Charlotte smirked.

"What?" Ruby's shoulders attacked her ears. "What?"

"It's nothing. Never mind. Why not take the pills?"

"I'd rather drink." She cashed the first glass and returned it to the counter for a refill. "I can't drink and take the pills." She held up the bottle on the counter. "I'd rather drink."

"Then throw them out. Can you imagine if someone came and found them? What are you keeping them for?"

"I may need them sometime."

Charlotte nodded. That made sense. It paid to be prepared. Life could be messy.

*****

Emma Eaken arrived at the gate to the Everett estate around seven-thirty. It was the first time she'd ever needed to be buzzed in from the road to anyone's home. With much trepidation, she shifted her car into gear and rolled slowly up the tree-lined drive. Fall bloomed around her. A few leaves had already given in to defeat and fallen to the ground. She drove over them, thinking that was what happened when defeat won out.

When the drive opened onto the square where she was expected to park, Emma paused. The home was enormous, a pretentious kickback to plantation living. The structure had probably been around since the civil war but had most obviously undertaken some major renovations. The peaks and gables rose majestically into the skyline. A small veranda perched above the front doors, which were surrounded by giant stone columns. Emma considered turning back before deciding to ring the bell.

"Right this way," a tall elderly gentleman greeted her with indifference.

"Thank you," she whispered, hoping to find her voice again soon.

"Ms. Eaken," he announced before bowing and leaving her under a magnificent archway at the end of a short wide hall.

"Ms. Eaken." A tall thin woman in designer apparel stood at once and met her in the doorway. "Come in, please, make yourself at home."

Emma would never feel at home there, regardless of the amount of time she stayed. She did, however, sit on the edge of a small settee and cross her ankles the way her mother once insisted.

"Thank you for having me, Mrs. Everett."

"Ms. Everett. Actually, why not call me Helena."

"Thank you, Helena." Emma smiled. "I'm sorry to be coming around for the reason I am, but I'm doing some research and it has led me to you."

"Hmm. Yes, well I think this will go far better than I had anticipated, then. How can I be of assistance to you?"

"I'm looking into the life of a local girl found dead at the Church of Hope. Her name was Daisy Douglas."

"I assumed that much correctly then," she answered gravely.

"You're familiar with your connection to the girl then?"

"Unfortunately. Can I get you some tea, Ms. Eaken?" Before Emma could object, she'd already called the old man to her door.

"Please, call me Emma."

Helena ordered tea for two and the gentleman disappeared once more.

"Emma, this young woman ruined my marriage." She looked much less jovial with each word. "I'm afraid I said some awful things about her and even wished the worst upon her. It sickens me to see what fate has done. You can imagine."

Emma let the words settle in. Earning her position as investigative reporter for Channel 3 was rough. She'd had instance to be underhanded many times and the stress brought out the worst in her. If all the people she wished dead would die, it'd be much quieter in Montrose Hills.

"Yes. Can you tell me anything about the girl?"

"Only that she was everything I had once been, according to my ex-husband. They met at the mall or the pool, or some other place a man his age shouldn't have been, and she made him feel young. In exchange, he bought her things. It was symbiotic, except for the marriage wrecking. I posed a problem in their little escapades. So he announced his affair, professed his love for her and left. Threw caution to the wind and asked for nothing in the divorce."

"He asked for nothing?" Emma thought she'd been following along fairly well, but still reasoned she missed something.

"Yes. This," she gestured upwards, "is all mine. The money comes from my family, and he had his freedom to use it as he chose. He could have asked for something, but he didn't. He would have lost, but he didn't ask. All he wanted was her and she dumped him."

"For another man?"

"For lack of cash, I'm guessing. So yes, for a man with more to offer."

"I see."

So there were more. A local Lolita. It would have been a great story if she weren't dead. Maybe it would be great because she died, but Emma wasn't sure she could bring herself to slander the young woman posthumously. It was a tough call though because the way she died, suspiciously, and with a well-known pastor, made for great news. Not happy news, but an excellent story.

"I'm sorry. I didn't mean to bring up anything painful."

Obviously Helena must've know when Emma arrived the conversation would be uncomfortable. Something clicked in Emma's mind. "When I arrived, you seemed relieved I wasn't here for something else. Would you mind telling me?"

"I'd assumed you were trying to get the gruesome details of the divorce proceedings. Anytime a local with money gets a divorce, it usually ends up in the paper. Rich people interest everyone. We irritate the snot out of those who have less and we're great gossip for one another at the club." A sad but true smile appeared under her eyes.

The tea arrived and Emma was compelled to stay a while. It seemed beyond rude to bring up something painful and then leave. She wasn't sure staying was nice, either. "Do you know anything about the girl?" Emma sipped tea from a tiny cream and rose colored cup.

Helena pursed her lips and her eyes pinched at the corners. "You mean, did I have her followed? Yes. I hired a private investigator after my ex-husband confessed his love for her. I wanted to see if he was being scammed. I have my estate to protect."

"Was this a scam?" Emma was hopeful and a little guilty for it. A private investigator was an unexpected bonus.

"Not beyond the typical father figure infatuation. She had a history of pairing herself with older men since high school. No locatable father in her life until high school, and her mother had little to offer along the lines of finances or instruction. The men filled a void, a psychologist would say, and they bought her things she couldn't have had otherwise. It's difficult to say whether she was the predator or the prey really."

"You're not angry with her?" Shock registered in Emma's voice.

"No. I'm very sad for her actually. I'm angry at my idiot of a husband. Ex-husband."

It occurred to Emma this woman had plenty of reasons to want the girl dead and being sorry for her might or might not be true at all. Also, she might not be alone. "You say she had a history of this?"

"According to my private investigator." She held up a finger and moved across the room. "I'm admittedly biased here, so I'm going to give you the number of the gentleman who worked with me on this. She returned with a business card. "I'll give the office a call in the morning to let them know I've consented to release the details. I only ask you leave my name out of anything that comes to print as a result."

"Of course." Emma's heart-rate spiked. She was happy with the information she had already gleaned. This act of generosity stole her breath away. Internally, she squealed and clapped. Outwardly, she sipped tea from a cup she worried might break without warning and balanced on a settee she knew would stain if that happened.

When the tea was finished, Emma pretended to receive a text while Helena stood to call the gentleman to retrieve the tray.

"I'm sorry. I need to go. I don't mean to be so abrupt."

"It's fine. Please see Emma to the door."

"Thank you again, Helena. I'm indebted to you and will hold to our agreement completely." Emma meant every word. This little white card could break her career into the big league. She owed Mrs. Everett. Walking to her car, her mind reeled, a mixture of befuddled and elated. Too bad she had to wait all night to call the number on the card.

CHAPTER FIFTEEN

The first and grandest of many bridal showers was held at the Walsh home. Ruby couldn't contain her excitement. Her first show! She arrived three hours early to tend to the details and manage their execution. But pulling into the Walshes' drive put her in a foul disposition. The drive was double the width of hers and shiny black asphalt all the winding way. If that wasn't enough, the huge manor, if that's what they called it, sat atop a great precipice to the rear of the picturesque property.

Ruby exited her van in a huff. What sort of grand view would an estate like this overlook? She stamped around to the rear of the van, not needing to see what was back there. She knew what the soft tick she heard in the distance meant. Golf. In a man's eye, this enormous structure atop a great cliff would only be perfect if the view from half the home was of a golf course. The scowl on her face hurt. She imagined it creating new wrinkles as it sat there.

"Mrs. Russell!"

Ruby groaned when she heard the eager voice.

"Good morning, Sophia." Ruby sighed, and Sophia's hopeful grin sagged.

"We're setting up in the kitchen. Please, let me help you." Without permission, Sophia gathered things right out of Ruby's van. There were no words to describe how Sophia's presumptuous actions affected her.

When Sophia spun and headed towards her home, Ruby followed. The door stood twice as tall as necessary and was adorned in every direction by equally outstanding transoms. The entranceway soared above them. An elaborate mahogany staircase twisted upward toward a chandelier probably handmade by fairies and tiny forest creatures.

If Ruby could have left, she would have. She imagined throwing her hands in the air and walking out.

"Mrs. Russell, this is Antoine. He's here to assist you in any way you need. I'll let him show you around while I get the rest of your things." Sophia disappeared and Ruby shut her mouth, hoping not to draw attention to the fact she'd left it hanging open. Antoine bowed.

For a man at least ten years Ruby's senior, tall and dashing still described him to a "t". He was dressed in black from his shoes to his apron, and she swallowed hard. The sight of his apron heated places inside her she didn't like to think about.

"I'm Ruby Russell," she said as properly as she could manage.

"Very nice to meet you." His reply was too brief and Ruby shifted on her feet.

"They shouldn't have hired anyone to assist me. I have everything planned. I wish they would have asked." Her eyes ogled the kitchen as he led her through a maze of unnecessary rooms. The setup mirrored her own, if on a 10/1 scale.

"The Walshes employ me on retainer. I assist at all of

their events."

Ruby registered that immediately and stared. Antoine wasn't the staff she had in mind when Michael offered one. Rather, she imagined a couple stout old women with flour in their hair. His hair held no flour. His apron held a little beefcake. Ruby smiled.

"I've been with the family since Miss Sophia started grade school."

Miss Sophia. Ruby closed her eyes because she couldn't stop them from rolling otherwise. She wondered if Michael addressed her highness in any special way. Before her mind and mouth got together, she slapped her purse onto the counter and went to work. Antoine followed suit.

"I've put the table things in the dining area and courtyard. The decorator took the rest." Sophia leaned against the door jamb breathing hard.

"Thank you, Sophia." Ruby's mood fell from spectacularly triumphant and boss-like to being one more member of an abundant staff. The wedding reception was to be held at the Russell home. When compared to this posh setting, Ruby feared the guests would probably feel as if they were slumming it. She imagined them worrying about their safety.

When Ruby had done all Antoine would permit her, she went to find the courtyard. It wasn't difficult. A set of French doors off the kitchen took her directly there. The courtyard was a large, square, open area at the center of the home. Double doors opened onto it from the kitchen, dining room, rear hallway and study. A fountain rose up in its center.

"Hello." A tiny man in a white suit stood fluffing flowers on a table.

"Hello."

"You must be Michael's mother. He told me you'd arrived." The small man wore a brilliant silk scarf around his neck the color of emeralds, a white sport coat, and his black hair was gelled into form. His accent seemed to be German.

"Michael's here?"

"But of course, darling." The man glanced up from his work, and tipped his head toward the study.

Behind French doors, Sophia laughed in Michael's arms. His face lit up like a Christmas tree. His hands stroked her long hair and she was charmed right down to her toes. A mix of hostility and pride battled within Ruby. Michael seemed so at home. She'd already lost him. As if to confirm this as fact, he leaned down and kissed his future bride in a very intimate way. Though the act was more sweet than sensual, Ruby looked away. Meanwhile, she was thankful for such a large event. It would afford her the opportunity to blend into the crowd.

*****

Dr. Kessler hadn't slept in days. He and Meredith were at odds for the first time in a decade. Since the imagined threat on her life, Meredith had become very concerned about her husband's behavior and asked him about it continually. He worked long hours, spending entire evenings locked in his study. He grew edgy and stopped sleeping. Life's logic and predictability were gone. All symptoms led back to Ruby.

"Mark. Sweetie. Mark?" Meredith shoved at his slumped shoulder. He awoke to find himself at his desk again. She acted as if it were a personal slight. He groaned in remembrance. Tension returned.

CRACK!

"What the…?" His torso flipped upward as if on strings. His eyes were wild.

Meredith turned and left. He looked at the floor. She had dropped a stack of books from the looks of things.

Mark Kessler rubbed his eyes and stared hard at the screen before him. He'd poured over files from Heartland Behavioral Health all night. At first, he'd felt guilty asking for information on Ruby. He didn't anymore. He knew the bean dip was a threat. She must have seen the book on castor bean poisoning. The puzzle pieces came together. He'd tried to get his things in order before she arrived, but that one small book, hidden from him by files, lay completely exposed to her. *A deadly mistake.*

As the physician in charge of Ruby's care following her initial release five years ago, he should have requested her files then. Instead, he had chosen to approach her on a weekly basis. No reason to delve into her history had ever presented itself. She had attended every session, unquestionably on the upswing. Ruby had seemed fully recovered when she stopped making appointments, so Mark let her go. He found no reason to continue if Ruby had nothing more to say. He could see now how very wrong he'd been. As Dr. Shrieve pointed out, the judicial system had its limitations, and a good attorney and local laws had set Ruby free. Continued therapy was more a formality than a requirement.

All these years, without therapy, without medication, had allowed her to regress. This time she wasn't a mother mourning an empty nest. This time she came to therapy with a pleasant smile. She went through the motions each week and then poisoned people on her days off. Of course, she covered the evidence. Ken's autopsy cited drug interactions and heart failure. Ruby's neighbor and her Bridge club had no connection to Ruby, aside from proximity. She obviously hated Reverend Flynn, but he had a faulty furnace. For every theory he devised about Ruby, there was at least one major hole in his plot.

Mark opened his desk drawer and took a handful of

pills he prescribed himself under a pseudo name. He washed them down with a dollop of scotch left in the glass on his bureau. His head and eyes ached. His neck and back were stiff. The right thing to do was make up with his wife, stretch his muscles, take a hot shower and ask Meredith if he could take her out to breakfast. That would have been the better option. But he knew it wasn't the option he was going to choose.

Mark's eyes stuck to the screen. He rolled his head a few times and went back to work. Ruby Russell had more than enough reasons to need medication. He needed to uncover her dastardly deeds and find proof soon, before Michael's wedding. Ruby wouldn't survive the event without a complete break. He imagined her setting fire to the whole shebang. He pictured guests dropping around the champagne fountain, like cult members drinking Kool-Aid. A bride doused in pig's blood was the most harmless scenario that crossed his tired, anxious, medicated mind. *I have to stop her.*

*****

The Lake Shore Community Center bustled with activity. There had never been an event so large in the history of Montrose Hills. More than two-thousand people had already come through. The community center was normally used for high school playoff games or the occasional conference, but never a funeral.

Following Reverend Flynn's unexpected death, people from all around flocked to Montrose Hills to support the community. Everyone wanted to help the church or get involved in Glenn's outreach ministries. Some even came to raise awareness of carbon monoxide – the silent killer. Each for their own reasons, the building holding his memorial was practically bursting at the seams.

Ruby found a small bistro-style table near the kitchen

and listened. She had her suit from Kenneth's funeral cleaned and repurposed it for espionage. Her tiny veil hid her face, and in such a large crowd, it was easy to blend.

She hated herself for attending, but she couldn't leave. Yes, her being there seemed to make a mockery of his death, considering it was her best friend who killed him and all. However, Charlotte claimed there was always a clue left behind. So, Ruby was on reconnaissance. If Charlotte was right, then someone in the crowd may have heard or seen something. Her gaze picked over the knots and clusters of people in the cavernous room. How many onlookers did Daisy tell about Ruby's alleged suicide. Her fingers twitched. Well Daisy was dead and Ruby was not, so that was something.

Most of the gossip near the kitchen centered on Daisy. All of it was grotesque and none of it of any interest to Ruby. From the sounds of things, that young lady would have died from some form of sexual disease eventually. She hadn't lived an honorable life. Sad. She was young enough to have made a difference if she'd lived a better life. It occurred to Ruby she should get involved in programs to mentor young women. She'd be as good at that.

The reverend, on the other hand, seemed to have been truly loved. Not a single word uttered meant to harm his stellar reputation. In fact, most assumed the two were in a counseling session, not a tryst as the media suggested. Perhaps they hadn't heard about the pills and prophylactics. They had created a story that suited them without having all of the evidence.

Ruby shook her head and moved along the back quarter of the room, avoiding news cameras, but not chairs. She often tripped and ran headlong into the furniture. Caterers jammed too many of everything into the space. Accommodating so many people proved an impossible task.

She understood that. Kenneth's wake had been just as tricky. Now, managing the wedding events and coordinating the reception gave her even greater insight. Her chin lifted. Pride puffed her chest.

From her vantage point, Ruby watched the Channel 3 cameras float above the masses. The cameras rode high upon the cameramen's shoulders, but Ruby couldn't see which reporter moved with them. Terminally frustrated, she stretched up to her toes and moved in slow stealth motion. The act incited her vertigo. She bobbed and weaved in a sea of strangers, unable to stay on point, until a final whack of her toe sent her hopping. She sat in the nearest chair, to stop the room from tipping.

"I know you," a woman in the seat next to her said. "Well," she shrugged, "I don't *know* you. I've seen you around."

Ruby stared at the heavyset woman in her sixties with wide saucer eyes. Certainly she was drunk. This woman couldn't have seen Ruby anywhere. She was completely disheveled. Her gray hair swept into a messy ponytail, much too long for her age. Her clothes more appropriate for a power walk than a funeral. The frown on Ruby's face sent the woman stammering for clarity.

"I've seen you at the Partridge Parish." Confidence firmed her tone of voice. "I saw you with Reverend Flynn."

"Oh," Ruby apologized. Of course, she wouldn't have noticed her at any other point. "Yes, the mission is a very nice addition for the city, isn't it? Do you eat there often?" Ruby's eyes moved back to the cameras.

"I vol-un-teer at the mission," she corrected. "How did you know Reverend Flynn? Or was it the girl you knew?" Her eyes narrowed on her new tablemate.

Ruby balked at the inference she had known the wanton child. "Reverend Flynn performed my husband's funeral."

Ruby held her head high. She was a widow and deserved respect for the great ordeal she'd come through. She eyed the other woman's ensemble, and wondered silently if she lived on the street. She didn't speak again. It came as no surprise that the woman left shortly thereafter.

Ruby never understood why people were so sensitive. That lady would probably go home and bury herself at the bottom of a chocolate pie. It'd be a nice trip, but unlikely to ease the pain of her portly figure. Ruby knew. She spent her share of time that way. Lately, though, she preferred wine.

A gush of sweet relief blew over her lips. Ruby didn't recognize the young beauty before the Channel 3 cameras. It wasn't Emma Eaken, a welcomed blessing. It wasn't a good time for any additional stressors. Unbelievably, the event was dry and Ruby's hands were already slipping against everything they landed upon. *A wine flask will be a worthy investment.* Ruby made her way a bit deeper into the crowd and sat with her back to the larger picture. She'd wasted her time. No new information there.

The annoying twang of the nosey urchin woman raised the hair on Ruby's arms. She was back in earshot. The woman's voice was as unmistakable as her looks. Ruby leaned in on an elbow and snuck a peek over her shoulder, hoping for time to escape a second conversation. The woman spoke to a pair Ruby recognized. Bunny and Sophia stood elbow to elbow, nodding politely.

As far as Ruby knew, the little trollop hadn't had time to confess her sins to Sophia. That meant Ruby shouldn't be seen attending the day's event without cause. Ruby couldn't think of a suitable reason to know either of them, so she panicked. Fight or flight kicked in. Never one for fighting, Ruby jumped. In her haste, she smashed her knee into the underside of the table, and it smarted. The metal braces keeping the table together clanged and dug into the meat above her kneecap. Holding her leg with one hand and biting hard on her lip, Ruby hopped away under cover of a severely overdone floral arrangement. The stage nearby wasn't yet in use. The podium offered refuge. She sat, nursing her wound and listening as the conversation unfolded.

"Did you know the reverend well?" the homeless woman pried.

"No, ma'am," Sophia's voice was subdued and respectful, even to her.

"My daughter and I knew Daisy for many years."

Ruby peeked around the podium to see Bunny stroke Sophia's perfectly manicured hair. A pretty silk headband tied her look together well. She wore cream and navy. The skirt fell below the knee and the jacket buttoned neatly to reveal only the silk blouse beneath it.

Ruby rolled her eyes and rested against the podium.

"Then you must have heard all the gossip," the woman rudely interjected. Ruby scooted closer.

"She was a nice girl," Bunny spoke with authority. "She had a tough time, harder than you'll ever know, and she did the best she could. She had a good heart and a good head on her shoulders. Children learn what they see, and she made the most of what shreds she had to work with."

"Well, then you probably know the words whispered about her and Reverend Flynn are the truth."

"I don't know anything of the sort." Sophia's voice came low and harsh. Was she offended? How good could she truly be if she protected the honor of a Jezebel so fervently?

"I'm only surprised she moved on so quickly." The taunting voice egged on. Ruby wished she'd been more rude. Then the woman would have left before meeting with the Walshes. Though she didn't like them, Michael did and that had her feeling protective.

"She was seeing that other man."

Ruby stopped breathing.

"Kenneth, something, until he died, then, BOOM, she's on to the reverend. She had no shame."

"Kenneth, you say?" Ruby could tell Bunny's intuition perked.

"Yeah. He was like twice her age. It was shameful and she brought him to church with her, too. The two of them sat right in the front row, not ten feet from the pastor every Sunday. Pfft. They sat there beside her father half the time."

"You don't remember his last name?"

"No."

"Let's go, Mama, please." Sophia begged, tears present in her voice, if not yet upon her cheeks.

"Sophie," Bunny spoke under her breath, but loud enough for Ruby to hear, as the two walked away from the angry woman. "What was Michael's father's name?"

Ruby hobbled down the long corridor to the parking lot at top speed. Blood spilt between her fingers as she dragged and hopped, clamping one palm over her knee as she went. Crowds of people stared as she pushed her way outside and into the sun.

Momentarily blinded, she held her small clutch as a visor above her head. It took several moments to get oriented, and then she scurried on. Her van was parked as far from the door as possible to avoid being spotted if anyone looking for her showed up. She climbed inside and headed straight for safety. She needed to be consoled and probably a few stitches as well.

Charlotte's house was dark despite the daylight. Her blinds were drawn and no sounds came from inside. Ruby pounded hard against the door. Several minutes passed, and Ruby sat against it to catch her breath and examine the damage to her knee and suit. Without so much as footsteps for warning, the door pulled open. Ruby fell in, throwing her swollen ankles into the air.

"Damn kids!" Charlotte screamed, waving a fist over her head. Ruby's head hit her feet.

Screaming ensued and Charlotte collapsed.

"Charlotte!" Ruby yelled into her friend's face, swatting her cheeks without compassion.

She came around as Ruby dragged her out of the way of the door. There was more screaming then, but one-sided this time.

"Am I dead!" Charlotte cried as she thrashed on her floor.

"Why on earth would you be dead? Be serious, Charlotte. You only opened the door. Does door opening equal death in your head now?" Ruby crawled to the nearest wall and leaned against it.

"You-you were dead," she reasoned. "You're bleeding and someone left you at my doorstep as a threat. I'm next." She rolled over onto her face and sobbed.

"Get up. There's not a thing wrong with you, except you've been holed up in this house all day watching junk, and getting your underpants in a bunch. Get over here and help me. I think I need stitches."

Charlotte peeked at Ruby who was covered in blood.

"I hit my knee under a table and it opened the skin above my knee cap. It's deep and bleeding. I tried holding it with my hand, but I was sweaty, so I switched hands back and forth."

Charlotte gawked.

"I wiped my hands on myself to keep them dry so they'd stay put. I made a mess. I know that, and I'll have to burn this suit or the dry cleaner will think I committed a murder in it."

Charlotte stumbled to the kitchen and washed her hands. She gathered her first aid equipment. "I wasn't watching junk."

"*Crime Scene Reality, Thelma and Louise, Unsolved Murders, Arsenic and Old Lace*?" Ruby raised an eyebrow as she ticked off the DVD titles beside Charlotte's television.

"Research! I wasn't having a movie day for crying out loud. I was doing research, and I love Cary Grant."

"Research on what?"

The two women exchanged a long, clueless stare.

"On what? Ruby, we're fugitives!" She swatted her forehead with one palm. "We need to see how we can get out of this country and if we can't, then we have to cover out tracks."

"What happened to Fiji?"

Charlotte shook her head looking defeated. "There's extradition there. I thought we could fly over to Europe where everything is connected with trains and make an escape. If we buy tickets to one place, they can only follow us that far. Then we can take the train to a country without extradition policies."

"I like Europe," Ruby whispered, feeling like a child in Charlotte's care.

Charlotte cleaned the wound with feather soft touches and dressed it securely in gauze and cotton. "Me, too, but unless you want to live in Moldova…"

"Where?"

"Right. As it turns out, I don't want to live anywhere that doesn't have extradition. So, we're going to have to clean this all up and then maybe just change our names and move somewhere we want to live."

"Thanks." Ruby touched Charlotte's arm.

"No problem. You don't need stitches, but you'll be sore for a while. Your knee will look awful in a day or two, then worse before it's better."

Ruby stretched and bent her leg a few times to check mobility. Charlotte was right. It really was sore and quite swollen. It was easier to see now with the blood cleaned off.

"I think we're caught. I went to the vigil for Reverend Flynn and Daisy Douglas, and…"

"What!" Charlotte covered her mouth, motioning like she were going to be sick. Her eyes flew wide and round like a deer's. She shook her head without saying a word.

"What?" Ruby looked around for what she missed.

"The perp always goes back to the scene of the crime," she mumbled from behind her hand. "You've practically implicated yourself by simply being there."

"What?"

Charlotte bobbed her head in confirmation.

"What in the devil is a perp? Also, I didn't kill them. You did, remember? It wasn't the scene of any crime. It was a remembrance luncheon with two-thousand people. Are they all suspects now?"

"You're a perp, Ruby Russell. Unsub, perp, killer, whatever you choose to call yourself. You are."

"I'm not a perp, and you swore if I told you about that time in the Poconos, you'd never bring it up again." Ruby's eyes shut and her cheeks flamed. "Unsub sounds like something you made up, or got from one of your silly movies. I'm not a killer."

"No?"

"No. You are."

"What?"

Ruby's lips puckered and her lids slid downward. "You, Charlotte Mason, killed those two. I had no idea that was even an idea in your mind."

"Neither did I. I didn't plan it. I already told you. I was trying to help you."

"Well, thanks for nothing. Now my future in-laws were at the lunch event because they knew Daisy Douglas. Some homeless woman told them Daisy was seeing 'Kenneth someone' before the reverend, and now Bunny is two blinks away from fingering me for this."

"I knew you'd get caught." Charlotte's voice came pensive and despondent.

"I. Did. Not. Do. This."

The look on her face told Ruby Charlotte held her responsible whether she had been there or not. It seemed the two were at an impasse. One couldn't escape without the other. The friendship of fellowship was transforming into one of necessity and blackmail. She'd have to smooth things over so they could get on with it. Charlotte might be formulating a plan.

"Fine. What did Cary Grant teach you about getting a new identity?"

CHAPTER SIXTEEN

"Dr. Kessler, you can use this room, if you'd like." A nurse motioned him inside and turned on the lights. Mark Kessler spent more and more time at Heartland Behavioral Health reviewing Ruby's files. Meredith forbade him to do it at home any longer. All in all, his research was costing him money. He saw fewer appointments each week because he spent so much time out of the office. Eventually his escapades would catch up with him and Meredith wouldn't be happy. Until then, he hoped to finish his investigation before the money situation caught up.

The archives at Heartland were vast and complete. It was daunting, but he persevered. Day by day, he followed leads from file to file, trying to recreate a glimpse of Ruby's time there. She was somehow less chatty then than even now. Notes from her meetings with therapists were useless.

He prepared to give up when a reference to her mother set Mark's wheels on solid ground again. Ruby's mother, Violet, had had her own set of issues. Violet Graybill, a one-time caterer and proprietor of Graybill's Graces

Confectionary, had been crazy. Call it what they might, Dr. Kessler saw it as clearly as if it were written in watermark behind every sentence. Nuts. Nuts. Nuts.

It was a great anomaly in her day to own a business, if you were a woman. Brilliant and unstable. What had Dr. Shrieve called Ruby? A fox. His heart raced as he thumbed over details in the file. Her husband, a common laborer, refused to be of any help in her success. He resented her for it and drank his way through it. A couple of children later, he drank more than he worked, and Violet's business had all but failed. She started to work from home, while caring for her children and nursing the thumps he gave her, but they barely got by.

The nearest doctor was a town over from Montrose Hills, and the Graybill income was supplemented by Violet's knowledge of herbal remedy. Her garden was as much a source of joy to her as her own daughters who worked hard to follow in their mother's footsteps, for a while.

The girls were very young when tragedy struck. The money was nearly gone, and the garden was used more and more to sustain them than for profit. Ruby and Rose, her little sister, were forced outside as their parents discussed at length where the next meal would come from. That was the day Rose, small and hungry, ate her mother's castor beans, while Ruby pulled weeds and picked the handful of peapods remaining on the vine.

"Why would her mother grow castor beans?" Mark asked himself a dozen times. Of course, they were used to induce vomiting in the event of a poisoning, but they themselves were deadly. Shouldn't they have been grown under lock and key somewhere? Parents today would never dream of such irresponsibility. That decision had been the beginning of the end for everyone involved.

Rose died. Ruby found her sister when they were called

inside a while later. In Ruby's recount, they were talking one minute and Rose was gone the next. She believed Rose hid among the corn, tempting Ruby to join in tomfoolery instead of tending the garden. Ruby's father blamed her and Violet. Violet blamed herself. Ruby floundered and then overcompensated.

As Violet detached from the world, following the loss of her baby, Ruby rose to the position of caretaker.

"Ruby," Dr. Kessler cut to the chase at their very next appointment. "Tell me about Rose."

"Rose." Ruby repeated the name in a whisper.

"Ruby, do you blame yourself for her death?" Dr. Kessler leaned toward her as if he might will the answers from her mouth.

"No."

"No?" He slumped, wondering if he were wrong, or if she were playing coy. Both were viable possibilities.

"I do have some guilt for not being very sad about it," she said after some thought.

"You weren't sad to lose your baby sister?".

"No. In all of the ways I can see, she had it much better than we did. She was never hungry again, never sick, never sad. She never saw Daddy hit Mama, or Mama staring out into the garden as if she'd return home at any minute. She never had a heartbreak or betrayal set her back. She'd had enough trials and tribulations in her few short years. She didn't deserve anymore, and I was only sad for me when she died. I missed having a playmate and a sister. It was only for me."

That was the most she'd ever said to Dr. Kessler at one time. It occurred to him she seemed more human in her short soliloquy than he'd ever imagined her to be. Until that moment, Ruby Russell was more of a conundrum, an enigma, or an anomaly for him to dissect until she made sense. She never had.

"What do you know about Rose?" she asked.

"I know you had a very difficult upbringing."

Ruby crossed and uncrossed her ankles, seeming to choose her next words carefully. Dr. Kessler never knew if she'd change the subject or indulge him. This time, he hoped for indulgence. "I became the head of the household at twelve." She stared him down as if in blatant defiance.

"You cared for your father while your mother was away?"

"My father left when mother didn't bounce back after Rose's death. I cared for her until she was hospitalized, but when the state took her, he left all together. It was his moment. Carpe diem." Her mouth twisted up.

"And you?"

"I took care of things until she came home, and then I took care of her until she died."

"Did she live with you after you married?" Dr. Kessler tried to imagine Ruby and Ken and Violet. It was difficult. Then after Michael came along, it must have been overwhelming.

"No, Dr. Kessler," she spoke softly, as if to allow him in on a secret with her. "Mother didn't make it that long."

Did she just wink at him? He pulled in a long breath and moved away from her slowly. His mind raced with the message she was trying to send. Had she killed her mother? Did she believe she, too, was better off, as she did her baby sister? He ran his hand over his forehead and shoved his fingers into his graying hair.

"Ruby, thank you for your candor." Dr. Kessler could barely look at her. He looked at his glass of water with question. The room tilted.

"You couldn't be satisfied to deal with each day as it

came. You had to know *all* about me. You had to know about Rose and Mother. I won't speak of the dead."

"Ruby, it's my job to help you. You never open up, so I was forced to try to understand you some other way."

"By invading my privacy and drudging up the most painful moments of my life? You call them defining moments." She nodded her head, mocking his terms. "How would you feel, Doctor, if I invaded your privacy, dug into your personal history and family affairs?"

Dr. Kessler slid one finger into his collar and pulled a bit. His brow grew warmer than he could justify. Memories of his college panic attacks flitted just this side of his consciousness. Had she poisoned him in his own office? He needed something to take the edge off. Reluctantly, he took several sips of his water, to get a hold of himself. Ruby watched.

"Your mother," he choked out, finally, desperate to know.

"Died of a broken heart."

That was an old timer's saying for suicide after the death of a spouse, but Ruby applied it to the loss of her child. Dr. Kessler thought Ruby might have had a hand in the outcome.

"Did you have a nice childhood, Doctor?" Accusation saturated the words.

"Yes."

"Were you loved? Is that how you developed the confidence to become a doctor? You probably are the result of two loving parents, who never threw things or harmed you. You never went hungry and you never doubted your ability to change the world. Am I close, Doctor?"

"Ruby, are you doing alright? Is there anything you want to talk about with me, now that you're talking to me?"

"I'd appreciate it if you'd leave the past where it is." She toyed with her watch.

"What about the present?" He was certain they'd made a breakthrough and was frightened by that realization.

"Sophia wants a mojito and burrito luncheon for her shower." She changed the subject seamlessly, as if it were normal. She stuck her pointy tongue out at the idea. "Mrs. Walsh and I are in agreement. This is a childish notion, but she's still the bride, so I must come up with some way to add class to the circus." Ruby rolled her eyes and Dr. Kessler considered a dissociative identity disorder for the first time.

"The bridal shower? That's what's on your mind right now?" he asked sarcastically.

"I only have a few days to get things together before we meet again, Bunny, Sophia and I. Actually, Sophia might need to call in or show up on that Internet camera of hers. Classes are back in session."

"Uh-huh." Dr. Kessler zoned out for the remaining thirty minutes. Ruby was long gone anyway. Only chatter filled the time, nothing more. "Ruby," he interrupted a rant about color schemes and fabric availability. "Are you taking the medication I've been giving you?"

"Of course. It's made such a difference."

Seventeen minutes later, Mark watched Ruby through the slats of his office mini blinds. The moment her taillights were out of sight, he cleared his calendar and drove home with abandon. The traffic infuriated him. He punched the gas at every green light and stood on the brake pedal at every red. His hands alternated between drumming against the wheel and assaulting his thick grey hair. Mark never saw a thing, aside from lights, the entire way home.

He replayed hundreds of conversations with Ruby Russell. *She did it. She did it. She did it.* Mark rocked in his seat as his car inched towards home. Another handful of pills was sure to help with the traffic. He kept them locked in his glove box and briefcase, never at home. Meredith was on to him, nagging and chastising him. Soon she would see. She would understand.

"Damn." She was home. Meredith's Prius was parked in the driveway. She would lecture about him leaving early, no doubt.

He closed his door gently and slid like an apparition into their home. Clutching his bag to his chest, he darted towards the study, towards freedom. He kicked the door open and dove in behind it. The lock snapped into place. He was safe.

Castor beans were the answer. Ruby thought she was so clever with the bean dip threat, but in fact, she'd given him her secret. Bean dip was made with beans. Castor beans were poisonous, ba-da-bing, ba-da-boom. Killer.

"Mark?" Meredith's voice echoed down the hall.

Ricin was poison extracted from bean pulp. A simple task for Ruby. She knew her way around the kitchen and garden. Her mother had probably made castor oil to treat patients long ago. Ruby would know. Her sister probably died the same way. She hadn't given specifics and there was no autopsy on file. He'd checked. Records before the 1970s weren't plentiful in Montrose Hills. That was it!

The knob to his door twisted and stopped. Thump. Thump. Thump. "Mark!" Meredith's small fist worried his large oak door.

Her mother would have blamed herself for Rose's death. Ruby would have an affinity for such a method because it was in her knowledge base and personal history. Mark's pulse raced. His hands jumped on his desktop and his clarity was stellar. He clutched the edge of his desk when Meredith pounded one last time before storming away. She would see. He was solving murders.

*****

Emma followed her leads smartly. She'd been in three towns and online for days. Daisy Douglas had quite a lucrative business going for her. The doorman at Daisy's building let Emma inside in exchange for a new fifty dollar bill. The building was a major step up from her mother's ashtray of a homestead. Daisy's longest-standing engagement provided her the address and keys. Emma only had to agree to keep his name out of the paper.

Apartment 1200 was at the top. She had a penthouse view of Montrose Hills. It wasn't much of a view, but it probably felt prestigious to a girl from the trailer park. Emma moved with purpose through the apartment, clicking on lights as she went. Simple white carpeting, beige walls, cream-colored furniture and little else filled the space. Her kitchen was clean, fridge was bare, but the bathroom overflowed with hygiene and beauty products of every imaginable sort. Everything looked painfully ordinary. Until she swung open the door at the end of the hall. The bedroom behind it caused Emma a case of the giggles.

Daisy's bedroom boasted hot pink satin sheets, Hello Kitty pillowcases and a camera on a tripod. The oddity shocked Emma. Then comprehension sickened her. She fished a tissue from her purse and pushed the buttons on the camera. She played back the footage without touching the buttons. As she should have expected, Daisy appeared on the little screen dressed as a school girl. Pigtails and minimal makeup left her looking closer to twelve than twenty.

Dressed as a child, Daisy performed numerous adult activities, including some with partners, but mostly self-exercised. Emma took a pen from her pocket and began to shove things around Daisy's desk looking for evidence. She was careful not to touch things or leave prints. Her stomach churned with grief for the lost girl.

Her laptop was still on, and Emma only needed to seek in order to find. Daisy had a Web site where she collected five dollars a minute by credit card for viewing her performances. The more financially savvy pervert could pay a hundred dollars an hour instead. Emma doubted anyone viewing the material needed an entire hour.

Daisy's desktop was covered in files and icons. She had more naked pictures of herself than Paris Hinton. Her desk drawer brimmed with accessories and tools of her trade. Her closet spilled over with costumes. Emma focused on Daisy's computer. Lives were documented digitally these days. A file entitled "Love" caught her eye and she held her breath as she clicked it open. Inside were hundreds of photographs of her with men.

Apparently Daisy had covered her act by documenting her time with these fellows. She kept a log of time spent with each, their approximate net worth and marital situation. At her time of death, she was seeing two men, neither of them were the reverend. In fact, there was no record of her involvement with him. She had better records than the local courthouse, but not one word about her most current lover. It didn't make sense.

Emma scrolled through the Love file. She jotted down names and dates of men from the past year. If any one of them had been involved in her death, it would be a great story. It would be sad, but newsworthy. Then, as her nerves pressed her to leave before she was charged with trespassing, a name from the list caught her eye. She didn't recognize the face in the photo, but the name rang a bell so large Quasimodo himself couldn't have stopped it.

Emma's shock twisted into a sneer and then settled on fortitude. She stood, shut the windows she'd opened and placed her notebook into her bag. One last look over her shoulder at the creepy bedroom, and she was ready to take her investigation in a whole new direction. She no longer needed to call the Montrose Hills Boys and Girls Club about that basket. She knew where it had really come from.

*****

"Hello." Michael was out of breath. He'd been on the treadmill for nearly an hour and hated to be interrupted, but with the wedding right around the corner, he never knew. It was becoming more and more commonplace to diffuse Sophia's hysterics after speaking with her mother or his in regards to the wedding.

"Michael Russell?" the charming and familiar voice asked.

"Yes." Michael dabbed sweat from his brow and wiped his hands with a small white towel. "This is Michael."

"Michael, my name is Emma Eaken. I work for Channel 3 News in Montrose Hills. I believe that's your hometown."

*****

"Mark?" Meredith called his name before he managed to get the keys from his pocket.

"I'm here, darling." He shoved a stack of Ruby Russell's files into a thick leather satchel and unlocked the door.

"Mark," Meredith wrapped her arms around him and kissed his cheek. "Sweetheart, we've been invited to a wedding."

Uh-oh.

"Really? Whose? Hasn't everyone we know gotten married, at least twice by now?"

The attempt at humor was lost on his audience. She placed the opalescent envelope flat against his chest and held it in place until he took possession of it. He didn't need to look, but he wanted to keep up the façade.

"Michael Russell is getting married next month. We're invited. Were you aware of this?"

He was caught.

"Yes." He decided quickly less was more. If he remained silent, she'd believe he was a liar. If he spoke, she'd be certain of it.

"Are you still seeing her? Did you break your promise to me?"

He didn't have time to answer before she went on. "This is why you've been so uneasy lately. This is why you're keeping your distance, skipping work and locking yourself in the study. This is why we haven't had sex in eleven days."

"What?" Mark moved to a safer distance behind his desk.

"You know you've been lying to me, and you've been staying busy, too busy to come to bed with me. Then you're gone before I finish my yoga in the morning. You've been much more than 'busy.' You've been avoiding me because you've been lying to me." Her slight frame seemed a foot taller. She loomed in his personal space, evoking his fight or flight mechanism.

He could neither fight her nor run from her, so he sat in the nearest chair and confessed.

"What exactly were you hoping to accomplish? Did you aspire to solve the murders yourself? You hoped to lock her up? Did you think the people in charge of that needed a two hundred dollar an hour psychotherapist to assist them?"

"I wanted the truth. I like facts. I like piecing together the things that make us who we are. You know this. These days, I only talk with angry teens and neglected housewives. Ruby added a little spice to my week." His eyes landed tellingly on his briefcase. A slight tremor played over his hands, and he shoved them in his pockets.

"The kind of spice you thought was in the bean dip?" She hadn't yet gotten over the embarrassment he had caused her on that one. "Tax payers will pay for that overreaction for a decade. Not to mention, at least half those women will never visit me again."

"Can we go?" His eyes burned holes in the invitation.

"Are you serious? First, you think this woman is a murderer. Then you think she's trying to kill me, or us, whichever. Now you want to go to her son's wedding?"

"Meredith, I'd love to see her in her element. She's always so out of context at the office.

"She'd not a lioness on the savannah." She narrowed her eyes on his. "Are you sleeping?"

He shuffled his feet beneath his chair, one knee bounced erratically.

"Are you eating? I can't tell if you're thinner. I haven't seen you in less than a turtleneck and trousers in eleven days."

"Please," he countered, unable to think of anything else until she agreed to attend with him.

"I'll go, but I don't condone this behavior. You're acting squirrely." She stared at his toe tapping wildly and it stopped. "You have a responsibility to our marriage and to your health before your career. After this, you need to make some decisions about what's most important to you. I won't continue to be the other woman to some nut job sociopath."

"Agreed." He smiled a wide toothy smile. Meredith left. Immediately, Mark shoved the RSVP card into his bag. He would hand it to Ruby himself.

His hands shook anew with anticipation, and he almost ran to his study to write down all he'd come to understand so far. He created a timeline of events to put a visual aid to his work. The line stretched across the back of his cork board facing the wall.

He rolled the board into the space beside his desk and cleared a space to pin the invitation above a photograph of Michael and the announcement of their engagement, which he'd clipped from the local paper. The entire west side of his office looked like a crime investigation. He had copies of portions of past files. Clippings of deaths where he suspected Ruby as the culprit, and most recently, he added photographs of her home he'd taken for reasons he didn't understand.

Excessive, yes, but hobbies were healthy and he often recommended them to men bored with their line of work. His hobby was cheaper than golf and more exciting than fishing, plus Meredith wouldn't want him fishing for actual fish. The moment Ruby slipped up, he'd turn her in for her crimes, and he'd be a hero.

CHAPTER SEVENTEEN

The phone rang a dozen times that afternoon. The final bridal shower was just two days away, and Ruby had no time for phone calls. She had plenty to make, but no time to accept any incoming. No time for small talk.

Ruby zeroed in on the main course. She'd prepared a plethora of pastries in advance. Those snuggled safely in her freezer, and appetizer preparations weren't necessary until the day before. Drinks came together the morning of. Ruby had a checklist on a clipboard hanging beside her sink. She never missed a mark on her schedule. The only possible hold up in sight lay with the vendors. If the linens and tables didn't arrive on time she'd kill them. The Ashland Community Center where the Walshes volunteered had agreed to host this event, so Ruby knew Antoine wouldn't be in her way. She was grateful to carry the full burden this time, without the distraction of his tall, dark and manliness.

When her doorbell rang, Ruby was elbow deep in guacamole. Impossible timing. She really needed to finish what she started before she did anything else. Meanwhile the doorbell continued and Ruby's nerves frazzled. Answering the bell was not an option.

"Mom!" Michael's voice echoed in her ears.

"Michael?" She scrubbed her hands roughly and resolved to begin again at midnight when everyone else slept.

Michael bounded into the kitchen as she shut off the water. "Why didn't you answer the door?"

"I'm getting things together for Sophia's shower." Her blouse stuck to her chest and her hands trembled. "Why are you here?"

"That was rude." An unprecedented tension in his voice increased her tremors. "You don't seem like yourself, Mom. I noticed it at Dad's funeral, but who's really themself at a funeral?"

Ruby took a step back. He took a step forward.

"Are you feeling alright?"

"Yes." She breathed deeply. "I'm fine. I'm surprised to see you. The last time we spoke, you said you were unable to come home for this. You said you'd be home early for the wedding, but not the final shower."

"Mmm. The last time we talked. When was that? We used to talk every day."

"I've been busy trying to please you." Tears formed in her eyes. The tension was unbearable. She fumbled to turn her back on him and pour a glass of wine.

"Drinking again?"

Condescension. Really? She didn't like it. Ruby imagined what it might feel like to retrieve her stepladder from the pantry and climb upon it long enough to slap him.

"You say I'm not myself." She choked, swigging from the wineglass. "What about you? What's wrong with you? You're like a pond person."

"A pod person. Not a pond person. You're right. I'm not

myself. I'm angry and I'm almost never angry. You taught me not to get angry."

"That's right. The good book says we should turn the other cheek, and it shows good character to overlook another's shortcomings. Getting angry only shows your own backside." Ruby refilled her glass.

"How about you? Do you get angry?" He leaned against the counter and looked her over carefully.

"Yes," she whispered, barely audible even in the silence.

Michael's hard expression cracked. He stepped to her and wrapped his arm around her shoulders before kissing her head. "Come on, Mom, we need to talk."

They sat in the sunroom and evaluated one another. Neither of them was themselves, and it was an unfamiliar dynamic between two previously compatible souls.

"Is there anything you want to tell me about Dad?"

Ruby clutched the underneath of her chair and crossed her ankles beneath her. She'd never lied to Michael before, and she resented being put in a position to do so. Tears swam beneath her lids, and she wished she'd had the forethought to bring her glass with her as they walked.

"Was he," Michael paused and Ruby knew he knew. Somehow, he'd discovered what she'd hoped to never speak of again. "Was Dad seeing someone else?"

Ruby's face contorted. Her lips rolled in on themselves. She closed her eyes and prayed when she opened them, he'd be gone. He wasn't.

Ding dong.

Michael jumped. Ruby was already on her feet, knocking her chair backwards behind her. "Doorbell. Can we talk about this later?" She didn't wait to see if he agreed.

"Ruby! I've got it!" Charlotte beamed as she strode through the front door, knocking Ruby aside. "Cuba!"

"Hello, Mrs. Mason." Michael stepped out from the

sunroom and Charlotte froze. Her eyes tracked between the two similar faces. Her eyes widened and her fingers covered her mouth. When she began to chew her lips, Michael invited her in for a seat.

Ruby grabbed the wine bottle and followed them with all the enthusiasm of a funeral procession. She tipped the bottle as she rounded the corner. Her life had come to this. She was drinking directly from the bottle like a wino. No reason to bother with the formality of a glass.

"What a surprise," Charlotte finally said.

Ruby took another drink, and Charlotte gave her the stink eye. Ruby shook her head.

"I thought Mom could use some help," he said, "but I'd forgotten she has you to lean on in a pickle."

Charlotte's forehead climbed her hair to the crown. "Of course."

"You know Sophia knew the girl who visited with the pastor a while back? Daisy Douglas."

"Mmm hmm."

Ruby stifled a giggle. The wine made everything better and more complicated all at once.

"Well, it seems Daisy Douglas was quite a little tart."

The women eyed one another cautiously. Michael fiddled with his phone. He turned it on them and Ruby went to find her glasses. She had never seen such a small television in her life. It was ridiculous that people couldn't wait to see whatever it was on their proper computer or television.

When she returned, a little girl in pigtails wielding a massive lollipop skipped out, onto the screen revealing her backside beneath a three-inch white tennis skirt. Her middle was bare and her small bosoms were pushed into a nearly sheer top with a pink teddy bear on it.

"What's this?" Concern colored Charlotte's voice.

"Wait."

"Who's this child?" The girl in question began to rub the skirt between her thighs. "Oh dear."

The rubbing continued and her legs parted further, revealing things Ruby had never seen in her life. Her mouth hung open and sounds fell out. None of them coherent.

The girl rubbed her shirt until it spontaneously rolled upward, revealing her bare breasts and a silver ring in one taut nipple. The sounds she made caused the women to gasp and Ruby struck the little phone.

"God's grace!" Ruby exclaimed. "You're addicted to pornography?" She stood and began to pace crazily. "You cannot marry that sweet Sophia until you've gotten this under control. We need to call St. Sebastian's. They have a program."

Michael picked up the phone and paused the video. "Mom, this isn't my problem. It's yours."

Charlotte's head hit the table firmly.

"Oh, you've caused Charlotte to pass out again. She has a terrible time staying upright under stress. You know that. Help me move her to the sofa."

Michael hoisted her over his shoulder and turned to his mother. "Look, carefully." He handed her the phone.

It was against her better judgment, but Michael asked very little of her, and she did want to help. Inside the little screen was a child kneeling on a bed. She had long brown hair and olive skin. She reminded Ruby of someone.

*****

Michael sat between the women and waited. Charlotte looked comfortable on the couch. His mother lay on the floor. He had propped her head with a pillow, and finished her wine. Their inability to remain conscious was a solid confirmation of their guilt. They'd recognized Daisy Douglas. They knew why he had showed them the video.

They knew that he knew. Now he knew they knew that he knew. So, what should he do?

"Ruby?" Charlotte roused first and nearly rolled onto the floor when she saw Michael. "Oh."

"Oh," he repeated. "Would you like to explain some things to me?" He hoped Mrs. Mason would be more accommodating and forthright than his mother, who he knew would take her secrets to the grave.

"I'm not sure what you mean."

"Do you think you can tell me why Emma Eaken from Channel 3 News called me across the country?" He'd wait for the cows to come home if that was how long it took her to speak.

"I have no idea why she would have called."

"You have some idea."

"What did she say?" She looked at Ruby, who was still out cold.

"She said my father knew the woman in the video I showed you. I know it's true because she came here a while back, while we were having tea with the Walshes. She was with Reverend Flynn. I offered them muffins."

"Oh?'

"You were here, Mrs. Mason. Remember? So was I."

"Oh."

"You knew about her and my father. So did my mom. Why keep that from me?"

Ruby groaned and threw her palm over her forehead.

"I didn't want to ruin your image of him." Ruby's voice was weak and shy. "I only found out just before he died. We never even had a chance to fight about it, and then he was gone."

"What was she doing here?" He struggled to speak and process at the same time. If he didn't keep Ruby talking, he'd never get any answers. Michael was a bit thankful for the wine.

"She said she came to apologize. She said she didn't know I was alive. Your father told her I died after you left for college."

"Emma Eaken called him." Charlotte interjected.

"Emma Eaken called you?" Ruby looked as if she may need to lie back down.

"Yes. She was the one who told me about Daisy and gave me the Web address of her little business. If you'd like to see more, it'll cost you."

"You're not angry?" Confusion crumpled Ruby's brow.

"At Dad, sure, but I'm not angry with you. I'm a little peeved you didn't confide in me. You've been through so much. I could have been an asset to you." He examined his mother closely as she rolled left and right, trying to sit up. "You didn't let me help." He stretched out a hand to her. "Then again, I sidelined you with the engagement." He looked out the bay window as he spoke.

"What else did Emma Eaken say?" Charlotte asked.

"A lot. She told me about the Bridge club next door and more than I wanted to know about Daisy and her family. She told me about the men at the Channel 3 station and the homeless people at Partridge Parish and then Daisy and the reverend. There's been a lot going on in Montrose Hills this year."

"Why did she tell you all of that?" Ruby's voice cracked as she looked discretely in Charlotte's direction.

"She thinks you're involved in it."

"In what?" Charlotte's voice rose.

Ruby reached for the wine, but it was empty. Michael shook the bottle and gave her a crooked smile. Ruby scooted around on her bottom, trying to get up. Michael extended a hand to her and she left to retrieve bottle number two. She split it with her son, wino style.

"Why don't you tell me?" He looked at the women. This was more a command than a request. Ruby turned her face away, naturally secretive, and protective of her baby. Charlotte began at the beginning. She released the full details of the chocolate mousse.

"Mom!" Ruby smashed her eyes shut. Michael pulled her to his chest and she sobbed very lightly. "I'm so sorry."

"Sorry?" She wiped her nose with a handkerchief and blotted at her eyes.

"I should have been here for you. I wish you would have told me."

"Well, she didn't, and it just got worse," Charlotte said.

"What do you mean?"

Ruby kept her head wedged against his chest as Charlotte explained the ugly truth about the Bridge club and their illegal entry to the Tanner home, wherein Emma Eaken had arrived.

A light whistle sound, like a bomb falling, came from Michael's lips. "Okay. She's got nothing on either case. You're going to be fine."

The silence warned him that might not be true.

"Is there more?"

Silence.

"What else?"

"The poisoning at the station was supposed to throw her off the trail."

Michael swallowed hard as he let that resonate. "The reverend?"

"Which time do you mean?" Ruby asked into his shirt.

"Which time what?" Michael tried to pull her from him, but she clung on tighter.

"I sent the basket of cakes."

"But he donated those to the Partridge Parish," Charlotte added.

Michael covered his eyes with his palm. "I meant the carbon monoxide."

"That was me," Charlotte said.

Michael tipped the bottle to the sky. He stared and the ladies stewed before him.

"Michael?" Ruby peeked at him with one large blue eye.

"Maybe you should sit," Charlotte suggested. Michael nodded once and shuffled to the sofa, shoving his mother along with him.

"Can I get you some water?" Charlotte offered.

Another nod and a double swig of the wine bottle, then he fell over on the couch. His lips vibrated one on top of the other. Michael pulled a pillow over his face.

"What should we do?" Ruby asked Charlotte.

"Michael?" Ruby tugged on his arm.

"I-I'm just trying to do the math," he cried from beneath the pillow.

"Oh, dear, don't. It's not important, and it's sure to make matters worse," Charlotte offered sound advice.

Michael's legs swung over the edge and he was upright again. "I thought you've been seeing Dr. Kessler again."

"I have!" Ruby promised. "I started right after your father died.

"What does he say about all of this?"

"Well, I don't tell him, of course. How could I? We just make small talk and I leave for a week in between."

"You don't think he knows? You see him every week and he's trained to see psychosis. You don't think he's on to you?" Michael's face flushed. His hands trembled and his voice rose a few octaves higher than popular culture considered masculine.

"I don't talk much, and I warned him about being too nosey."

"What's that? You told your therapist not to be nosey?

Well, that's not at all suspicious," Charlotte interrupted.

Ruby guffawed at Charlotte. "Sarcasm isn't very becoming."

"Mom."

"He was reading about food poisoning. Ricin poisoning is done with castor beans and he had a book on his desk about it."

"Like Aunt Rose," Michael murmured and fell over once more. "Right."

"You say you warned him. How did you do that, precisely?" Charlotte asked.

"That's a story for another time. He understood he should drop it and he has. I'm certain. It's that nosey Emma Eaken who's giving me problems now. Maybe Bunny, too."

"What?" Michael was back up. Ruby explained what she overheard at the remembrance luncheon and Michael went to make a phone call.

*****

"What do you think?" Charlotte asked when the coast was clear.

"He's a good boy." Ruby tried to eavesdrop on his call.

"I'm going to see the Walshes." He grabbed his hooded sweatshirt.

"Wait. We're not done here. What about Emma Eaken?"

"She's going to be a thorn. I need some time to think about it. I came here to ask for the truth about Dad. I didn't expect to hear all of this. I need time to process it all. I'm still hoping this is a dream, or an alternate reality where nice old ladies kill reverends and homeless people."

"We're not old," Charlotte said. "We're barely twice your age."

Michael rolled his eyes and called over his shoulder as he blew past them, "Try not to kill anyone else while I'm away."

"Don't be smarmy."

Michael pulled open the front door with a burst and checked his pockets for keys.

"Well, that went well."

"I don't think so." Ruby wiped down the wine bottle with a look that could have been a thousand miles away.

Michael sent them both one last warning glance, and then he was gone.

CHAPTER EIGHTEEN

Autumn burst over Montrose Hills changing prim green lawns to color splattered rectangles of leaves and mums. Busting a bad guy made for the Channel 3 headlines, but finding one who masqueraded as a neat-nik ninny of a suburban housewife was sure to blow Emma's career all the way to the *Today Show*. Emma hounded Michael, waiting for an angle, a slip, a break. She even went so far as to travel to his home and try to question him. Unfortunately, the trip had resulted in a wasted paycheck.

Emma, who had been thwarted at every turn, was more determined than ever to land a story. She wasn't sure what it was, and she didn't care, but she knew Ruby Russell was guilty of something. Emma wanted out of her small life. Michael Russell could help her with that, but he wouldn't budge.

If he would have agreed to talk with her, she probably wouldn't have called the local hospitals. It was only out of sheer desperation and boredom that she had. A well-meaning candy striper answered and found Ruby Russell's name in the computer. Ruby had stayed for a week a few years prior, not from food poisoning, which Emma expected, but from psychosis.

Emma arrived at the hospital in under ten minutes. The candy striper allowed her access to the computer in medical records. A handshake agreement to get her some time on air during a future exposé about young volunteers sealed the deal.

It didn't take long to find two leads. The name of Ruby's assigned follow-up hospital, and the name of the facility she'd been transferred to, Heartland Behavioral Health. The story didn't seem like much for news, but Emma was running on fumes and mush. Nothing else substantial had panned out thus far, so what else could she do? She made the trip to Heartland.

The beautiful retreat surprised her, hardly resembling a hospital of any kind. The large oaks and apple trees shaded lines of flowering bushes. The leaves were raked into neat piles and wooden benches leaned against elaborate stone walls. If it weren't for the gates and guards, she would have imagined herself wandering in a park.

At the door, she was buzzed in and ushered towards a library where a mostly gray-haired man sat puzzling over some files.

"Do you work here," she asked hesitantly, "or, live here?" One foot remained in the doorframe at her side.

"I… neither." He stood and reached for her.

Emma took a step back and the gentleman smiled.

"I'm Dr. Mark Kessler. I have a private practice in town. I'm here doing research. Can I help you, Miss Eaken?"

"You know me? You were expecting me?" Perhaps she had arrived in wonderland.

"I live in Montrose Hills. Who wouldn't know you?"

Emma smiled back. She liked being recognized. "What

are you working on?"

"Ah, doctor patient confidentiality." He waved his bifocals over the files and shrugged. His disheveled appearance caused Emma to wonder if he really was who he said he was.

"You?"

"I'm looking for Dr. Samuel Shrieve. He was the doctor assigned to a patient here a few years back. I'm looking into something about her now."

"Her?" Dr. Kessler's hand twitched.

"Ruby Russell."

Dr. Kessler sat back roughly in his seat. "Ruby Russell."

"You know her?"

When he didn't respond, Emma considered offering to get someone for him. "I'm looking into a series of strange deaths in Montrose Hills and they all seem to have a link to this woman. I know it's a small world and there are only so many degrees of separation for any of us, but still." Emma watched the alleged doctor. He went completely still apart from a hand tremor and eye twitch. He knew something, too, just like Michael Russell. What was it that she wasn't privy to and why would a doctor hide it?

Emma stirred the pot. "Her husband was sleeping with Daisy Douglas. I have proof, photographic and written. I've had the good fortune of being able to access Daisy's home computer." Emma wasn't sure fortune was the right word, but it sounded nicer than admitting the whole truth on that score.

"You're sure?"

"So you do know her." Emma smiled.

"What do you know about her?" Dr. Kessler stood and gathered his things.

"Kenneth Russell was having an affair with the girl who died with Reverend Flynn." Emma smiled slyly and waited.

"That would give her reason to want them both dead."

"Well, that's presumptuous, not to mention melodramatic," he croaked, tugging at his collar. He placed a hand on the back of his chair when he stood.

"Did you know Ruby or only Kenneth?"

"I've heard she's a magnificent baker." Dr. Kessler's smile became wild and unsettling to Emma. Then he turned and was gone.

Emma watched him stumble along the railing in the hall towards the cafeteria.

She definitely had her fingers around a thread. Now, it was time to pull.

*****

It was late in the day when Michael returned. Ruby and Charlotte waited on pins and needles. Telling him might have been their worst mistake of all. Ruby slumped over the arm of her rocker wallowing in pity when she saw his headlights pull in behind Charlotte's car.

"He's come home!" The announcement brought Charlotte to life and they met him at the door.

"How did it go?" They asked in unison.

Michael made his way to the kitchen and drew a glass of water from the sink. He turned to rest his back against Ruby's counter. "I need to think," he said.

"Where've you been?"

He opened the cabinet where his mother once kept aspirin and pulled out a freezer-sized bag of pink and blue capsules.

"Those are mine, but I don't take them." Ruby rushed in to pull the bag from his hand. "Don't worry. I really don't take them. I only keep them, but I do have the prescription refilled, so everything is fine."

"In what reality is everything fine?" The shock in his voice made him seem years younger.

"Michael, I've sheltered you far too long. The world is not the safe and loving place I've always made it out to be. "

"Mother." Michael grabbed the large bag from her hand and held it over her head for inspection. "Have you ever considered that m-a-y-b-e you should take these?"

"Pish-posh. I'm fine. Those pills are just to make Dr. Kessler feel better."

"I don't think so."

"Put them back in the cupboard, please. I'll get you some aspirin."

Michael obeyed and went to sit on the sofa with Charlotte. She smiled. "I went to visit Bunny. It was a courtesy to let her know I'm in town. I had dinner with her and let her catch me up on the wedding details. Eventually we got around to what she was told about Dad." He let his head fall.

"Is she going to the authorities?" Ruby returned with the aspirin and more water.

"Is she going to be a problem?" Charlotte mirrored the sentiment in her own way.

"Why would she go to the authorities? Please try to think like someone who's not on a,...Ack." He hacked a throaty noise at them.

"I just told one woman more lies than I ever have in my whole life. I did that on behalf of the woman who taught me not to lie. What's happening?" Michael rubbed his face and sighed.

"What did she say? You're being cryptic." Ruby tsked.

"She said she heard Dad might have known Daisy. She was mortified to tell me. I assured her she was mistaken. I said you two had the perfect marriage and Dad adored you. I said you and he were deeply in love and you'd be devastated with such lies."

"Did she believe you?"

"I hope my word meant more to her than a stranger's, but then again, I was the one lying, wasn't I?" Michael's chin flipped up, allowing his head to hang back over the couch.

"You did good." Charlotte patted his knee. "She won't be asking any more questions. She only thinks there's a rumor about an affair, nothing more, and that's personal."

"Oh, yes." Michael rolled his head back and forth. "*That* is personal."

"Besides, there's no one left who knew for sure."

"You're angry," Ruby fretted.

"Mom!" He gasped. "Seriously? Are you kidding me?"

"Oh dear."

Michael softened. "Why? I can't get it in my head. Why?"

"Well, your father," she began.

"I know." He held his hand up like a policeman stopping traffic. "I understand. That was very sad. I know you had no way to predict what would happen. How could you?"

"Thank you," Ruby mouthed the words. Michael kept his hand in place.

"What about the rest? You're sure you had no idea Mrs. Tanner was diabetic? You wanted her approval? Why? And the muffins for Reverend Flynn. You tried to make him sick. I can't understand it. You know better. You taught me better than to care what people think or to try to hurt others. Then Emma and that cheesecake." He groaned and closed his eyes exasperated."

"It all got a bit out of control, dear. I wanted to teach Tillie a lesson. I was grieving and angry and impetuous. I wanted recognition. The others were in the wrong place at the wrong time. I didn't know they were diabetic." Ruby pleaded.

"They're dead, Mom. Then you tried to kill Emma Eaken

on purpose."

She hid her mouth behind her hand. "I should have tried harder."

"I can still hear you. Do you hear yourself?"

"She's causing problems," Charlotte said.

Michael spun around to stare at her. "Please. Tell me there is hope of inspiring clarity here. Stop encouraging one another. How are you both so calm?"

"We're not, honey."

"We yell a lot." Charlotte frowned.

"Mom, those men at the news station. They had families and lives."

"They were thieves. The note on that box said it was for Emma."

"Are you all done now? Or should I move back to Montrose Hills so I can break one of those capsules into your wine every evening?"

"Oh, she shouldn't be taking those and drinking," Charlotte said.

"Thank you." Michael stared.

"Well, of course, we're finished, but I'd love to have you home, sweetie."

"Of course."

Ruby could hear Michael's disapproval.

"Except," Charlotte held up one finger and they both looked at her. "Emma's a bit of a problem. If she suspects us of all we've done, and I think she does, it won't be long before she eventually pieces it together."

"I don't know. She was really fishing when she spoke with me. She threw out all the unusual stories in this community. She was trying to find something to run with. I don't know if she has any idea how it fits, or if it does. I think she'd take any lead and run."

"Maybe give her a new lead?" Charlotte asked and Ruby

bounded clumsily to her side. Her hands folded together at her sternum.

"What new lead?" she asked excitedly.

Michael stepped to them. He looked a bit menacing, and the women stopped.

"Charlotte has been doing research." Ruby's eyes were on the floor.

"Emma's the prime candidate. She's been in contact with everyone and following leads."

"Like a guilty person." Ruby remembered being told this tidbit. She turned to Michael who looked like a doe in the forest at hunting season. "Guilty people like to get attention for it, watch at the scenes, and see people's reactions."

"You two need to stop. You need to stop. Do you understand me? Please give me until the wedding to think. Okay? Please, promise me you won't do anything else until after the wedding. Please?" His voice wilted at the last plea.

The women exchanged a silent glance and then nodded without words. Michael placed his glass on the counter and walked methodically up the stairs to his old room.

*****

The fact that they hadn't actually promised had not gone unnoticed, and Michael rubbed his chest. He was too young to get an ulcer.

"Thank you for seeing me." Michael was shocked to have gotten in to see Dr. Kessler with absolutely no notice.

"Come. Sit." The doctor motioned him to a chair, where he had to first clear files from the seat.

The office was a mess. His desk vomited paperwork and the floor was stacked with books, files and newspapers. It reminded Michael of the newsroom at his college. He doubted anyone with problems left there feeling any better.

He imagined his mother cleaning the place before she could even sit.

"You're getting married." Dr. Kessler smiled wildly.

"Yes."

"How's your mother handling that?"

"Well, actually, she approves of the family and the girl, my Sophia."

"But..." Dr. Kessler waited expectantly.

"I suppose she wishes I'd wait until she dies to get married." Michael slid his feet on the papers beneath them. "She doesn't share well."

"She doesn't like change." Dr. Kessler bounced an ink pen on his lips.

"Who does?"

"So, what brings you here today?"

"I wanted to get your opinion on how she's doing. I live too far away to tell for sure and with the wedding coming, she's not herself."

"I can't say." Dr. Kessler paused. "She barely speaks to me and her behavior has always been quite distinct from every other patient I've had."

"Do you think the medication is helping?"

"Honestly, I'm not sure she's taking it."

"Why do you say that?"

"Well, I don't know. She seems exactly the same, every time, but," Dr. Kessler didn't look well.

"But?"

"I'm not sure. She opened up about her childhood earlier. That was a breakthrough, but it wasn't as if she were taking me into her confidence after all these years. It was more like she was making a justification or maybe it was a rant? It wasn't right."

"You think she's not right?"

"I can't say. She's being less than forthright, and I legally cannot say." He winked at Michael.

"If she weren't right," Michael treaded lightly. "If she were a danger to herself, or to anyone, what would happen, given her history?"

Dr. Kessler perked up. "Given her history, I suppose any attorney would get her an insanity verdict and she'd live out her years in an institution. I'm not sure justice would be served, but it's the likely outcome."

"Justice?" Michael's intuition stirred. As he waited for the answer, he looked more carefully at the stacks and piles around him. He remembered his mother's mentioning the bean book.

"Well, a number of individuals plead insanity when, in truth, they knew full well what they were doing." Dr. Kessler fiddled with his desk calendar and Michael continued to survey.

Each of the books and all of the files were carefully turned away from his chair. The books' spines faced the doctor. The files stacked tabs down. Michael wondered which of them was more anxious. He hoped he didn't look as bad as the good doctor.

"I'm concerned about her health. You seem worried about something else. Insanity pleas? Attorneys? Are you trying to tell me something?"

"No. Are you?"

"No."

"Looks like you're working on some major research here." Michael spoke in his best academic voice. Perhaps they could meet on similar ground. "I worked in the research lab all through undergrad. Maybe I could help?"

"Why could you help?" Dr. Kessler tilted his head. "Because you did research in college?" His eyes narrowed.

"Sure. I could be an extra set of hands."

"You have a wedding coming up. Why would you want

to help me with a pet project?"

"A pet project?"

The two men stood then, eyeballing one another.

"Something of a personal interest to me." Dr. Kessler's shirt wasn't tucked into his trousers and he was wearing tennis shoes with his ensemble.

"You don't look well, Doctor."

"Tell your mother I said 'hello'." Dr. Kessler pulled his door open as he spoke. "Give her this, would you?"

Michael recognized an RSVP for his wedding.

"Thank you for your time." Michael took the envelope from Dr. Kessler's grip. He listened for the door to close behind him. It didn't until he was clear of the waiting room.

At home, Michael didn't notice the strange car on the curb. He barreled inside, stressed out from a two-way trip in traffic and his suspicions about Dr. Kessler.

"Mom." He swung the door open and closed it behind him. "You invited Dr. K…"

"Hello, dear!" Ruby's shrill voice cracked the silence like a fresh farm egg against her shining granite counter.

Michael stopped to see Ruby's red face looking helplessly at him from the kitchen.

"Mom?"

"We have a guest," she said quietly. The look on her face told him it could very well be the grim reaper behind her. It nearly was.

"Hello, Michael." Emma Eaken stepped around Ruby and lifted a tall glass of sweet tea into the air.

"Out!" Michael looked around for her things. A tiny coat hung on the coat tree and a large bag lay beside the front door. "Out!"

"Michael," Ruby gasped.

He strode across the room and traded Emma her tea for

the coat and bag. Then he looked crossly at his mother, who shook her head at him. He knew she wouldn't poison anyone in her home, again. That would be careless.

"You have no right to be here." He placed the coat over her shoulders and steered her towards the front door. "You're a crazy, nutty, woman and I don't need anything messing up my wedding day. Take your loony conspiracy theories and fairytales somewhere else. Check yourself in while you're there." Michael pulled the front door open again and shoved Emma out onto the porch.

"Somewhere like Heartland Behavioral Health?" Emma asked as the heavy wooden door closed in her face.

Ruby gasped and pointed frantically at the door. "You gave her my bag." She held a tiny black clutch in her hand.

Michael opened the window beside the door and tossed the clutch onto the porch. "Leave Mother's bag on the mat." Then he secured the window and locked it as well.

"What was she doing here?" He turned to Ruby who gawked.

"Meddling, I suppose, but she'd only just gotten here when you came in."

"Why would you let her in?" He rubbed his chest, hoping not to have a heart attack before he could marry Sophia.

"What was I supposed to do?"

"Not let her in. You were supposed to not let her in." Michael began to pace.

"How was Dr. Kessler?" Ruby looked concerned and already past the Emma issue.

"He looked like he could use some medication. He's a mess over there. I'd find a new therapist if I were you."

"I don't need a therapist. It's only for appearances and a good therapist would ask too many questions. Dr. Kessler is just beginning to settle down."

"Yeah? It looks like he's going mad."

"Exactly."

"Who are you?"

She offered him tea.

*****

The rehearsal went off without a hitch. Ruby kept a flask in her purse and sat as often as she thought acceptable. The Walshes didn't show any sign of suspicion. Sophia was as charming as ever. The dinner exceeded her expectations.

Ruby insisted on catering the event along with the next day's reception. The work kept her mind off other things for two straight weeks. The execution of such an important meal was something to be carefully planned. It was an experience to be treasured. Every last detail occurred in perfect order and Ruby glowed with pleasure.

"Thank you so much, Mrs. Russell," Sophia said as she left. Ruby hated to like her, but she did. Then Sophia hugged her and Ruby saw, over the girl's shoulder, the look of pride on Michael's face.

"You're very welcome, dear. Michael has chosen a very lovely young woman for his bride."

"Thank you." Sophia blushed and returned to Michael's side.

The remaining crowd dissipated slowly, leaving only Ruby and Charlotte to clean up. It would be a very long night.

"Tomorrow's the big day," Charlotte said.

"He's not my baby anymore. He's someone else's husband, all grown up, and no longer in need of parenting." Tears squeezed out from behind Ruby's lids.

"Not that. Ruby, your young man is twenty-five years old. He hasn't needed parenting in a decade."

Clearly Charlotte wasn't a mother.

"What I meant was tomorrow is the wedding. Michael

said after the wedding, we're free to handle things our way. As far as I've seen, he hasn't done a thing."

"He's been busy. He's getting married tomorrow."

"No." Charlotte shoved a stack of table linens in Ruby's direction. "You've been busy. He has been," she paused. "I have no idea what he's been doing, but he hasn't fixed this mess, so I will."

CHAPTER NINETEEN

The next morning, Emma donned her nicest party dress and slipped her silk pashmina around her shoulders. Wedding crashing was one way to get her story and a good reporter wouldn't stop until she had it. Silver heels, clutch and a baby blue beaded gown would make her the belle of the ball. She primped in the mirror, certain that she looked perfect. Emma rarely wore her hair up, and she'd forgotten how striking she looked that way. Today her life was going to change.

Thanks to her friends at the Techno Shack, she was wired with a microphone and a mini camera. No one would suspect it in such a slinky dress. She'd done enough research to get in without an invitation. No one looked at those anyway. The church secretary told her the wedding was at six o'clock. She knew she could corner the groom easily an hour before. Only one lonely Town Car stood at the curb near the front door of the majestic old cathedral when she arrived.

Emma climbed the stairs stealthily, using all her

composure not to run. She'd waited for this moment for so long. The fact she would get her big break in a church was all the more reason to know it was her destiny. She, herself, hadn't been to church in years.

Inside she headed straight to the dressing rooms. The halls were long, and the marble ceilings rose to meet the sky. Shiny white marble illuminated the scarlet carpets. The effect was stunning. It was the most grandiose of the cathedrals in Ashland. Incense scented the corridors and flowers sprung up from every vase and pew. Emma breathed in the coming victory.

She found Michael inside the large room marked for the groom.

"Mr. Russell," she said in her most smoky voice. Her eyes already claiming victory.

"Get out."

"I was hoping you'd tell me how your mother killed Daisy Douglas, or maybe even your father."

"Get out!"

Emma slipped into the room and pulled the door shut behind her. "Just say it. I already know everything."

"You're insane. If it wouldn't throw my wedding off schedule, I'd call the police and issue a restraining order against you."

"You wouldn't do that." Emma didn't know how to get Michael to admit his mother was a murderer, but she planned to try everything. "I've spoken to everyone."

Michael stared at her in silence.

"I've spoken with Charlotte Mason and your neighbors. I've been to Treeline a dozen times." She smiled. Michael smiled in return and her confidence wavered.

"I've been to the Tanner house," she tried to erase his smug smile, testing, looking for what it was that would move him. "I've been to the Partridge Parish and to the

Church of Hope. There's a lot of gossip going around about your mother."

"Emma," he said coldly. "I remember you from school. You don't recognize me. That's obvious. I guess it's because you're several years older than I am. I remember how you are. You were always a cheerleader, but never the flyer. You dated the athletes, but never the captain. You were on the prom court," He walked up close to her. She stood her ground.

"Never the Queen."

"You think you know so much." She swallowed anger, still affected by the triviality of high school, though she was closer to thirty than eighteen.

"You went to college. It was only a state school." He shrugged. "I'll bet your ten-year reunion is coming soon. I suppose everyone around here knows you made it to the local news, but not the anchor desk."

"Your mother is a murderer." Her fingers shook from anger and embarrassment. "I've been to Heartland Behavioral Health. I've spoken with Dr. Mark Kessler and Dr. Samuel Shrieve." She stepped closer to him now. Chest to chest, the hate rolled off him in waves. The standoff could have collapsed the great church around them.

"You. Know. Nothing." Each word was its own sentence, emphasized and oozing with threat.

"It would be so much less messy if you'd just tell me. If you don't, things are going to get ugly."

"You lose, Emma." Michael snorted, dismissing her.

Her jaw clenched and released. The grip on her beaded silver clutch was damaging her manicure. She imagined throwing it at him.

"We'll see. Have it your way, I'll keep asking, keep pushing. I'm sure plenty of your guests are only here for the spectacle. They know all about your mother. She's bat-shit crazy. Dangerous too, only no one's ever been able to prove it. That's all." She turned and walked out the door. "Until now."

Ruby Russell stood outside the dressing room, her face as white as snow. Her mouth hung open. Ruby had probably heard enough to want to cause Emma bodily harm, and Emma believed Ruby was the woman for the job. Her steps hastened. Alone in a church with Ruby Russell was not where she wanted to be. Emma exited through the side entrance, hoping to find guests arriving early, or at the very least, her cameraman.

In the lot, she shaded her eyes from the setting sun. She could clearly see the Channel 3 van ahead of her, and she ran for it.

*****

"Emma!" As soon as Michael realized how angry Sophia would be at any spectacle Emma might make, he chased her. His mother stood across the sanctuary and he hoped she hadn't overheard any of their conversation. He wasn't proud of the way he'd talked to Emma. He'd belittled her. He was better than that.

Ruby's expression contorted. He could thank Emma Eaken for causing him more work. Now, he'd have to comfort his mother along with the bride. Hopefully Emma wouldn't make a scene.

She shoved open the side door and light came flooding in, blinding him temporarily and animating thousands of tiny silver particles in the air. Guests would arrive soon. The timing was horrendous.

"Emma!" Finally, she looked over her shoulder from a distance in the parking lot somewhere between Michael and the news van.

SMACK!

Emma Eaken disappeared beneath the large white

vehicle and then reappeared as the van returned to its spot. Michael froze statue still in the warm red glow of the vanishing sun.

"Michael!" Ruby called from outside the front of the church. "Michael!" She motioned for him to come to her, but he stood unable to understand.

The van sat, engine quiet in the parking spot ten feet from where Emma lay bleeding and motionless. Charlotte climbed down from the driver's seat and walked away from the van and church.

Slowly, Michael turned and jogged to Ruby. "Come on, Michael." She hurried him back inside the front door.

The attendants trickled in a few moments later. Michael couldn't speak. No one seemed to notice. The hustle and bustle increased until it was time to wait at the altar for his bride.

He noticed many things from his vantage. One, the side entrance was now padlocked. Two, Charlotte sat next to his mother, looking the part of the proud aunt. Three, Dr. Kessler occupied a pew near the back on the bride's side of the auditorium, watching his mother. Four, a man in a Channel 3 jacket paced the rear of the church looking aggravated. Finally, everyone else seemed thrilled to attend a wedding of this stature. Every respected member of the community was in their place, waiting to see the marriage spectacle, totally unaware a news reporter had been run down by her own truck an hour before.

Michael didn't expect to remember most of what transpired during his wedding ceremony. His mind shut down to protect itself, except for the bride's approach and the final kiss. The rest was automatic response, the actions of a detached mind and a body on auto pilot.

In the Town Car, he noticed a large spot in the side lot resembling an oil spill. His mother stood on the steps laughing and visiting with the four-hundred or so guests. Charlotte was at her side.

"Michael," Sophia whispered into his ear. "I love you." She kissed his cheek sweetly, one hand beneath his chin.

Alone in the car with his bride, he tried to absorb the beauty with him. She was a princess in white. Her gown hung loosely all around, covering the seat and much of the floor. Her toenails were petal pink and her French manicure had a subtle shimmer in the topcoat. Her hair was up, adorned by a tiara of rhinestones and her blush against perfect white skin was roses on cream.

Michael wrapped his arms around Sophia's tiny waist and kissed her as if it might be the last. He loved her with a complete love, and he had to protect her from the horror that was happening all around her, on her wedding day.

"You are the most precious treasure on earth. I'm the luckiest man alive."

The cuddling was exactly what Michael needed. He filled up on the sincerity and peace all the way home. They drove around long enough for guests to arrive at the reception. His mother had set up the entire back and side yards with tents and tables. Everything was gorgeous, picture perfect by any standard.

Michael climbed out of the car and lifted Sophia with him. He spun her gently and nuzzled her cheek once more before he had to deal with his mother.

Sophia's feet barely touched the ground before she was whisked away by her entourage of bridesmaids. Michael headed for the kitchen.

"Michael?" Bunny's voice stopped him. "Michael, have you seen the gown's bag?"

"What?"

"I can't find the bag I brought Sophia's gown to the church in. I left it in the dressing room and then I didn't see it when we left the church. Oh bother. I wanted to have it cleaned and preserved while you two were on your honeymoon. I hate to take it anywhere without a proper garment bag." Bunny rubbed her temples, trying to think.

Michael didn't have to.

"I'll ask my mother and Mrs. Mason. I'll let you know as soon as we find it. Promise." He squeezed her hand and she walked off in the direction Sophia had gone with her girls.

Ruby was in the kitchen drinking.

"Don't you look at me that way. You said we had until today for you to handle things." She waved a finger at him with one hand and lifted a bottle with the other.

Michael needed to think of Sophia. None of it was right, but he couldn't stop his mother. The best he could do was tend to his wife, and hope it all worked out. "Bunny's looking for a garment bag." He sifted through some storage containers on the counter. He recognized them from the church. Mostly they were filled with flowers and vases.

"It isn't there."

"You remembered the guest book, but you lost a six foot garment bag?" Michael was getting angry.

"Didn't forget it." Her lips formed the words around a mouthful of hand-dipped strawberries. "Tell Bunny to leave the gown in the guest room when Sophia changes. I'll get it to the shop in the morning. I know where it's headed."

"Why is she leaving it here?" Michael poured a flute of champagne.

"She'll change into her trousseau for your honeymoon."

"What's a trousseau?"

"A dress, probably."

"She has a second dress for leaving?"

Ruby rolled her eyes and popped another strawberry into her mouth. "We're going to need your help." She dusted her hands together and took one more sip of wine.

"With what?"

"Thank goodness, Ruby," Bunny's voice interrupted. "I see the garment bag in your van. I tried the doors, but they're locked. I don't mean to bother you, but I've been just sick, thinking it was gone."

Ruby's eyes widened and a nearly audible click sounded in Michael's head. Ruby began to choke on her strawberry. While Bunny poured a glass of water, Michael watched Charlotte taking the garment bag out of the van. It flopped heavily onto the sidewalk, out of Michael's view. Bunny glanced up, wondering if he planned to help his mother. He did.

"That was Mother's bag. She couldn't decide what to wear so we ended up bringing about half a dozen suits to the church. I loaded it myself. It helps to know what Sophia's bag looks like, though. I'll be better able to locate it."

"Enjoy the food and we'll be right there." Ruby struggled for air. Always the hostess.

"I suppose it is silly," she shrugged impishly. "What a lovely day, and I'm fussing over a garment bag. Alright, alright," she tossed her palms up. "I'm going to go enjoy my daughter and my husband. I'll see you two later." Bunny smiled and left.

A knock on the mudroom door sent Ruby flying. Charlotte whispered frantically for Michael to help. Ruby needed to begin serving appetizers and mingling. They each took action.

"I can't drag it anymore without damaging the bag," Charlotte seemed ashamed at her lack of strength, not the fact she'd run a woman down and stuffed her into a garment bag, then hung her in a van, like a suit, and drove her to a wedding reception.

Michael lifted the bag with little effort and tried with all his might to imagine it filled with the suits he'd suggested. He followed Charlotte into the small gardening shed in the back of their yard where the property bordered the woods. The shed had been empty for years. *Now it had renewed purpose.*

Walking back across the lawn, he noticed Dr. Kessler leaning against the corner of their home, glancing haphazardly over his shoulder in their direction. Charlotte appeared to notice, too. "Excuse me," she said. "I need to make a run to the bakery."

The world was on its head. Ruby baked enough desserts for a thousand people, and Charlotte was going to buy some more. He watched her disappear into the mass of cars, and he went straight to find Dr. Kessler.

The doctor sat with his wife at an otherwise empty table. "Dr. Kessler, I'm so glad you could make it." He watched Mrs. Kessler's reaction. She looked like she'd have preferred to be at a root canal.

"Thank you. This is my wife, Meredith."

"Hello." It was easy to see they were fighting.

"Your mother has a lovely garden." He threw his chin towards the place he'd just been.

"Are you enjoying the appetizers?"

Dr. Kessler stopped chewing to appraise the inquiry.

"Michael?" Ruby called and he left.

*****

"Did you hear that? He threatened me. It's because I caught them."

"Shut up." Meredith chugged her third glass of champagne.

"I saw them carrying a garment bag to the shed. Why would they do that?"

"Who cares?" she spat.

"Aren't you even curious?" He begged her to see what

he saw, but she refused. His eyes twitched from nerves, and he contemplated his ability to escape his wife's presence long enough to get inside that shed. "Fine. I'll be back."

"Where are you going?"

"To the men's room." He looked in the crowd for Ruby or Michael. When he was certain they weren't watching him, he went to the shed for confirmation of something criminal.

*****

"This will fix him." Ruby tossed back cream puffs and cracked open a number of pretty capsules into a tray of dips and breads.

"What are you doing?" Michael stubbed his toe against the counter and let an oath slip.

"Watch your mouth." She busily dumped drugs into the cucumber and dill dip.

"Have you gone completely over the edge? You can't do that here, now."

She wiped her hands on her kitchen towel. "I certainly can. I must." She turned to walk away and Michael grabbed her arm tightly.

"No, you won't."

Ruby stared for a count of two and then stomped her heel into Michael's toes.

"Ouch! Damn it, Mom!"

Ruby grabbed his face hard with her free hand. With the other she balanced her deadly dip. "I told you to watch it."

"Done." Charlotte's voice bounded through the front door.

"Good." Ruby set the platter down and went to see Charlotte. Michael followed.

"What's done?" He imagined Charlotte digging a six foot grave in the last twenty-five minutes.

"Will you please go and enjoy your wedding reception?" Ruby insisted.

"Oh." Charlotte made a tiny sound. Michael saw the reason. A white Channel 3 van was pulling into the crowd of cars on the cul-de-sac.

"Crackers," Ruby cursed.

"Yeah," Michael agreed. "Crackers."

Michael rushed out the front door to meet the man exiting the van. He also saw Dr. Kessler returning from the shed in the backyard. His heart sputtered in his chest.

"Hi, I'm Michael Russell, the groom." Michael smiled broadly at the man who smiled in return.

"Hey, I'm Clint. Emma asked me to do her a favor today and help cover your wedding. I almost never work with her and I'm not sure what I'm doing."

"Hi Clint, I'm Mark." Dr. Kessler walked up and extended his hand to Clint.

"Hey, man. Nice to meet you." He looked back to Michael. "I was supposed to meet her at the church, but she never showed. I think. I can't be sure, but I thought her car was there. She wasn't. So I came here thinking I got my messages mixed, but I definitely don't see her car here. Have you seen her?"

"No. I haven't seen Emma today."

"Do you normally keep your shed padlocked?" Dr. Kessler asked.

"I'm taking off." Clint was clearly annoyed at the apparent runaround.

"Do you normally go through private outbuildings when you're invited to someone's home?"

"If you see her, maybe mention I was here?" Clint raised a hand as he rounded the van and slid back into the driver's seat.

"I'll do that," Michael called.

Dr. Kessler stared.

*****

"Mark!" Meredith appeared at the outskirts of the party area. "Get back here. The appetizers are being served."

Michael broke into a run, and Mark followed. Meredith caught him by his elbow as he tried to slide past. "Let's go!"

"No!" He tried to shake free of her grip.

"Fine. Take me home then. First, you make it impossible to back out of this wedding. Now, you leave me sitting alone at the table for half an hour. What's going on with you? You know what, never mind. Take me home."

Michael had disappeared into the crowd and Mark slumped his shoulders. "I saw Michael carrying a garment bag to the shed."

"Stop."

"Listen. I checked it out and the shed's locked." Mark made a face at Meredith and she folded her arms over her chest.

"So is ours."

"The Channel 3 camera man was here looking for Emma Eaken, who was looking into Ruby Russell's past a few weeks ago."

"You're ranting." Meredith stamped towards their car. "I shouldn't be driving."

"Come on. You said appetizers."

She skulked behind her husband back to their table. "I should eat something, but then you'll take me home."

Mark's head bobbed. His eyes were already searching for their table.

Michael was leaving it as they arrived. He carried a tray in one hand.

"Hey, is that our appetizers?" Mark asked loudly.

Meredith jumped between them. "I'm so sorry. This was a mistake. Let's go, okay? Please?"

"No way!" Mark shouted. "Give me that tray of dip!"

People grew quiet as Dr. Kessler caused a spectacle. When he saw he had an audience, he spoke louder. "Why are you taking our appetizers?"

"Your table was empty. We assumed you'd gone." Everyone stared. "It's a mayonnaise base, and it shouldn't sit." Michael looked apologetically into the crowd.

"Because mayonnaise can cause food poisoning?" His eyebrows rose.

"I don't know. Why let it sit?"

"Because we're here." Dr. Kessler held his arms open wide. He looked around at the masses. When he looked back at Michael, Charlotte was leaving with a tray like theirs.

"Here you go, Dr. Kessler. We have a new tray for you. It's still chilled and I'm sure you'll enjoy it."

Dr. Kessler shoved passed Michael and ran into the kitchen, shouting for the original tray.

"Mark, stop." Meredith trailed behind him.

"Ma'am," Officer O'Leary strolled into the kitchen, tipping his hat in Ruby's direction. "I'm sorry I have to be here. You've had an awful time of it these past few months and now this joker's ruining your son's wedding reception. Congratulations, by the way, young man." He nodded to Michael.

O'Leary's partner took Dr. Kessler by the collar out onto the porch.

"Thank you for your generous contribution to the policeman's ball this year. We do remember those who support us." He turned to leave. As the door came open, the shouting pierced the hush inside.

"She's a killer! She poisons everyone with her fancy muffins and dips. Dips! She's serving poisoned dips! Don't eat the dips!"

Meredith tipped back another glass of champagne and looked sullenly at Ruby. "I guess I should call a cab."

CHAPTER TWENTY

"Michael!" Sophia ran into his arms. "What happened?"

Michael kissed her head. "Dr. Kessler had too much champagne, I think. What a shame. I'm so sorry for the outburst." He pulled her tight to his side. "I promise to make it up to you, starting right now."

Michael led his bride onto the dance floor beneath a cascade of twinkle lights and pink roses. "Maestro." He nodded to the small orchestra seated on the newly erected stage.

Together they danced until the crowd demanded they eat cake and throw garters. Then they watched their friends and family have the time of their lives. The moment was perfect. The evening, as a whole, sucked eggs.

"Psst. Psst." Hissing sounds came from the rear of the house, and Michael wasn't surprised to see his mother motioning for him again. He hadn't seen her in at least an hour. It was hard to guess what she'd been up to.

Michael excused himself, kissing his new bride and disappearing into the shadows beyond the house.

"We need you to move the bag," Ruby said in a hush.

The bag.

"Where?"

"To the Tanner house." Ruby led her son to the shed and then across the side lawn to the neighbor's empty house.

"What are we doing here?"

"We're leaving her for the realtor." Ruby opened the door.

"You have a key?"

Charlotte was already inside. "This way."

They moved down the stairs into the spacious walkout basement. "This is beautiful," Ruby said quietly.

"Here. Leave her here." Charlotte pointed to a small chair and ottoman.

Together they unzipped the bag and placed Emma on her throne. Charlotte smashed the soiled bag into a cinch sack and handed Michael a new garment bag.

"Here. This is from Doodle Brothers. It's exactly like Sophia's. Tell Bunny you found it in one of the boxes from the church." She ripped the price tag off and slid it out of the plastic for him. "Okay, go on before they realize you're gone. We'll be over in a few minutes."

Michael stared at Emma. He looked into each of the eager faces standing beside him. They might as well have been redecorating for all the concern they showed. "You cleaned her up?"

"Where did you think we've been? We're not monsters. Charlotte bandaged her head and I did what I could to remove any evidence from the lot."

"They have special lights," Charlotte interjected. "They can tell if people are moved."

"She'll be okay. Though we are hoping for extensive memory loss." Ruby rubbed Michael's arm.

"She's alive?" Breathe caught in his chest. His mind

whirled with relief and fear. "I thought…you hung her in the shed! She's been in a bag for hours."

"I gave her a little something to help her rest." Charlotte stroked bangs from Emma's forehead. "She won't remember the shed."

"Now, get back to your bride. She'll miss you soon. If I don't have a chance to tell you before you leave, have a magical honey moon." Ruby pulled her son into a tight embrace and sniffled into his tuxedo. "I love you."

"I love you too, Mom." Michael raised a hand toward Charlotte and kissed his mother's head. Then climbed the stairs to the Tanner kitchen and slid out into the night.

*****

"Did you get the other thing?" Ruby asked.

"Yep." The "p" popped on her lips. She lifted a bag from behind the chair. Treeline Bakery was written on the front.

"She was hit by a truck. Someone's bound to notice that," Ruby complained.

Charlotte huffed and tore open another box. "This is a staged scene. Don't be daft. Of course she was hit by a truck. Someone's making a point here." She raised her eyebrows high. "She was abducted."

"Oh. What point are you making exactly?" Ruby didn't want to have to ask, but Charlotte was the one who watched all those movies. Surely she didn't expect Ruby to know anything about being a criminal.

"Ah!" Charlotte threw her hands into the air. "It's not me making a point. Keep up. Whoever was behind all those Treeline poisonings and cover-ups is punishing her. It's a warning for people to drop the case or they'll end up like this. You know," she paused for a moment, "like the horse head in those mob movies."

Ruby nodded without understanding. Charlotte had thought this through, and Ruby was thankful. That's all that mattered.

"Everyone knows Emma's been looking into the murders and putting pressure on Treeline, plus that man, she called him Stuart, was with her here before. He'll point that out once she's found here. Hopefully, authorities will follow this long enough for us to get settled somewhere far away."

The women dotted Emma's mouth with crumbs and frosting. They laid out the remainder of the pastries as if she had been enjoying a delectable spread. The scene was certain to keep tongues wagging and authorities busy. After all, Emma was hit with her own van. No one had seen her at the church or the reception. The mess seemed to be coming together very neatly, finally.

Ruby and Charlotte pulled the door shut behind them and went back to the reception. It was a shame Emma had to ruin a perfectly delightful reception. Ruby regretted Michael's wedding day wasn't as perfect as her son, but she simply couldn't control everything.

*****

"She's crazy!" Mark Kessler screamed into the soft white walls. "Crazy!" He banged his head into the fabric and sobbed. "They did this together. He helped her. The family. The whole family."

He heard the orderly outside his door snickering, "I used to work for that guy."

"Yeah," another voice agreed. "Working in mental health isn't great for your mental health."

"She does it with the bean dip," he hollered pathetically, hoping someone on the other side would believe him. "She uses muffins and beans." Tears streamed down his once noble face.

He knew what happened. It was all right there in front of them, but they refused to look. She had the police in her pocket. He hoped Emma Eaken wouldn't give up. As soon as he got out of there, he was headed straight to Dr. Shrieve with this. He knew. Shrieve knew about Ruby. Once she was behind bars or under observation, Dr. Kessler would offer Shrieve, or Emma, or whomever, a byline in the capture. Meredith would see then. He would be a hero. A hero.

The sedative kicked in as Mark imagined seeing Ruby for therapy during her in-patient time. They would work through her issues. He could help her see that what she had done was wrong. "It's not right to do this, Ruby." His voice quieted with each word, and soon, he slept soundly for the first time in weeks.

*****

"Well, what do you think?" Charlotte peered at the sun.

"Cutie's Cupcakes has a whole new meaning when we're the cuties." Ruby giggled.

The women stood ankle deep in the sand, staring up at the small wooden sign. Cutie's Cupcakes had just gone Caribbean. It was nothing like the sprawling warehouse in Montrose, but it was theirs.

"Do you suppose natives eat cupcakes?"

"Everyone eats cupcakes." Ruby's expression told Charlotte to be sensible.

"There are plenty of tourists." Charlotte nodded.

"They aren't natives." Ruby eyed Charlotte disapprovingly. "We need to try and fit in. They're called locals."

"Are you sure we can call it Cutie's?" Charlotte asked for the umpteenth time since they landed. "Isn't that trademarked, or something?"

"No." Ruby brushed the bangs from her eyes. "There's nothing like that here. That's all in the states, Charlotte."

"You own Cutie's Cupcakes."

It was a small sea-green hut, just large enough to sell her

pastries. She'd still have to make most of them at home, but home was very close.

"We need a car," Ruby said. No way she could carry her baked goods safely every day.

"A golf cart," Charlotte amended. "Cars need registration."

"Oh."

"What about Michael?"

"He's telling anyone who asks they had a lovely honeymoon and when he got back, I was gone. We bought those burner phones you taught me about, so we can keep up with our chats. Maybe we'll get our story on one of those missing person shows."

"You'll need to remember sunscreen." Charlotte arranged her large hat carefully.

"You should open a first aid stand."

"Oh, that would be nice! Do you think I'd need a license for that here? I never finished my degree."

"No, not here. There aren't any rules here like in the states. It's practically a third world country."

Ruby looked up and down the beach, sizing up their future. Barbados wasn't beyond extradition, but it was beautiful.

As the women admired their new business, a crowd of rowdy middle-aged hipsters stumbled past, snickering and calling to the ladies in the surf. The hair on Ruby's arms stood on end. She imagined their wives at home somewhere, caring for their children while they made bacon in the Caribbean.

"Ruby?"

Men all over the world chased young girls. She couldn't exactly hide from that.

"Ruby?"

One of the men waved a bottle of island rum into the air.

Surely they realized how ridiculous they looked.

"What will be your new signature muffin?" Charlotte dug her feet deeper into the sand and watched sandpipers running from the waves.

"Coconut?" Charlotte pressed.

"Go away!" One of the girls called, pulling a cover-up around her small suit.

"How old *are* you?" another chided, and the girls ran off together as the men drank up.

Exactly on cue, the women answered Charlotte's question together, "Rum."

Cutie's Cupcakes of the Caribbean was officially open for business.

No, Ruby's life was not a fairytale, but her kingdom had grown and her new castle served cupcakes. In this new land, white knights still seemed unlikely, but maybe she could finally offer a few offenders the stocks.

THE END

ABOUT THE AUTHOR

As an only child Julie had plenty of time to people watch and make things up. When she didn't think she could make a living at the latter, her love of people led her to a BA in Psychology instead. A few years and three kids later, she discovered the thrill of writing. Hopelessly caffeine addicted and bouncing through life, writing became a harness for her seemingly endless supply of energy and enthusiasm. Best of all, writing created something of value in the wake.

You can find her day or night on social media sties like Facebook and Twitter@JulieALindsey or blogging her journey to publication at Musings From the Slush Pile, where she shares tips on writing, author interviews, and industry buzz from the web.

Visit
www.knightromancepublishing.com

For more updates on

The Killer Confection Series
by
Julie Anne Lindsey

Death by Chocolate (Book 1)

Coming Soon!

Drop Dead Delicious (Book 2)
Return of The Cupcake Killers (Book 3)

12474981R00157

Made in the USA
Charleston, SC
07 May 2012